oLivia LunGed a...
drove him dow...
enouGh to knoc...

Trying to catch his breath, he glared up into those feral eyes and saw not a trace of the girl with whom he had hatched this plan. Olivia growled and raised a talon above him.

Jack drove his right fist up into her throat. The Prowler reared back, clutching at her neck, and he sat up and drove punches into her abdomen, once, twice, three times, like working a heavy bag at the gym. Jack was a little bit more than average height, but he had been hard at work in the pub his entire life, and there was power in his arms and shoulders, enough to really hurt this beast.

He hesitated.

A massive Prowler hand flashed down, a single claw tore the skin on his right cheek. Jack hissed in pain as Olivia leaned in to whisper to him. The words were raw and gutteral from her bestial throat.

"Don't hold back."

Available from Pocket Books

PROWLERS

WILD THINGS

CHRISTOPHER GOLDEN

POCKET
BOOKS

LONDON • SYDNEY • NEW YORK • TOKYO • SINGAPORE • TORONTO

For Rick Hautala

This book is a work of fiction. Names, characters, places and incidents are products of the author's imagination or are used fictitiously. Any resemblance to actual events or locales or persons, living or dead, is entirely coincidental.

First POCKET BOOKS edition April 2003
Copyright © 2002 by Christopher Golden
POCKET BOOKS
an imprint of Simon & Schuster UK Ltd.
Africa House
64–78 Kingsway
London
WC1B 6AH

www.simonsays.co.uk

ISBN: 0-7434-4017-X
10 9 8 7 6 5 4 3 2 1

POCKET BOOKS and colophon are trademarks of Simon & Schuster

A CIP catalogue record for this book is available from the British Library

acknowledgements

Thanks, as always, to Connie and my boys, and to Lori Perkins, Lisa Clancy, Micol Ostow, Tom Sniegoski, and Peter Donaldson.

PROLOGUE

Alone in the dark.

Chet Douglas lay on a bedroll in the cab of his rig and stared up at the ceiling in the dark. Whenever he was on a long haul like this one—the trailer filled with electronics parts on their way from Alabama to Albany, New York—he split the drive up with two- and three-hour catnaps. It had taken some getting used to, but it got the load there faster, got the pay in the bank sooner.

He was young, after all. There would be time to sleep later.

In his mind all those excuses seemed completely reasonable. But there was another reason Chet tried not to sleep too much on a long haul. Sometimes the rest areas along America's midnight highways were full of truckers trading beers and stories, and some of the diners had their share of lot lizards—the sad-eyed women who so often hooked up with men who were just pass-

1

ing through. And that was okay, that camaraderie and companionship.

But sometimes . . . sometimes the rest areas were empty, the lot abandoned, even the highway quiet. Chet prided himself on his safety record, held his head up high whenever the subject came up. He was not going to be a statistic, another one of those long-haul boys who fell asleep at the wheel and took out some grandmother or a couple from Iowa with three kids in the car. So when he was tired, he stopped. He rested. But he never liked those darkened spots, bereft of any life, save for whatever rustled in the trees beyond the pavement.

Chet Douglas hated to be alone in the dark.

Of course, he never would have admitted that to his wife, Sally, or anyone else. It made him feel foolish. He was a grown man, after all. But whenever he was alone on the roadside, Chet made absolutely certain that the curtain was drawn tight to separate the rear of the cab from the front so that he could not see the night-blacked windows. At home, in his own bed, he slept soundly and peacefully enough. But now, there in the truck, he felt like a child again. If the curtains were open, he might be able to peer out through the windshield at the gathering dark, at the trees that swayed with the wind, at the shadows.

And he knew, absolutely, that if he dared to look, he would see things moving there in the dark, shifting in the shadows, just as he always had as a little boy. Faces at the window, talons scratching the glass.

Ridiculous, but inescapably true.

WILD THINGS

Sometimes Chet didn't get any sleep at all on those long hauls. At least, not until dawn. But now dawn was hours off, and he had to lie there and force himself to close his eyes, try to keep his mind from turning again to the dark. He hummed to himself, soft and low, one of the old Bonnie Raitt tunes he and Sally had sung to the kids every night until the boys announced they were too big for lullabies.

As though he had been drinking, he felt the world slipping away from him, a haze falling over his consciousness. Exhaustion finally catching up with him, and Chet gave himself over to it willingly. The sweet melody still in his head, he drifted toward oblivion, his chest rising and falling in a soothing rhythm, his breath slowing. Outside, the muffled sound of the wind.

The wind, soothing, gently rocking . . .

Chet opened his eyes, suddenly awake. For a moment he was confused, lost in that realm between sleep and consciousness. Something had roused him, had reached in from the night and touched him. A loud engine passing by on the highway?

Then it came again, distant and muffled as the wind, a shriek of terror and anguish, a desperate cry that made him freeze, eyes wide. His heart began to hammer in his chest and his breathing became ragged.

"Jesus," Chet whispered, there in the dark.

Get up. Get in the driver's seat, fire the big bitch up, and haul ass out of here, he commanded himself.

A third time the voice cried out, somewhere in the night beyond the metal cradle of the cab of his semi.

This time it was closer and there were smaller sounds accompanying it, little squeals of fear that sounded more than a little like surrender.

A woman. Maybe a girl.

But where had she come from? As he lay there unmoving—as though somehow whatever peril lurked out there in the shadows might not notice him if he remained completely still—that was the one question that rose up in Chet's mind. If a truck had pulled in, he would have heard the rumble of the engine, the hiss of hydraulic brakes. Even a car engine coming up that close would have woken him.

From the woods, Chet thought. *She came from the woods.*

It was ridiculous, of course. Chances were the woman had run out of gas along the highway somewhere and had started walking. But that did not explain her frightened screams.

Now there was only the wind and the low hum of a few cars passing down on the highway. Chet swallowed and found his throat was dry. A voice screamed within him, telling him to keep his head down, to stay out of it. You never knew what was going to be out there in the dark, in the woods.

Get out of here!

Suddenly he was in motion. He sat up, threw the curtain back, and climbed into his seat. Chet scrambled to get the keys out of his pocket, fumbling to force his hand in at that angle because his beer belly got in the way and the denim was frayed and faded and shrunken. The keys jangled as he pulled them out, listening hard for any sound outside the truck that should not have been there.

But he would not look out the window. He dared not peer out through the glass into the shifting shadows until he had turned the key, worked the clutch, and fired the engine up. It roared thunderously, bellowing like some great beast. Chet knew it ought to have comforted him, the power of the machine. And perhaps it would have, if not for the noises he had heard just before the engine caught, the sound of footfalls on pavement and of a soft voice crying out for God or anyone to help.

The engine roared and at last Chet looked out the window to his left, where the sounds had come from. Out there in the darkened lot, by the trees. He saw her then, a dark-haired woman stumbling toward the truck, dark streaks on her face that might have been mascara or dirt or blood, one arm hanging limply at her side.

In that moment Chet Douglas hated himself.

Coward, he thought.

Here was this woman, maybe barely old enough for him to call her that, injured and in trouble. If she came from the woods, she had likely been camping and gotten lost. He had no idea how she had come by her injuries, maybe an angry boyfriend or a pissed-off bear, or possibly just a bad step and a fall down some ravine.

No. Not that last one. Not with the way she whimpered now, and the way her huge eyes gleamed with starlight and terror. She was running away from something, that much was obvious.

And you were gonna take off on her. Coward. What a child, he scolded himself. *Afraid of the dark.* There would be more recriminations later, more guilt, of that he was sure. But that was for later.

Chet killed the engine and reached behind the seat to grab an aluminium baseball bat he kept back there for when things got a little too rowdy on the road. A lot of guys he knew carried guns, but that was dicey business when you travelled interstate nearly every day of your life.

The paint on the bat was faded and the metal scarred, not from parking-lot scraps, but from playing ball with his boys. The metal was cold against his skin and its weight felt good. He hefted the bat, popped the lock on the door, and stepped down out of the truck. Chet sucked in a breath of cold October night air and lifted his chin, stood a bit straighter.

The girl—he could see now that she was no more than sixteen or seventeen—ran right at him, staggering the last few feet.

"Oh God, oh Jesus, thank you," she whispered, breath coming in ragged gasps.

Chet could practically smell the blood on her face and clothes. Her eyes were wild with terror, half blind with it as her gaze darted around at the truck, the darkness, at Chet himself, trying to focus, maybe just to make sense of it all.

"What happened to you, honey?" he asked, voice a tired rasp.

She threw her arms around him and buried her face in his shirt. But the girl did not cry. Her shoulders heaved and her breath came hard and fast and she twitched there in his arms, but she did not cry. Chet held her away from him and stepped by her, brandishing the aluminium bat. He stared out across the darkened lot, into the nighttime shadows of the forest.

"Where is the son of a bitch?" Chet asked, feeling the adrenaline pumping through him now, feeling brave.

Brave, because he wasn't alone in the dark now. It wasn't his own safety that concerned him, but the girl's. And he could be brave for her, if not for himself.

The girl continued to breathe hard, to mutter under her breath, and he wondered if she was in shock or something.

"Come on out!" Chet shouted into the dark, sure now that it must be her husband or boyfriend. "I'll give you a taste of what you did to her!"

The terrified girl began to laugh softly, madly. *Poor thing really has snapped,* Chet thought. He squinted his eyes and thought he saw someone else moving in the trees, in the woods, and he was surprised that the guy had the guts to come out now and face him. Chet might have a few extra pounds on him, but he was a big man, and he had the bat.

"Come on," he muttered to the figure in the woods. "I'll give you a taste."

Then, as Chet watched, the man stepped out of the woods. No, that wasn't right. The man stumbled out. Even in the dark, with only a sliver moon and the stars above, Chet could see that he had been hurt, that his face was ravaged and his clothes hung in strips from his body.

"What the . . ." Chet began.

The man collapsed in a heap on the tar and did not move.

Beside him the girl laughed again, a bit louder now, a sharp edge to it. Chet turned to look at her . . . and the girl began to change. As though it had consumed her from within, a monster tore its way out of her skin, a sleek, slavering thing with sable fur and glistening needle teeth. As if the darkness itself had claws, it reached for him.

Alone again, alone in the dark, Chet had time only to think that all along he had been right about the night and the shadows and the faces at the window.

Then it was upon him.

The baseball bat clanged to the ground, leaving only the whispers of the wind and the low, contented growling of the darkness.

CHAPTER 1

Red and gold neon lights gleamed off puddles left behind in the road by rain showers that had passed through Boston on and off all day long. But it was night now, and the rain had passed. A chill wind swept in off the ocean and weaved its way through the streets, even far away from the harbour. Jack Dwyer could taste the tang of salt on the air, the influence of the sea reaching deep into the city to touch him where he walked side by side with Bill Cantwell on a narrow Chinatown street.

Jack shivered and zipped his scuffed and battered black leather coat. His burly companion had only a light cotton jacket but did not seem to be bothered by the chilly night at all. Not that Jack was surprised. Bill was far more than he seemed. The big, bearded man was the bartender at Bridget's Irish Rose Pub, which twenty-year-old Jack and his older sister, Courtney, owned and managed. Bill was also Courtney's boyfriend.

But he wasn't human.

A delivery truck was parked halfway on the sidewalk up ahead, and they had to walk out into the street to go around it. Jack had no idea what was being delivered to a Chinese corner grocery store at ten o'clock on a Wednesday night, but he figured it was useless trying to figure it out. Though the entire neighbourhood was only a few short blocks, walking through Chinatown was a journey through another world.

It was bordered by other neighbourhoods, by towers that housed some of the best medical research, treatment, and education facilities in the world, but also by what little remained of the sex trade in what had once been Boston's Combat Zone. In truth, it hardly warranted being called a town at all, but Chinatown was a kind of island in the midst of the city, isolated without walls.

Neon signs blazed in the elegant symbols that made up the Chinese language. Jack knew enough from previous visits that most of the people who lived in this tiny community kept all their business to themselves. They owned the shops and bars and restaurants, and it was a matter of pride that they gave nearly all of their trade to Chinese-owned businesses within a three-block radius.

Chinatown was as insular as they could manage, and yet their economy was not as self-supporting as they might wish. The tailors and cobblers, many of the restaurants and bars, even some of the markets and other businesses, relied not merely upon neighbourhood trade, but clientele from beyond Chinatown. And all day long small buses shuttled people from these streets to jobs at Chinese restaurants all over the greater Boston area. The reality was that despite appearances—and many wishes—to the contrary, Chinatown was a part of the city.

Jack knew that. But it did not change the way he felt as he walked beside Bill along that foreign street. There was something wonderfully exotic about the place, a kind of electric current that charged the air with mystery. Young Chinese men and women cruised slowly by in their cars, engines growling low and dangerous. A middle-aged man and a white-haired old woman exchanged pleasantries on a corner, angry voices shouted inside a bar, all in a clipped language that seemed more sounds than words, just as when written it seemed more symbols than letters.

Bars and restaurants lined the street, interrupted by a Laundromat, a video store, and a dozen other small businesses, some of which Jack could only guess at because most of the signs were painted in Chinese characters. Most, but not all. On one of those signs amidst the words he could not read was a single word in English: *Lotus*. Even as he and Bill drew closer to the unremarkable brick front of the building, the door opened and a Caucasian man emerged. He was short, yet powerfully built, and his hair was cropped to a quarter-inch of stubble. Dark glasses wrapped around his eyes, though it was long after dark.

Strange music and unfamiliar odours poured out the

door in the moments before it clicked shut again behind the man. He glanced up once at Jack and Bill, nostrils flaring, and then he turned his back to them and started off in the opposite direction. Bill paused a moment outside the door of the Lotus, as though waiting for the other man to put some more distance between them. Then he glanced at Jack.

"Remember what I said."

Jack nodded once, more than happy to keep quiet and follow his friend's lead. Bill knew this place. He didn't. That was reason enough. Bill nodded in return, then rapped hard on the thick wooden door of the Lotus Club. A moment later there was a *click* and the door pushed in several inches. Jack reached for it, but Bill shot him a cold look and he pulled back just as it swung open.

Within there stood an Asian man so large he dwarfed even Bill. His head was shaved bald, and the image of a tiger was tattooed on the left side of his skull. Beyond him was a stairwell that led down into the cellar club, and it was from there that the odd music thumped. Multicoloured lights strobed the walls.

The huge doorman narrowed his gaze and glanced from Bill to Jack and back again.

"Good evening, Lao. I'm afraid we're a few minutes late," Bill said.

Lao did not take his eyes off Bill again, but he sniffed at the air and his upper lip curled back in distaste. His teeth looked too long, too sharp, and even though Jack had expected that, still he shuddered at the sight.

"You brought a new face, Guillaume," the creature

known as Lao intoned. "Winter's not going to like that."

"Winter owes me, Lao," Bill replied. "Are you going to turn me away from the Lotus? With all the other threats to our kind, would you make me an enemy?"

Lao lifted his chin and took a long, audible breath. Jack watched the two huge men-who-were-not-men, and he felt the rhythm of the music below pounding into his chest, and he inhaled the rich aromas of mint and cinnamon and coffee and so many other things from below. With eyes narrowed, Lao studied him again.

"What is your name?" the doorman demanded.

If he speaks to you, answer immediately and truthfully, Bill had said. *If you lie or you become afraid, he'll smell it on you.*

"Jack Dwyer."

When Lao raised his eyebrows in surprise, the tiger at his temple seemed to crouch as if it were about to strike. A sound came from his chest; a kind of rumble, either of contemplation or anger, Jack could not determine which. Then Lao leaned forward, practically bending over, to stare at him eye to eye.

"You don't look like much, boy," the doorman grunted.

Jack said nothing. He steeled himself, gazed back defiantly, and simply waited.

"You know there are those downstairs who'd like to kill you just to prove you're not as dangerous as the whispers say you are."

This time Jack could not help a tiny flinch, not of fear but of surprise. He had no doubt, any time he was within any real proximity to Prowlers, that they would be happy to kill him. Most of them were savage. So that information was hardly news to him. But the idea that he was considered dangerous, that they whispered about him . . . that he had become some kind of bogey-man to these monsters who lurked in the shadows of the night . . .

Jack found that he liked that. He liked it a lot.

But he did not allow that pleasure to show, did not crack the tiniest smile.

"He wants peace, Lao. Live and let live. Same as you do," Bill explained. "Nobody who comes to the Lotus has anything to fear from Jack or from me. Come on, old friend. We're not here to start any trouble."

A car passed by with pop music turned up loud, somehow out of place here. A short way up the street a girl stepped out from the darkness of a recessed door-way and strode toward the car as it pulled to a stop. She wore a white shirt tied at the waist to bare her belly, and a plaid skirt that would have looked like a school uni-form if it had not been so short. She bent to speak softly to the man in the car and then walked around to climb into the passenger's side.

The distraction caught Jack's attention for mere sec-onds. When he glanced back at Lao, he realized that both the doorman and Bill were staring at him.

"Is he brave or stupid?" Lao asked.

Bill chuckled softly. "A little of both sometimes."

Jack frowned, not liking this turn in the conversation.

"You turned your back on me, boy. I might have had your life just now," Lao told him.

"Not if you wanted to survive the night," Jack replied curtly, remembering too late Bill's admonition to keep silent.

But Lao only smiled and nodded and stepped aside. "Go in, Guillaume. Remember this, though. If there is a mess, you will be the one to clean it up."

"Agreed."

With that, Bill led Jack farther inside. The door closed behind them and Lao locked it with a metallic *clank*. The music grew louder the moment they began to descend the stairs, and as they entered the club the swirl of coloured light seemed to mute and diffuse everything, so that at first Jack could not see well at all. Slowly his eyes began to adjust.

As they moved through the establishment Jack found himself disappointed. Down the centre of the club was a long oval bar that appeared to be constructed entirely of stainless steel. On one side was a small dance floor, upon which several dozen gyrated slowly to techno-punk—or whatever the music was that pumped from the speakers. On the other side, tables and booths where clubgoers sat and drank, perhaps ate something off the traditional Chinese menu.

Jack had expected something else entirely. He had read stories and heard things about some of the wilder clubs in Manhattan, and even a few illegal after-hours things in Boston, where people played bondage games, hurt each other for pleasure, or sat and watched perverse floor shows. He had no idea what he had thought the Lotus would be like, but this was not it.

The clientele was mostly, but not exclusively, Asian. And though there was a kind of grinding, insinuating flavour to the place, as Bill led him around tables and past the bar Jack at first thought that there was nothing really extraordinary about it.

Then his eyes adjusted further and the music seemed to grow louder and the lights blurred into one red haze glittering off the eyes of the clientele in the Lotus Club. As he passed, one by one they sniffed the air and turned to gaze at him. Some of them reacted physically, crouching just slightly as though on guard. Jack felt the hairs on the back of his head prickle, and his breathing slowed. He could practically feel all their eyes on him, all those predators.

And he the prey.

Then he remembered what Lao had said, and he knew that the roles of predator and prey could easily be reversed, and he felt better. Most of the customers in the Lotus were not even people, but Prowlers, members of an ancient race of shape-shifting monsters who could look human, but who would never *be* human. Their numbers were comparatively few now, and the great packs of olden times had dissipated far and wide, hunting the fringes of human society, many Prowlers hunting alone.

But Bill was proof that there were also those who had given up the old ways, whose only interest was surviving the spread of humanity, living peacefully within that society as best they could. Even for those, however, there was an urge to gather. Perhaps there was no pack for them now, not really, but they felt a desire to draw together, to be among their own for a time.

The Lotus Club was the place where they could do precisely that. Jack knew from his friendship with Bill that there were Prowlers who were not savage killers, but he had never imagined there could be so many of them existing beneath the notice of their human counterparts. So many of the Prowlers in the club were Asian that he had to wonder if the Lotus was the only such place in Boston. And what of the other cities in America . . . and around the world? The implications of that line of thought were staggering to him.

Bill led the way to a booth in the rear corner of the club, far from the bar and partially shielded from the swirling lights of the dance floor. A thin black man with a white streak in his hair glanced up at them from the booth as they approached. He clutched a tumbler of whiskey and ice in one hand and rapped the table in time with the music with the other. He wore a dark silk shirt, without any visible adornment on his clothes or body. And yet there was something about him, the way the bartender and waiters looked his way, and the fact that there was no one seated at the adjacent tables, that spoke volumes about the man's power.

At the edge of the booth Bill paused, and Jack followed his lead. They stood there as the thin man studied them, a slim smile on his face.

"Hello, Guillaume."

"Winter," Bill replied.

The Prowler's dark gaze swung toward Jack. "Why do I think you're Jack Dwyer?"

You already know I am, Jack wanted to say. He could sense it. Someone had told Winter he was there, or the man had seen him before somehow, but it was not a guess. Winter *knew* who he was. But this time Jack remembered Bill's admonition and kept silent.

"Sit," Winter told them. Though he gave them an enigmatic smile, the word was not an invitation. The skin at the edges of the man's eyes crinkled slightly with that smile. Winter sat back in the booth, leather sighing as he moved, and he regarded them.

"Thank you for coming," Bill said. "I would not have asked you to look into this if I knew of any other way. It's been nearly two months since Dallas died, and I've tapped all my sources in the underground trying to track Olivia down. She just disappeared, Winter. I couldn't turn to anyone else."

Bill's tone was almost reverent. Jack had never heard him speak that way to anyone before. Though Bill had told Lao that Winter owed him, clearly it seemed he was not about to remind the other Prowler of that debt.

Winter barely acknowledged Bill's words. Instead he focused on Jack, who forced himself not to squirm under the intensity of that scrutiny.

"You really killed Tanzer?"

Tanzer. The leader of a vicious pack that had ranged

up and down the eastern seaboard slaughtering humans with abandon. It had been many months ago now, but the memory was still fresh.

Jack nodded. "Not alone, but yeah, I killed him."

"And you took out the sanctuary up in Vermont?"

Again Jack inclined his head, but more slowly this time, less willing to lay claim to that particular feat.

Winter laughed softly. "I wonder how long your luck is going to hold out, Jack. Jack the Giant-Killer."

The dark-skinned man's eyes were almost mesmerising. Much as he wanted to tear his gaze away, though, Jack would not. A dozen retorts came to mind, but he kept his teeth clamped down on all of them and simply stared back at him expectantly.

At last Winter looked away, turned his focus on Bill.

"Guillaume, I owe you my life," Winter said kindly, almost sadly. "And when I had an opportunity to save your sister's, I failed in that. No matter how far I wander or how many people whisper about me, I will never forget that. You have never called upon me before because you did not want to."

Bill began to protest, but Winter waved his words away.

"I understand. Truly, I do. I walk a line between this underground world and the surviving packs, and yet somehow I stay alive. Somehow." He smiled, and there were a thousand secrets in the lines of his face. "But you should know that you could call upon me forever and my debt would not be paid. Claudia's death is a dark cloud upon my heart, just as it is upon yours."

Winter paused, glanced at Jack, and then looked to Bill again.

"When her mother died and she realised her father was not ever going to behave toward her the way a father should, Olivia stayed for quite some time with your mother's pack in Quebec. In April of last year she simply left without a word. Weeks later she turned up in New York. She made friends in the underground quickly enough, and word from the wild there is that she wanted to make it in the music business. She played clubs, met all the right people, joined that scene.

"Six months ago she disappeared. Whispers in the wild say something went bad with the music thing, but I think that's just a cover."

Bill stared at Winter as though at a loss for words.

Jack wasn't. "Why?" he asked.

Winter shot him a questioning glance.

"I mean, why do you think that?"

The thin Prowler tapped his fingers in time with the music, and when he spoke again, it was to both of them.

"Jasmine," Winter said calmly.

"Shit," Jack whispered. Jasmine had been Tanzer's mate, one of the few survivors from the pack he and his friends had destroyed. He knew that she had had a vendetta against them ever since.

"Jasmine has gathered a new pack in Manhattan," Winter continued. "She hired Dallas to kill both of you and your loved ones. Dallas was concerned for Olivia. Jasmine told him she might be able to help him locate the girl. Maybe that was just blowing smoke, hoping to guarantee his allegiance. But what if it wasn't?"

"Then Jasmine knows where she is," Jack replied. "No disrespect intended, but we knew that already. It isn't like Jasmine's just going to tell us."

At his side Bill shuddered. Jack glanced at his friend and saw that the big man had covered his face with his hands. He ran his fingers through his beard and then turned to Jack.

"You're missing the point. Just like I missed the point. What Winter's saying is that he thinks Jasmine *has* Olivia. Took her on purpose, an insurance against me."

Winter nodded slowly, thoughtfully, fingers still tapping rhythm.

"Either that," he said, "or Jasmine already killed her."

The kitchen at Bridget's Irish Rose Pub closed at ten o'clock, but half an hour later there were still a few tables at which patrons lingered over their meals or simply laughed together and shared drinks, not wanting the night to end. The staff, on the other hand, couldn't wait. They had long since begun to wipe down tables and roll utensils inside clean napkins for the next day, careful all the while to avoid making the remaining customers feel rushed.

Molly Hatcher used a clean rag to polish the brass railings around a corner booth and watched as her friend Kiera Dunphy approached a fortyish couple to ask—for what had to be at least the third time—if there was anything else she could get them. Molly smiled and shook her head. Kiera had a new boyfriend, and it was obvious she wanted to get home to him, but if Courtney saw her hovering around customers like that, Kiera was liable to get an earful.

The bar was still buzzing, though not nearly as packed as it would have been on the weekend, or in midsummer. Nobody had gone so far as to turn the lights up in the restaurant, but by eleven, if any of the tables were still occupied, Courtney would do just that. As it was, the music on the sound system—usually Enya or the Chieftains, something along those lines—had been traded in for an ancient recording by the Allman Brothers Band.

Molly moved to another booth and sprayed the railing that separated it from the next. She polished it enough that she could see a gleaming, twisted funhouse reflection of herself. A long streak, probably from some child's greasy fingers, remained, and she rubbed at it.

"Don't get all crazy, Hatcher," came a familiar voice.

With a soft laugh she turned to find Courtney Dwyer eyeing her curiously. Along with her brother, Jack, Courtney had owned and managed the pub since their mother's death ten years before, and yet despite the stress she lived with day to day, it never seemed to show on her face. Though Courtney was a decade older than she was, Molly thought she would still have looked twenty if not for the lion's-head cane she relied upon to get around.

"Hey, it's your place," Molly said. "I just work here."

"And live here," Courtney corrected. "And always give two hundred percent."

Molly shrugged, sheepish. Though she and the Dwyers had a great relationship—they were closer to her than any blood relations she had—it was unusual for them to dish out straight compliments without a little sarcasm or teasing to go along with them.

Courtney smiled, crinkles forming at the corners of her eyes and on her nose, where a light spray of freckles lent to the illusion of youth.

"The rest of the brass can wait. I need a minute," she said. Then she turned and started off toward the back of the restaurant.

What's this all about? Molly thought. But she picked up her rag and the polish she had been using, and followed. Courtney led the way to a curved booth in the rear corner where the head hostess, Wendy Bartlett, sipped from a glass of soda. As they reached the table, Tim Dunphy pushed through the swinging doors from the kitchen, a dishrag in his hands. He wiped them dry as he approached.

"Hey, boss," he said, running a hand over the stubble on his shaved head. "You wanted to see me?"

Courtney smiled. "Have a seat, Tim. You too, Molly."

They did as they were asked. Molly glanced around the table and saw from the expression on their faces that Wendy and Tim seemed to be just as much in the dark as she was. Courtney was the last to sit, sliding in beside Tim and resting her cane against the table's edge so the metallic eyes of the lion seemed to glare hungrily at them.

Molly tried not to look at it.

There was a moment's pause as Courtney took a breath. Molly let her gaze wander to the colourful tattoos on Tim's arms before she glanced back up at her friend and employer.

"I'm just going to get to it," Courtney announced. She pushed a lock of hair behind her ear and smiled. "No happy preamble, no pep talk about how great all of you are at your jobs and how much Jack and I appreciate the effort you put in here. Which we do. I should have done this one-on-one, but to be honest with you, I don't have a lot of time for protocol these days. So here's the thing. . . ."

Courtney hesitated a second, and Tim jumped right in.

"There some kinda problem?" he asked, eyes narrowed, South Boston accent weighted with concern.

With a mischievous smile, Courtney nodded. "Oh, yeah, Tim. You're all fired. What with you having the kitchen under your tyrannical rule, and Molly and Wendy pretty much running the place without Jack and I having to worry about it, I figured the fastest way to bring this place into bankruptcy was to get rid of you guys. And you know, it's always fun to fire someone who lives under the same roof."

Courtney glanced at Molly and rolled her eyes.

"You got a wicked sarcastic side, Dwyer," Tim drawled.

The boss brightened. "Don't I?"

"So you were telling us how wonderful we are," Molly prodded. "Please continue."

At that, Courtney sat back in the booth as if a great burden had been lifted from her. She settled in comfortably and took them all in with a glance.

"It's no secret that Jack and I have been letting some of the day-to-day stuff fall to others. After everything that's happened, well . . . other things take up our attention sometimes. Bill manages the bar, and he's got a couple of responsible guys working with him. But with us not spending every single waking hour on the floor of the restaurant these days, we've decided to promote Molly to manager."

Molly blinked and stared at her, mouth open in surprise. Neither Courtney nor Jack had breathed a word about this to her, and repercussions swirled in her mind. She had been working as a waitress at Bridget's for six months. Not even. There would undoubtedly be people who thought she did not deserve the promotion, who wondered if she had gotten it by merit or simply because she was so friendly with the owners. Beyond that, there was her own self-doubt. *Do I even have the knowledge and the confidence to manage this place?*

"Hey! Way to go, Hatcher," Tim said. He leaned forward and patted her hand with a conspiratorial wink. "I guess I'll have to watch the flirting now, huh? Don't want to get in trouble."

Courtney's expression was grave. "As you all know, it's not often you'll find a time when both Jack and I are off the premises, but it does happen. As we get involved in other things it's also possible that there may be times when neither Molly nor Bill is here. Beyond that, it'd just be nice to know that when we're not on the clock, there are people riding herd on those shifts who can answer questions and make decisions without us. That in mind, I'd like to offer both of you, Tim and Wendy, positions as assistant managers. Not that you haven't been pretty much doing that job all along, but we thought it would carry more weight if it was official."

Tim seemed genuinely stunned. Molly knew him well enough that she understood. He was a Southie boy, born and bred, a tough Irish guy from a neighbourhood that churned them out by the dozens. There was more to Tim than that, evidenced by the way the kitchen staff looked up to him, but he had never graduated from high school and thought of himself, quite simply, as a cook. It was nice to see the light in his eyes when it really sank in what Courtney was asking.

"No argument here, boss," he said. "I appreciate it."

Wendy was not so quick to respond. A line of concern had appeared on her forehead. With her new short haircut she looked severe, almost angry. Then she smiled, her face softening.

"Thanks, Courtney. It's nice to be asked. I just . . . I don't want to be difficult, but what does that mean exactly? You know, with pay and hours and all that?"

Courtney laughed. "Straight up? It means more hours on some shifts. If, by rare chance, none of us is on duty, I'd expect you to stay until closing. Tim already has a key and all the security system info. I'll get one for you, Wendy, but this isn't going to happen very often. On the other hand, when you're on duty, like I said, I'd expect you to handle issues that arise, particularly between employees, disputes with customers, urgent orders that need to be filled. Whatever it might be.

"There *would* be more money, but not nearly as much as I wish I could give you," she finished. Then she leaned forward and folded her hands on the table, studying Wendy. "What do you think?"

Wendy took a breath, let it out, and then shrugged, a sweet sort of smile on her face. "I'm in. And thanks."

Abruptly, almost as though the business at hand had been forgotten the moment Wendy said yes, Courtney grabbed her cane and stood up. Then she turned to face them again.

"It's a relief to know that we can count on you. I'll talk to you all individually tomorrow, work out the details on your pay increases. I'm going to post an announcement on the bulletin board tomorrow morning, but consider the promotions effective immediately."

Though she claimed to be relieved, all the lightness and good humour went out of Courtney then.

"Molly," she said. "Come upstairs with me. I want to go over some things with you."

With that, she turned and hobbled away on her cane, and Molly had a moment to think how much older Courtney looked when she couldn't see the light in the other woman's eyes. When all she saw was her handicap. Molly congratulated Tim and Wendy, then slid from the booth and started across the restaurant after Courtney. Together they went up the staircase that led to the apartment above the pub. As Courtney worked the key in the lock Molly nudged her.

"You could have warned me."

A flicker of a smile whispered across Courtney's face. "What would have been the fun of that?"

Then the key clicked in the lock and Courtney pushed it open. It was dark inside—Jack was still out with Bill—and the older woman turned the lights on while Molly locked the door behind them. Both of them stood very still a moment, listening to the sounds of the apartment, wary from painful experience of anything that might be out of place. After a moment they let out a collective breath, and Courtney led the way into her bedroom.

If not for the bed, the room would have passed for an office. Courtney had always lived simply, but in the months since Molly moved in with the Dwyers, what little personal flair had gone into decorating the small space had been overrun by bulletin boards tacked with newspaper articles and computer printouts. When there was no more room there, Courtney had begun tacking them to the bare walls.

The computer was on.

"What is it?" Molly asked as the tiny twist of unease that had been woken in her downstairs now grew into a dark, dreadful weight in her gut.

Courtney rested her cane against the wall and slid into the desk chair. She stared at the computer screen and hesitated a moment. Then she turned to face Molly again.

"Are we serious about this?"

"About what?"

"See, if we were serious, you wouldn't even ask me that," Courtney replied sharply.

Molly sighed. "All right. I'm sorry. Yes, we're serious. I just . . . it isn't exactly pleasant."

"No. No, it isn't." Courtney slid the computer's mouse across a blue pad and then clicked it, and a moment later the printer hummed to life on the desk beside the monitor. She stood up and went to the nearest bulletin board, limping badly without the cane. With her weight against the desk, she pointed to an article pinned to the board.

"Doug and Arlene Rausch. On the way back from eloping in Niagara Falls. Both in their fifties, both on their second marriage, the elopement wasn't a secret from anyone. They have grown children who thought it was sweet, romantic, all that sappy crap. But Doug and Arlene never got home. Last they were seen was in a bookstore just off Route Eighty-seven, a couple of hours south of the falls, where Doug used his credit card."

Molly frowned. "That could be anything."

"True." Courtney pointed to another piece of paper. "Jared Wilkes, fifteen-year-old runaway, found in the woods at a rest stop on Route Eighty-seven. All torn up. You don't need the details, but they'd sound familiar."

"All right," Molly said. "We know the signs. It was

probably a Prowler, but sad to say, one killing doesn't give us enough to go on. It could be a drifter or an isolated incident. No way to track the monster just on that."

When Courtney smiled, Molly shivered. The older woman used the wall to steady herself and then indicated a magazine article that looked to have been pulled from *Time* or *Newsweek*. There were several pages taped to the wall. The piece was about the safety record of the long-distance trucking industry.

"What am I missing?" Molly asked.

"Truckers fall asleep at the wheel enough to make people concerned, but not as often as the media wants us to think. Still, it happens. They crash, people die, shipments are destroyed. But there's a thirty-mile stretch of Route Eighty-seven in upstate New York that completely throws off the statistical curve. Incidences of trucking accidents are more than double the national average. But here's the kicker. Percentage of fatalities resulting from those accidents? Eighty-seven. Eighty-seven percent, Molly. Many of the bodies burned or crushed beyond recognition. What are the chances of that?"

The dread had spread all through Molly now. Images of mauled bodies and trucks ablaze with fire flashed through her mind.

Courtney sat back at the computer and pulled the new article out of the printer. She handed it to Molly.

"Chester Aaron Douglas. Independent trucker. Apparently crashed his rig on a hard curve south of

Albany. Dumped it in a ditch and the engine caught fire. Two bodies found inside, the authorities assume one of them was a hitchhiker. But Douglas's ex insists he would never have picked up a hitchhiker. And guess what else? His body was thrown from the cab during the crash. He didn't burn. His body was torn up, mauled, mutilated. New York State investigators believe it was bears that got to the body after the crash."

Molly stared at the piece of paper in her hand, but the words all blurred. A prickle of heat scurried like spiders' legs across the back of her neck.

"I guess Jack and I are going to New York."

CHAPTER 2

Jasmine ran along the paved paths of Central Park, the steel-and-glass towers of Manhattan dark silhouettes in the distance. The breeze carried the scent of decay, as the autumn leaves fell and plants withered. This time of year, when the shadows seemed most ominous, was joyous for Prowlers. So many humans carried the scent of fear on them. Jasmine's blood sang as she ran along the curving path, still wearing a human facade, a masque of weakness. A pretty one it was, though, she knew, with her milk-chocolate skin and copper-red hair, her eyes bright Halloween orange, mistaken every day for contact lenses.

She raised her face to the stars and breathed in the scents of the wild. Central Park was a most cherished gift to her, a kind of paradise. It was a bit of nature torn out of the heart of the most extraordinary urban forest in the world. An undercurrent of danger ran through the entire city, so that Manhattan was a sort of wilderness unto itself. Now that she had spent time here, the idea of building her new pack anywhere else seemed ridiculous.

Off in the bushes she caught the scent of a raccoon, fat and lazy, nature's little thief. Her stomach rumbled, but Jasmine would never taint herself with such simple, easy prey. She wanted to see terror in the eyes of her prey, wanted to hear it scream. The only animal that would satisfy her walked on two legs, not four.

Once upon a time, the park would have been empty this late at night, the province of vagrants and gang-bangers. But New York City had changed. Central Park was cleaner, the paths lined with lampposts, uniformed police strolling about. In the early evening it was common to see lovers walking hand in hand, bicyclists, and Rollerbladers. Slowly the vendors moved their hot dog and pretzel carts out of the green, heading home. The spectre of old violence and the shadow of the unknown remained, however, and as the hour grew later, fewer and fewer people could be found in the park.

But Jasmine was not alone there, even this late.

A homeless man with a winter hat and a scruffy beard lay on a bench with his hands beneath his head, surprisingly alert, staring up through tree branches at the stars. Jasmine bristled as she passed him, and her fingers curled into talons. But as prey, vagrants were less interesting and even less of a challenge than fat-bellied raccoons.

The path curved ahead and Jasmine ran faster, careful not to move *too* fast. Inhumanly fast. Laughter split the night, and she rounded the bend to see a quintet of casually dressed young people, three men and two women. The air was rich with their aromas, and Jasmine judged them instantly as college students down from Columbia or up from NYU, probably cutting through the park to get to a more convenient subway line.

Their laughter stopped when they saw her, and all of them glanced at her as she ran by. Soon, though, she had left them far behind. Moments later her eyes narrowed as she noticed a dark silhouette ahead of her on the path, a figure approaching in the shadows between pools of lamplight. Jasmine slowed only a bit, but then he stepped into the light, and she saw the gleaming badge of the policeman.

"Excuse me, miss," he said. "Do you really think you ought to be out here by yourself this late at night?"

Jasmine came to a stop just a few feet away and flashed him a coquettish smile. "Do you think I have something to be afraid of, Officer?" she asked.

The policeman looked up at her from beneath the brim of his hat, expression grimly serious. "You never know what kind of animals might be lurking about, miss."

"Ah, but that's what makes life interesting," Jasmine purred. She crossed the space separating them in one long, graceful stride. "The uniform is intriguing, Alec. Makes me want to tear the clothes right off you."

Alec growled softly and pulled her into his arms.

Jasmine folded into his embrace, relishing the way they fit, and wrapped one leg around behind him as though she might climb right up onto him. With a small, throaty laugh Alec removed his cap and slipped it onto her head.

"Don't do that," he whispered, punctuating his words with soft kisses on her forehead, her slightly parted lips, her throat. "I took all the trouble getting it off him without ripping it."

Jasmine sniffed the air, then touched the collar of the police uniform her lover wore. It was damp and sticky with fresh blood.

"This won't wash," she warned him.

"So I'll burn it," he replied, hands caressing her with obvious need. "Bad girl, running on ahead like that. Had to sprint through the bushes to get ahead of you."

"I like to keep you in pursuit," she confessed, gazing into his gleaming eyes. "It never hurts to remind you who leads this pack. Now, come on, I have a surprise for you."

With that, she darted forward and gently nipped his nose with her teeth, then turned from the path and sprinted across the green lawn. The land sloped gently upward there to a copse of trees, and Jasmine raced for it with abandon now, no longer worrying that she might be observed. She had to let the wild out. The heat rose in her and she felt herself begin to change. As she reached the seclusion of the trees her false flesh rippled and then tore away to be replaced by sleek copper fur. With a shake of her head she felt the sweet pain of her jaw distending, her face elongating into a snout. Teeth sprouted in long rows.

At the peak of the small hill she crouched, concealed from the rest of the park by trees. Her heart beat a new rhythm now, an ancient and primitive tempo like the cadence of paws rushing across hard-packed earth.

Excited, aroused, she turned to find Alec already at her side. His fur was sable black and thick. They sniffed and nipped at each other, and her long talons traced lines on his back.

"This is what you wanted to show me?" he asked, his voice the roll of distant thunder. "Not that I'm complaining."

"No," she said bluntly. "Listen. Don't you hear them? Inhale. Don't you smell them?"

His pointed ears twitched and Alec cocked his head. A moment later a light chuffing noise came from his throat; the laughter of a Prowler. Together they crept over the other side of the hill and down through the trees, finding themselves on an outcropping overlooking a wide paved road. A road that wound its way through Central Park.

It was quiet there, save for the *trip-trop* clack of hooves upon the asphalt as a tired horse drew a small carriage through the park. A driver sat at the front, clucking his tongue affectionately to urge the animal forward. In the back were a pair of young lovers who clung to each other beneath a blanket and nuzzled faces. From the look of them, they had time and money to burn.

"Oh, how you spoil me," Alec growled.

Jasmine ran her tongue across her needle teeth.

The horse began to hesitate as the carriage drew nearer, but the driver urged her on with soft entreaties. Jasmine crouched on the edge of the outcropping and sniffed the air for evidence of any other humans. Her fur bristled with anticipation. Alec began to move forward, but she glared at him and bared her fangs, and he shrank back.

There was love, and then there was instinct. She was Alpha, and Alec would heel to her commands or Jasmine would tear out his throat. When she saw that he was appropriately cowed, she glanced down at the carriage again.

Once more the beast of burden shied, its hooves clacking on the road as it tried to pull back, to turn. Again the driver kept rein over it, not trusting the animal's instincts. Humans had been part of the wild at the dawn of time, but nearly all of them had forgotten how to listen to the urgings that whispered at the back of their mind; the ancient knowledge they still retained was useless to them.

The lovers in the back of the carriage giggled like schoolchildren and kissed. Jasmine lunged from the outcropping, out over the road. Her claws came down, glittering in the starlight.

The horse neighed loudly in alarm, a scream all its own. Jasmine had already decided that it would be the only survivor.

◆◆◆

PROWLeRS

Saturday morning arrived with a cold northeast wind and a sky the crystalline blue of new snow at dawn. Winter was still a long way off, of course, but the air whispered its imminence and the night had left an early frost upon the city. Jack had been able to see his breath when he went to the fish market that morning, but now the hint of winter had abated, the wind had subsided, and the sun had begun to warm the brittle grass underfoot.

Allman's Farm was in Ipswich, a rural town forty minutes or so north of Boston, depending upon who was driving. The farm and orchards sprawled over a broad hillside, the acreage impressive enough that many of the families and couples who visited rode up and down the hill in hay-filled carts drawn by bellowing tractors. Earlier in the year the attraction would have been the apple trees, and before that the rows of corn. But this was October, and the wicked promise of Halloween lay ahead. On this beautiful fall weekend the lure was pumpkins.

Yet the farm had a great deal more to offer than its enormous pumpkin patch. There were pumpkin-carving classes and contests, all sorts of decorative gourds and bunches of Indian corn, and a small petting zoo. At the restored early-nineteenth-century barn there was a bakery, from which the most delicious odours drifted into combat with the animal smell of the farm. Apple and pumpkin pies, fresh muffins, cinnamon-coated cider doughnuts, and other homemade pastries were accompanied by fragrant coffees and hot apple cider.

Within the barn itself was a gift and crafts shop loaded with country knickknacks and special Halloween items.

But what drew Jack were the horses.

He and Molly had been to Allman's Farm on a high school outing for the junior and senior classes. During that visit the only thing he really wanted to do was ride one of the horses at the stable on the premises. Allman's offered guided horseback rides through the trails in the woods back behind the property, even down to the Ipswich River. But that had not been part of the Catholic school's idea of a field trip. Jack had always wanted to come back but never had a chance. He enjoyed reading when he had time for it, and his tastes ran mostly to biographies and Westerns.

Westerns. He knew that it was perhaps a bit childish, but the idea of the Western hero on horseback appealed to him greatly. And yet he had never ridden.

Now he leaned against the corral fence and gazed admiringly at the chestnut mare grazing there. Slowly he turned to smile at Molly. She stood half a dozen feet back from the fence, dressed in a burgundy sweater and blue jeans. Though her emerald eyes were bright, she had a wary look on her face as she tossed her unruly red hair out of her face and waved a finger at him.

"I am not getting up on the back of that horse."

Jack shrugged. "All right," he said. Then he pointed at a small pen nearby where children were being walked around in circles on the back of a pony. "What about that one?"

Her lips pressed together in a tight line as she tried

not to smile, and she crossed her arms and gazed at him defiantly. Jack went to her, gazed down into those eyes, and pushed a single errant strand of hair away from her face. He lifted her chin and bent down close to her until their mouths were scant inches apart. Molly's eyes closed and he heard her breath catch.

"You owe me, you devious wench," he whispered.

With a cry that was half laugh and half indignation she shoved him away. Jack reached for her, pulled her closer to him again, even though she struggled half-heartedly to be free, and though she baulked as he tried to kiss her for real, it was only a moment before she leaned into him and he pressed his lips to hers, felt the warmth of her breath in his mouth, and once again he was overwhelmed by her, as he was nearly every day.

Their relationship was complicated, and even that word was insufficient to describe the intricately tangled web of emotions that entrapped them. Half a year before, the Prowlers had killed Molly's boyfriend, Artie. Artie had been Jack's best friend. It would have been difficult enough for them to contend with the fondness and developing intimacy between them, but there was so much more to it than that.

Jack saw ghosts. He spoke to the lost souls of the dead. That included Artie. And though it had been nearly two months since the last time he had seen the ghost of the third member of this strange love triangle, and Artie himself wanted them to be together, he still haunted them.

Then there was Eden Hirsch, a rich girl from

Winchester who believed she had been reincarnated dozens of times throughout history, and who visited the spirit world in her dreams. She had helped them out in the past and had made it clear, in no uncertain terms, that she would like to get to know Jack better. Though he was very attracted to her, and it was cathartic for him to be able to talk to someone else who had contact with the lost souls of the dead, Jack did not feel for Eden the way he did about Molly.

Complicated.

But they were dealing with it.

Slowly, in the past handful of weeks, they had begun to spend more time together outside the pub. Dates. Real, actual boy-and-girl dates, sweet and romantic; the kind of thing Jack had never really made the time for in the past. There had been a great deal of kissing. Long, tender, almost ridiculously earnest kissing, and very little else. Jack and Molly both wanted to take things slow, to take their time. Particularly in moments like this, with her in his arms, curled up against him, lips brushing his, lingering, he did not mind in the least.

Her fingers twined in his, and she rested her head against his chest.

Then she gave him a hard shove, and he toppled onto his butt on the brittle grass. Molly stood over him with her hands on her hips.

"I am not riding a horse."

Jack laughed and stood, shaking his head. It was his turn now to wag an admonishing finger at her. "Listen, you. We spent more than half an hour looking at baskets and scarecrows and all that arty craft stuff in the barn back there, and I didn't say a word. That, sweetheart, is my idea of hell. Now you're going to tell me that you can't spend an equal amount of time riding a big, stupid, harmless animal at a walking pace with a guide making sure you don't get lost or go too fast?"

The chestnut mare whinnied as though taking offence at Jack's words. Molly only stood and stared at him in contemplation for a long moment as a family of five trundled by with a wagonload of pumpkins.

"You called me 'sweetheart,'" she said at last.

Jack frowned. "So?"

"It's so . . . Humphrey Bogart. So old-fashioned." Molly raised her eyebrows suggestively. "I think it's kinda sweet."

It was a standoff then, the two of them staring at each other. The pleasure of her company, the laughter in Jack's heart, were things Jack cherished, yet as the seconds ticked by he struggled in vain to keep them from being eclipsed by other concerns. They both had to work that night. Then, in the morning, they would be leaving for upstate New York to search for answers in a rash of mysterious deaths, to search for Prowlers.

Perhaps Molly saw a flicker of dread in his features, or perhaps, he thought, her own mind was travelling down the same road and she was willing to do anything to avoid thinking about it for a few hours longer. Whatever it was, she narrowed her eyes and studied him.

"We are going to buy a ton of pumpkins for the pub."

"I don't know about a *ton*," Jack countered. "How would we get them all back?"

"And there *will* be more cider doughnuts for Molly before we leave."

Jack smiled. "Are there fewer calories involved if Molly speaks about her appetite for doughnuts in the third person?"

She hit him, feigning a look of shock.

"Yes, yes, hoards of pumpkins and enough cider doughnuts for Molly," Jack said quickly, backing away with his hands in the air.

She stared at him a moment longer. Then Molly shrugged. "All right. Let's ride."

"No fair. I've always wanted to say that."

Courtney felt like a different person whenever she sat down in front of her computer. As long as there were no monsters about, the rest of her life was pretty predictable, and it all revolved around the pub. Not that she minded—Bridget's meant everything to her. But in her daily life people saw her as the boss, or the woman with the cane. A lot of men, despite what they said, had a hard time seeing past that length of oak.

Not that she had been all that concerned with what men thought since she and Bill had become involved. Still, she could not deny that for once it would be nice to be admired by a guy who didn't notice the cane first.

The computer, though . . . that was an entirely different story. The Internet had changed life so fast, in so many ways, that she found it difficult now to remember what it had been like *before*. Online shopping, airline tickets, news, rumors, a chat room for anything and everything, no matter how eccentric or perverse.

Which accounts for the perverts, she thought. For no matter what the topic was, there were always those men who took the opportunity to try to hit on her, some woman they knew nothing about who was just a name on a computer screen. Guys were so very strange.

In the past few months Courtney had spent more and more time surfing the Web for news and rumours about the Prowlers. Just like everything else online, the majority of what she found was useless, bits of myth and local legend, stories passed down that were likely no more true than classic campfire tales like "The Hook" or the one about alligators in the sewer.

A chill went through her as she stared at the screen. On the other hand, given what she knew about Prowlers, Courtney had begun to believe that many of the stories she read about them, even the most far-fetched, likely had some basis in reality. It made her wonder whether that was true of so many other urban myths as well.

"Don't get all freaky, Dwyer," she chided herself. Her life was freaky enough as it was.

Anytime she chatted online, or posted on a message board, it created a stir of strange emotions in her. There was a kind of anxiety that came from having seen too many bad movies and television series about people who were stalked or otherwise tormented by strangers who discovered vital information about them via computer. Not to mention the barrage of E-mail warnings about viruses that could cripple her computer and destroy her files. Though she spent a lot of time online now, she was nowhere near savvy enough to understand what was possible and what wasn't.

At the same time, the anonymity of it intrigued her, the idea that she did not have to behave or speak the way people who knew her in real life expected her to. *Probably why so many people act bizarre out here,* she thought. Courtney had never been to college, but she had heard stories of old friends changing completely during their freshman year. That sort of thing was possible when you were put into a situation without any expectations.

So Courtney was someone else: Prowlergrrl. When she thought of it independent of the online world, it seemed silly, almost embarrassing. But online, it got results. It was one thing to use search engines to find reports of mutilation murders, or where police suspected the involvement of animals, and to track down rumours about the Prowlers themselves. Another thing entirely to actually *speak* to people online. Especially when so many of those she contacted in her research were odd at best, and complete lunatics at worst.

Considering the subject matter, she was not at all surprised.

Wildside was different, though. Courtney had never met him in person, nor had she been able to establish any personal information about him, save that his real first name was Gregg and he lived somewhere in Alaska. In her journeys across the Internet, Courtney had not found a single source of information more reliable than Wildside's Web site, *undertheskin.com* When she stumbled across it in early September, it made her feel foolish to compare her meagre efforts with what had obviously been years of work on his part.

From the things she read on his site, she was certain Wildside had encountered Prowlers personally and lived to tell about it. Most of the posts on his message board were ridiculous, but from time to time there were those that sounded real, as if they might have come from witnesses, or even from Prowlers. The site reported sightings, suspicious disappearances, and deaths, and even outed public figures suspected of being Prowlers, including Senator Vaughn McKeckern of Illinois.

According to Wildside, he had received a number of death threats in connection with the site. That was how he knew for certain he was on the right path. But it was still up and running.

What had chilled Courtney was to discover that Under the Skin had rumour reports about the things Jack and Molly had done in Boston and Vermont, though thankfully there were no names attached. There was no way she was going to tell Wildside who Prowlergrrl really was, but she had told him enough that he believed she had first-hand experience.

Enough that he was willing to share information. And that was key.

Now she sat at the computer and stared at the

Instant Message window in which she was currently conversing with Wildside.

"I can't believe I missed all this Route 87 stuff," he typed.

"Neither can I. You're supposed to be the expert. :)"

"Nobody's an expert on this stuff."

Courtney swallowed and found that her throat was dry. She really knew nothing about this man—if he even was a man—but he was too valuable a resource not to pursue it further.

"I could use some help," she typed. *"Some friends of mine are going to look into it. Now that we've pinpointed this as a hot zone or whatever, could you see what else you can find out? It may be that there are suspects out there, or prime locations to start looking, that I haven't been able to figure out yet."*

There was a pause before Wildside replied.

"Wait. You mean your friends are GOING there?"

Courtney took a breath. Then typed: *"Yes. They've done this sort of thing before."*

"Then I won't try telling you how crazy that is. Look, I can do whatever you need. I'll get on it now. If it comes to it, I can access satellite images of every square block of the lower forty-eight. All right, kinda exaggerating, but if I can help, you just have to ask."

A smile stole across Courtney's features and she sat up a little straighter. *"You're something else."*

"No, trust me, I'm not. I'm all human."

"LOL. That's NOT what I meant, Wildside."

"Promise me one thing?" he wrote. *"When they come back, you'll tell me about it?"*

Courtney stiffened, concerned for all their privacy, for their lives. Then she relaxed. It was a reasonable request, and she could easily do that without giving too much away.

"I will."

"And think about visiting me in Alaska?"

"Men," Courtney muttered to herself. Then she typed: *"I told you I'm involved with someone."*

"Bring him," Wildside replied.

She smiled at that. *"Somehow I don't think you two would get along."*

They said their good-byes, and she shut down the computer. There were four cellular phones on the desk, and Courtney snatched one up and clipped it to her belt. All four were programmed with the other three numbers, and only those numbers. From now on, any time she and the people she loved were going to get involved with these animals, she was going to insist they each carry one of these phones and use them only for emergencies.

The phone felt heavy on her hip as she grabbed her cane and headed out of her room, then down the stairs into the restaurant. The phone weighed only a few ounces, but she knew that it would only ever ring if someone was in trouble, in danger. That was a burden that had nothing to do with physical weight.

Bill had been on autopilot ever since Wednesday night. Though he would not allow himself to believe that Olivia was dead, he was certain that his niece was in trouble. The beast in his heart wanted to lash out, to rip and tear, to draw blood and force answers along with pleas for life. In the garage beneath his apartment building he had an old Harley that practically screamed out to him. He could get on it, ride down to New York, hit the underground, and just start beating down doors and cracking heads until someone put him onto Jasmine or Olivia.

But he could not do that. He would alienate the underground, possibly get himself arrested, even get Olivia killed. Winter had prevailed upon his common sense. There was a better way to go about it, quieter, more diplomatic, and Winter had offered his help. Despite the primal urges within him to lash out, Bill had agreed. Yet with each hour that passed with no word from Winter, the tension grew within him, the predatory urges almost too powerful to combat.

A day and a half had passed with no word, and Bill spent that time dishing out beer and cocktails to customers he barely saw. He barked responses to other staff members. Only with Courtney was he calm. Her presence did not soothe the ferocity of his emotion and instincts, but seeing her brought him focus.

The Friday lunch crowd had thickened, and with Courtney upstairs, Bill had once more become sullen, almost surly. As he served pints of Samuel Adams to a pair of men talking technology at the bar, a third—a guy in a dark suit with close-cropped hair, a tan in October, and arrogance even in his posture—raised a finger and frowned.

"Excuse me!" the guy said loudly, as though offended that Bill had not been there to serve him within seconds of his bellying up to the bar.

The scent of him, the way he swaggered without even having to move, just set Bill off. He clacked the other customers' beers on the counter and stalked down the bar at the newcomer. Bill bared his teeth, a growl starting up from his throat that had been building in his chest since Wednesday night.

"Patience is a virtue, my friend," he snarled.

Most people would have sensed it right off, the threat of violence, the warning of danger that Bill knew must be coming off him in waves. Not this moron. He stood a little taller, righteous and offended. "Do you have some kind of problem?"

Bill grinned. There was nothing friendly or amusing about it. "I don't like your tone."

The guy actually snickered. "I don't much care if you like my tone. Now, what I'd like is a Crown Royal on the rocks. And if you have a problem, why don't you take it up with your employer, before I do."

Bill narrowed his eyes. Though he had spent years containing the beast, he could feel it straining to be free, the fur threatening to tear through his skin. His upper lip quivered. He was an eye blink away from tearing the smarmy little man's face off.

Then he caught the scent.

Furrowed his brow.

Lao.

People in the pub turned to stare at the huge Asian

as he walked through the front door and then across to the bar. But they stared because of his size and the tiger tattooed on the side of his bald head, not because they knew what he truly was. Lao stepped up to an empty stool but did not sit, merely stood behind it, waiting patiently, silently.

Bill focused again on the arrogant fool in front of him. He seemed to have faltered some when he realized he no longer had the bartender's full attention.

"Go away," Bill told him softly.

The guy still didn't understand that he was tempting fate. "You know what? I think, instead, I'll go talk to the manager."

"You do that." Bill spotted Courtney coming down the stairs from the apartment, and he pointed her out to the guy. "See that woman on the stairs? That's her. Go on. See if she'll fire me to keep you happy."

At last the guy looked unsettled. Bill's dismissal had thrown him off. He glanced over at Courtney and clearly was about to say something more, but Bill was done with him. He left the guy standing there and moved down to speak to Lao.

None of the humans would notice, or if they did, it would be nothing they could put words to, but the air in the pub was now charged with a kind of dark electricity. These two beasts, two old hunters, had never been friends, nor even really friendly. They were wary of each other, and yet the underground—and their acquaintance with Winter—made them unlikely allies. Lao seemed incredibly out of place to Bill, almost surreal as he stood there in the midst of middle-class tourists and local businessmen.

"Winter sent you?" Bill asked.

Lao nodded. "He has been unable to find any further information about your niece's whereabouts. As such, he has asked me to accompany you to New York and to introduce you to people there who might be able to aid you."

With a small chuckle Bill scratched at his beard and studied the other Prowler. "I hadn't expected to have company. You're sure a phone call wouldn't do for introductions?"

The throat of the tiger on Lao's skull—where the tattoo covered his temple—pulsed with his heartbeat, as if the cat were about to roar.

"Winter has asked me to accompany you. There are places you will not be welcome otherwise." Lao stared a moment longer, then nodded once. "We depart at midnight from the Lotus. You will drive."

Bill ground his teeth together. Here was another guy whose tone he did not like. But his mind went to Olivia, his only living family, and he knew that putting up with Lao was a small price to pay if he could get her back.

He nodded in return. "I'll see you there."

As Lao left the pub, once again drawing the stares of the patrons inside Bridget's, Courtney walked over. She looked more than a little confused as she glanced from Bill to the retreating form of Lao.

"You met my new friend?" the bartender asked her.

Courtney slid onto a stool. "The guy you wouldn't

serve? Yes. I just gave him lunch on the house. You want to tell me what that was about?"

Bill sighed, rested his hands on the countertop. "Sorry. This is your place, and I shouldn't take advantage of how we feel about each other like that. He was a jerk, and he caught me at a very bad time."

With a soft smile she reached out and covered his huge hands with her small, delicate ones. "I didn't like him either. But I don't want him spreading the word. On the other hand, you're my main concern. What's the story with that guy you were just talking to?"

"That's Lao. He's . . . well, he's supposed to help me find Olivia. With Jack and Molly leaving in the morning, I know the timing couldn't be worse, but I have to find her, or at least find out what happened to her."

Courtney reached up to stroke his face. "When do you have to leave?"

"Tonight at midnight."

He saw the sadness, the shadow of hurt that fell across her face, but then it was gone. "I guess we're going to find out if my new assistant managers can do the job."

"I shouldn't be gone more than a few days."

"Take as long as you need. I hope you find her. I hope she's all right," Courtney said. "But whatever you find down there, you come back to me when you're done, Bill Cantwell.

"You come home."

CHAPTER 3

Despite the half dozen or so Dumpsters in the alley that ran behind Bridget's and the other businesses on Nelson Street, the dark, narrow little passage never really smelled like garbage. Or, at least, it never *reeked* like Jack always imagined it should, given the sheer volume of trash back there, including the refuse from hundreds of meals a day. There was just something about the set of the buildings, these old, half-crumbling edifices that were laid stone upon stone when Boston was young. Somehow the angle of the alley caught the wind off the harbour perfectly, and the breeze caught most of the smells and whisked them away.

Yet on that fine Saturday morning, with the sky a rich shade of blue that seemed to exist only in October in New England, Jack stood outside the open door of his Jeep and he could clearly smell wood burning in a fireplace somewhere nearby. It seemed odd to him, almost impossible, that the wind could take the bitter, rotten smell of garbage and leave behind that warm, comforting fireside aroma. A tiny little miracle, in a way.

Why isn't life ever really like that? he thought. *Sweeping away the ugly, nasty stuff and leaving behind just the good?*

But that was a bit of fantasy, and he knew it. There were good things to be had, perfect, beautiful things, in his life. Jack understood that life was a balance, that light and darkness could only exist together. What he had, the people in his life he loved so much, were things worth braving the darkness for. So he would take the evil with the good. He would fight the monsters.

Even on a beautiful autumn day with the sun shining and the breeze blowing in all the scents of fall. Even then. Because that was the price he had to pay.

Molly sat inside the battered old Jeep with a map spread out on her lap. In the back was a wooden trunk with a heavy iron lock on it. The key to the lock was hidden inside the Jeep on the off chance that they might be pulled over for speeding. A quick search of the vehicle would reveal nothing out of the ordinary, but police would have to break the lock on the trunk to open it, and Jack figured most of them wouldn't go that far unless he and Molly gave them a reason, which he didn't plan on doing.

"I hate leaving you here alone," he said, running a hand through his spiky, close-cropped brown hair.

Courtney put her weight on her cane and stood a bit taller as she scowled at him. "I can take care of myself, little brother."

Their eyes met in silent communication. Both of them understood the reason for Jack's reluctance. It was not simply that he would be leaving her behind, or leaving the pub in her hands. There had been a great many conversations about such things over the previous months as the four of them had determined that they were going to pursue this crusade against the Prowlers in earnest. The staff at Bridget's could handle the additional responsibility and workload. Courtney would manage.

It wasn't about that. The wordless understanding between them now had to do with Bill. Courtney's eyes revealed the truth: She was terrified for him. A sudden departure the night before, a midnight rendezvous with Lao, and a trip down to Manhattan to try to find Olivia, knowing that Jasmine was lurking about somewhere, starting up a brand-new pack there. None of it boded well. They had no way of knowing when Bill would be back.

But he had promised to call her every morning, and had already done so today. That was something, at least. Jack gazed at his sister, saw the fear and uncertainty there, and he felt it within himself as well.

"He'll come back," Jack told her.

"Today?" Courtney asked.

Jack smiled. "Probably not today."

"Look, you take care of yourself. Check in regularly," she said as she stepped forward and gave him a quick hug. "But don't use that cell phone number unless it's an emergency, right?"

"Got it. You keep an eye out too."

Courtney glanced around as though someone might be listening, but they were alone in the alley. "I'm not all that concerned. I know we can never be sure, and we've had enough of them try to get at us here, but Bill told me he asked a couple of his friends to play guardian angel."

Jack frowned. "Friends" meant Prowlers. It was difficult enough for him, now that he understood what the underground was, to accept that there were dozens, maybe hundreds, of Prowlers in Boston that he had not known about. But the idea that some of them were supposed to be baby-sitting Courtney just did not sit well with him.

"Listen. If you have any trouble, call me, we'll come right home."

She promised she would, and they embraced once more before Jack climbed up into the Jeep. Courtney made Molly promise to bring him back in one piece. The girls had a good laugh with that one. A few moments later he drove down to the end of the alley, turned right, and left the pub behind. Again.

In the rearview mirror he saw his sister watching after them until they had turned out of sight.

As he navigated through the circuitous streets of Boston toward the highway, Jack reached out to take Molly's hand. She slipped her fingers into his without hesitation. Warmth, comfort.

"On the road again," Molly said.

"On the road," Jack echoed solemnly. "On the hunt."

The novelty of being away from home wore off for Jack pretty quick. The drive had taken them west on the Massachusetts Turnpike, deeper and deeper into the most rural parts of the state, until at last they simply ran out of Massachusetts and found themselves crossing the border into New York State. But in spite of Molly's company, Jack had grown impatient with the trip long before that. Boston radio stations had accompanied them through most of the drive on the Pike, but they reached a certain point around exit 8 or so when even the strongest of the familiar radio signals fizzled out.

It was as though some tether keeping him tied to home had snapped. A small thing, really, and yet it unnerved him in a way it never had before.

Jack spent nearly every day with Molly, and every night with her sleeping in a room just down the hall. He had no idea what would become of their feelings for each other, but he knew he loved her. Not in that desperate-to-see-her-naked way that guys back in high school had always equated with love—sometimes without words and sometimes with too many—but in the sense that he could not imagine his life without her. The touch of her hand, the lilt of her laugh, the tumble of her hair across her face, each of those things had a kind of sorcerous hold upon his heart.

Which was not to say he did not want to see her naked. Quite the contrary. But it meant that he was content to let their intimacy follow its own course with the lazy turns and rushing torrents of a mountain river.

The hours on the road passed slowly. They talked about the pub and about Bill's search for his missing niece. In a hesitant bit of conversation where each pretended it was no big deal, they talked about taking an actual vacation sometime, just the two of them. As a couple. The Jeep's tires hummed on the highway, and the vehicle rattled a bit if Jack edged it up much past seventy.

As they drove north toward Albany, Molly played with the radio and found a station she liked. A lot of Sting, Shawn Colvin, Matchbox 20, and not a single track from the viral epidemic of boy bands sweeping the earth in the early twenty-first century.

The farther north they drove, the less traffic there was, though he had a feeling that had more to do with its being Saturday afternoon than anything else. Nobody commuting today, and most of the people headed off for a trip were already well on their way to their destination. When the traffic thinned, Jack twined his fingers in Molly's, and for long periods they were just quiet, listening to the radio and the rattle of the Jeep, the rumbling of the road.

Trucks roared past them every few minutes, tractor-trailers with no business travelling at that speed. The terrain rose and fell in long slopes, hills and valleys, but the big rigs barely slowed, and often passed in the fast lane. Jack said nothing to Molly, but it occurred to him more than once as the Jeep shuddered in the wake of a passing eighteen-wheeler that this might not be Prowlers at all. Industry had its demands. He was wise enough to know that in business, competition often demanded compromise. But Jack was also stubborn enough to believe that safety should never be compromised, no matter what the competitor was doing.

Lulled by the journey, by the music and momentum, Jack suddenly felt as though he was waking from a kind of trance behind the wheel. He shook his head and glanced at the sign announcing that the exit half a mile ahead was for Hollingsworth. The name jarred him.

"Jack? Are you all right?"

He blinked, glanced sidelong at Molly. The Jeep swerved a little, but there was no one in the next lane. "Sorry. Just half asleep, I guess."

"As long as you're only half," she replied with a nervous laugh. "There'd be some seriously cruel irony in you rolling us into a ditch."

A thin smile spread across his features, but it felt pasted on. The exit for Hollingsworth came and went. Molly stared at the sign as they drove past and then glanced at him again.

"So this is supposed to be Prowler country? I have to say, it doesn't look any different from the rest of the highway we've been looking at all day."

Jack nodded. "I know. But it *feels* different."

"Does it? I don't . . . well, maybe it's you. I don't mean maybe it's in your head. I mean you can see into the Ghostlands, so I suppose it's possible you're picking up some kind of . . . vibe or whatever that other people would never notice. Have you seen any?"

Ghosts. That was the word she neglected to use at

the end of the sentence. Though they had frequently spoken about his talent—the ghost-sight, as he had jokingly called it several times—ever since Molly learned that Artie's spirit still wandered the world of the living, she was sometimes tentative when the subject came up.

Static hissed on the radio as they lost the station Molly had enjoyed so much on the drive north.

"Nothing. But I haven't really tried to see either. Figured it was kind of dangerous while driving. If they appear or whatever, that's one thing. But you know what I find really interesting?"

"What?"

"We've been on the road all day. Not once has either of us mentioned the Prowlers."

Silence descended upon the confines of the Jeep, save for the static on the radio and the roar of the engine. Jack had both hands on the wheel, but now he reached over to slip his fingers between Molly's yet again. A semi pulling a double trailer thundered by them with a squeal of metal that made Jack think of freight trains.

Molly leaned forward and used her free hand to switch off the radio. "I guess we've been postponing the inevitable."

"No more postponing."

Up ahead was another sign, this one for a rest area. They had passed a lot of them, on both sides of the road, but now that they were near Hollingsworth, they had entered the thirty-mile stretch of highway that Courtney had identified as a kind of blacktop Bermuda

Triangle, where people kept disappearing and far too many accidents seemed to happen.

The rest area ahead, just over the border into the town of Hollingsworth, was their first stop. The first of many. But it was already late in the day.

"We'll look around here, then figure out where the motel is. Tomorrow we can start hitting all the rest stops and roadhouses and whatever up and down this stretch."

Molly agreed, and Jack put the directional on to indicate that he was going to turn into the rest area. As he slowed the Jeep he glanced over at her again, and he was saddened to see the apprehension on her face.

"We'll be all right," he said quickly.

"Yeah," Molly replied softly. "I was just thinking that the reason we haven't talked about them? The reason we're feeling what we're feeling? It's that we both know that we're going to find something here. As much as I wish I could brush it off, Courtney found way too many stories about this area. I'm going to hope that it's just because this is some sort of migratory route for them. That's possible, by the way. We know some of the packs move frequently. Some are even nomadic.

"But I think we'll find them. And then we'll have to do something about it. Don't get me wrong, I want to destroy them. But I'm afraid, Jack. No matter how many times we fight one of these things and live through it, I think I'm always going to be afraid."

"That's good, Molly," he told her, fingers tightening

on the steering wheel. "That's how it should be."

"Afraid all the time? That's how it *should* be?" She sounded almost angry.

"Where they're concerned, yes. Not every minute of every day, but when you know there might be Prowlers around? Absolutely. Stay afraid. They're monsters, Molly. When we *stop* being afraid of them, that's when they'll get us for sure."

Jack drove into the wide rest area, a football field's worth of parking lot with a short row of portable bathrooms on the far side. Trash cans and a pair of rusting iron grilles rounded out the list of amenities available to the truckers who passed through, slept the night or day away in their rigs in that rest stop. There were three tractor-trailers there now, one whose engine was running. A card table and folding chairs were set up between two of the trucks, and a fortyish woman with weathered features sat with a cold beer in her hand, one foot on a plastic cooler, talking to a trio of tired-looking men, all of whom needed a shave.

"Anything?" Molly asked.

He parked alongside the nearest truck, as though the Jeep were just another metal dinosaur. Jack took a breath and focused, and his perception was instantly altered. He peered into the afterlife, the spirit world. The trucks and the parking lot and the trees beyond, even Molly there on the seat beside him, were drained of colour and substance. It was as though he sat in the midst of a dense fog and everything around him was just shadow, a world of brittle greys, like faded antique photographs. Where the world of flesh and blood seemed on fire with vivid life, this place was nothing but ash.

The Ghostlands.

"Nothing here," he told Molly, though it felt very much as though he were talking to himself. "If anyone was ever killed here, they've wandered off or they're just not lost anymore. They've moved on."

He felt an odd mixture of relief and disappointment as he closed his eyes and frowned. There had been times when he had looked into the Ghostlands and had some difficulty snapping his vision back to normal. When he opened his eyes now, though, his stomach did a little nauseous flip and the world was back to normal.

Jack killed the engine, then looked at Molly again. She took a deep breath and smiled.

"So, how exactly are we going to casually get into a conversation with a bunch of truckers about mysterious highway deaths?" Molly asked, a mischievous twinkle in her eye. "What excuse do we give for even saying hello to them, for stopping here longer than it takes to pee in the bushes?"

Jack rolled that one over in his head. He ducked forward and kissed her, briefly, his lips barely grazing hers. Then he popped open the door and climbed out.

"Screw excuses," he said, voice low.

Before he slammed his door, he heard Molly's response: "This should be interesting."

Together they strode straight over to the truck drivers at their card table. Jack made no move to cover it with a quick trip to the bushes, and Molly did not mention it again.

As they got closer Jack took a quick appraisal of the four people at that table. All four wore blue jeans in various stages of cleanliness and wear. At first glance it would be easy to assume that the woman was travelling with one of the men, but as Jack studied them he decided that was not the case. The two men closest to him had beards and blue eyes, and both wore tan work boots. They had enough similarity in their facial structure that he pegged them as brothers, likely travelling together, sharing the driving. That meant the woman in the white cable-knit sweater was driving her own rig, and the third man, a jarhead ex-military man by the look of his drastic crew-cut and the tattoo on his right forearm, drove the other one.

"You two lost?" asked one of the brothers.

"Not yet," Jack replied.

The brothers looked at him quizzically. The jarhead narrowed his gaze and sat up a bit straighter. *No sense of humour,* Jack thought. But the woman, whose tangle of dirty-blonde hair softened her looks up close, smiled at him.

"Can we help you folks with something?" she asked.

The other brother, bigger and broader than the first, popped the top of a can of Budweiser and brandished it at them as though it were some kind of ward against strange travelers. "Don't even think about asking us to buy you beer."

"Hank," the woman said, a warning in her voice.

"Don't talk to me like I'm your husband, Suzanne," Hank replied dismissively.

Molly arched an eyebrow and seemed about to interject when Jack shot her a look that silenced her. He knew the way her mind worked. Why this smelly, half-drunk oaf would think anyone would trawl rest stops looking for someone to buy beer was beyond him, but he did not want Molly to make the man feel stupid. Hank's brother, though, the one who had first spoken to them, looked intelligent enough. When Jack spoke again, his words were directed at the woman.

"We're not looking for directions," he said. "Last summer my cousin took off from home. Left Buffalo and hitched rides all across the state. I'm guessing he was planning to come to Boston to look me up. His name was Jared Wilkes. Blond kid, fifteen years old, big smile. Somewhere along the road he ran into the wrong people. Somebody killed Jared and tore him up like an animal."

The jarhead flinched and his nostrils flared in revulsion. Jack thought that was a good sign. The two brothers just gazed at him with blank expressions, clearly doing their best to be patient with the interruption until he and Molly left.

The woman was kind, though. "Aw, Jesus," she said. "That's awful. What are you doing up here?" A sudden understanding rippled across her face, and she gave a tiny shake of her head. "But you kids can't think you're gonna find anything up here yourselves. Especially not after all this time."

"Trail's colder'n a polar bear's ass," Hank muttered.

Jack stiffened. The younger brother fidgeted as though he had the good sense to be made uncomfortable by his brother's behaviour.

"He doesn't mean anything by it," the younger brother said. He stood up and offered his hand, first to Jack and then to Molly. They all shook.

"Jack Sears. And this is Molly Feehan," Jack lied.

"I'm Dave Krause," the man said. "Terrible thing about your cousin. I think I remember hearing about that on a run through here, maybe last fall. Found him at a rest area, didn't they?"

"That's right," Molly said.

All their eyes went to her. Jack didn't like the way Hank Krause looked at her, but there was nothing particularly monstrous about it. Just the normal, everyday beast that any pretty girl had to deal with. Still, he glared at the guy. Hank caught the look and gave him a sly grin, just between the two of them. Jack wanted desperately to hit him, but he figured unless he had a baseball bat, he had best just stand right where he was.

"Actually, it was *this* rest stop," Molly went on.

"Oh," Dave said, and a moment of silence fell upon them all as they looked around, apparently creeped out by the news. "Wow," he added. "Suzanne's right, though. Not sure what you hope to find after all this time."

Jack took a breath, stepped away from the card table, and stared out at the road. "Jared's mom still cries herself to sleep at night," he said, hating the taste of the lie in his mouth, wondering how good an actor he was. He turned around and studied them to see if they were buying it. It seemed like they were.

"When we saw this news piece about a trucker who got killed pretty much the same way up here, we just figured maybe it's the same guy. Maybe there's some connection between how this freak found Jared and how he ended up killing this other guy."

All four stared at him. The jarhead's gaze went back and forth from him to Molly. It had not been lost on Jack that the guy had yet to say a single word.

"What was the driver's name?" Suzanne asked.

Jack had forgotten completely. He glanced at Molly.

"Chester Douglas," she said. "Chet, I think people called him."

As though they were holding their breath, the drivers all glanced awkwardly at one another, searching each other's faces, clearly waiting for one among them to say, *Ah, poor Chet,* or something of the sort. Hank Krause tilted his can of Budweiser back and let it stream into his mouth, ignoring everyone else.

"Don't think I've ever heard of him," Suzanne said.

Dave shrugged.

The jarhead just stared at them.

Jack sighed and scratched the back of his head. He half turned to Molly, and she reached out to take his hand. *It's all right,* he thought as he slipped his hand into hers. *Let them see that. The frustration or whatever. Maybe it makes it all the more real.*

"Listen, we're sorry to have bothered you," Molly

said. "We really appreciate the time. The way we're thinking now is that if whoever killed Jared also killed Chet Douglas, he might have killed more people around here. Chet drove a truck, and the police say he often slept in rest stops along this road on his long runs. Jared was probably hitchhiking, and his body was left in a rest stop. If you think of anything else you've heard—even if it's only a rumour—that might be related, we'll be at the Riverside Motel in Fairbrook for a couple of days."

Dave slipped his hands in his pockets, glanced at Suzanne, and then looked back at them. "We're on the road, y'know? I mean, in a couple of hours none of us is going to be within fifty miles of here. But if I think of anything, well, I know where you are."

"Same goes for me," Suzanne said. "I'm headed for West Virginia, but I'll keep it in mind. And pass it on."

"Thanks," Jack said. "Much appreciated."

With that, he and Molly turned and went back to the Jeep. Behind them the drivers were silent, save for the sound of Hank popping another can of Budweiser. They climbed into the Jeep, and Jack started it up. He was about to pull out when Molly whispered his name. He looked up and saw the jarhead trotting toward them with a determined look on his face.

Wary, but curious, Jack rolled the window down.

"Hey," the jarhead said.

"You thought of something?" Jack asked.

The man blinked, then shook his head. "No. Just . . . I just wanted to make sure you knew how to get to that motel."

"Actually, we have terrible directions," Molly replied.

The jarhead actually smiled. "Take the next exit. Fairbrook, Dobbins Avenue, it says. Left at the bottom of the ramp, maybe two miles you'll pass this road-house called Capone's. The next intersection is Dobbins. Take a right there, and the motel's maybe a quarter of a mile up on the left."

Jack was astonished at how friendly the guy suddenly seemed. "Thanks," he said sincerely. "Drive safe out there."

But the guy did not back away. Instead, he leaned in closer to the window, and all the open, amiable warmth drained from his face.

"Pay attention, friend. I *know* you're full of shit," the jarhead said ominously. His eyes ticked past Jack to Molly, and then back again. "I remember the deal with that kid from Buffalo, and his mom killed herself not three months later. It was in the papers. You're not his cousin. I don't know what you're looking for, but I'll tell you this for free: Go home. Turn around and drive back to Boston. Now, if you're stupid, and you stay? Just watch yourselves."

"Why?" Jack prodded, heart racing. "You know there's more going on here. Why don't you just talk to us?"

The jarhead glanced over his shoulder, though the nearest trailer blocked his view of the other three. When he turned back to the Jeep, his eyes narrowed, and he stepped back a couple of feet. "Stay or go. If you have questions about this dead truck driver, ask Max at the Blueberry Diner in Hollingsworth. That guy talks to everyone. Sees everything. Makes some mean French toast, too."

He slapped the door. "Good luck."

Before Jack could thank him, he had rushed back around the truck to rejoin the other drivers.

"Well," Jack began. "That was . . ."

"Peculiar," Molly put in.

"One word for it. I was thinking more like 'freaky.'"

"That works too."

CHAPTER 4

From the moment he arrived in Manhattan—at just after five o'clock that morning—Bill had regretted not having ridden his Harley down. But Lao had insisted that Bill drive. It was his quest, his trip . . . his car and his money to fill the gas tank.

Lao was a less than ideal travelling companion. They had been acquainted with each other for centuries, and Bill had never been overly fond of the grim-faced Prowler. He spoke rarely and moved with a kind of cool confidence that seemed admirable in books and movies but was actually quite unnerving in real life. His reticence often caused people to make the mistake of thinking Lao was stupid, but one good look at his eyes would dispel that presumption. His mind was always working, taking the measure of any given situation, but Lao kept his own counsel.

Only the fact that Winter had instructed him to aid

in the search for Olivia gave Bill any faith in Lao's loyalty. The hunter, the warrior, had no love or fealty toward Bill or his family, but it was another thing entirely to betray Winter, who owed allegiance to no one and yet was venerated by all. The name itself had gotten them this far.

Since early that morning they had spoken to several members of the underground, who spoke to them only because they claimed to be affiliated with Winter. Several times that day Lao had tried to get in touch with Roger Martelle, a Prowler who was a music industry executive. By the end of the day they were dining with him at Birdland on the Upper West Side. Martelle gave them a lead, a music club on West Fourth Street in the Village called The Voodoo Lounge. Though the place was a hot spot in the city, it was owned by Prowlers, and at any given time a good portion of the clientele wasn't human. It was not a refuge for the underground, nor, according to Martelle, was it a haven for the savages.

But the word on the street was that Jasmine was recruiting, and the Voodoo Lounge was where she did her scouting.

The Oldsmobile had been in a garage on Seventy-second Street since shortly after breakfast, and Bill figured it would be best just to leave it there until it was needed again. With the parking situation in New York, it simply made more sense to take the subway or a taxi.

It was dusk as the yellow cab rolled up to the curb in front of the Voodoo Lounge. Lao climbed out first without a word or a glance, leaving Bill to pay the fare. He knew it should not bother him. Whether Winter put him up to it or not, the truth was that Lao was doing him a favour, and by rights Bill should be the one to pay the expenses involved. But there was something about Lao's attitude, the way he floated ghostlike through each new situation, barely even acknowledging that there was a fare to be paid, a bit of decorum to be observed, that raised Bill's hackles.

On the sidewalk they stood side by side and gazed at the facade of the Voodoo Lounge. The place was a study in downscale hip, the blacked-out windows painted with fluorescent musical notes and the sign quite purposefully and expensively crafted to appear as though it had been made from wood and rusted metal. The club was inconspicuous. If he had driven past it during the day, Bill probably would have thought that the place had been abandoned, closed down for months.

There would be no making that mistake after dark, however. A pair of bouncers stood on either side of the door, and Bill studied them, trying to determine if they were human. He tried to catch a scent, but the wind had kicked up. Live music blared so loud inside that they could hear it on the street, muffled but clear enough to make out some of the lyrics. It was a jazzy kind of blues that wasn't quite rock but sure as hell wasn't pop, and Bill felt his pulse drop into rhythm with the music.

He started for the door, and Lao stopped him.

wild things

Bill twitched, glared at the other Prowler. It was all he could do not to snarl. Lao withdrew his hand without a hint of apology.

"Stay here," the other Prowler said.

"Bullshit."

Lao's expression was impassive. "You are known, Guillaume. You wish to believe that this is not true, but it is. There are many among us who would have known you by sight even before you played football with the humans. If Jasmine is here, or even if her pack gathers here, there will undoubtedly be those who will recognize you. We are not here for a war. We are here to get in, find your niece, and get out as quickly as we can."

Without waiting for a response, Lao turned and went up the stairs and through the front door of the club, leaving Bill to stare after him. Much as he wanted to argue, what Lao said made sense. The bouncers were eyeing Bill closely now. He might have glared back at them, but Lao's words echoed in his mind, and instead he walked along the sidewalk until he was just out of sight of the entrance.

Cars slid by on the narrow Village street. A kid with too many piercings and a chain dangling from his pants rode a bicycle several years too small for him. Bill had spent so much time living among the humans that he was practiced at blending in, at being inconspicuous, in spite of what Lao had said. Still, there on the sidewalk he felt exposed and vulnerable, as out of place as a nervous thief hesitating in the parking lot before robbing a convenience store. A young lesbian couple passed, hand in hand. One of them, tall and lithe and blonde, smiled at him.

"You lost?" she asked.

"Just waiting for someone," he replied.

The urge to hurt his silent travelling companion grew.

The metal watch on his wrist ticked off the minutes, and each time Bill glanced at it, he was certain its hands were moving slower than before. The residents of the neighbourhood were an eclectic mix of faces and ages, from middle-aged business types to skateboard punks to hip, twentyish women dressed in what he thought of as ragged glamour. A man with greying hair and the attire of a male fashion model strode confidently along the sidewalk with a violin case in his hand.

With every tick of his watch, the sense of being out of place grew. Bill countered it with thoughts of Olivia. However vulnerable he felt, it was the smallest of sacrifices to make if it would lead to locating his niece, the beautiful girl he had held in his arms when she was just a baby. She had purred when he stroked her fur. She had grown up with a charisma and a kind of personal momentum that always reminded Bill of her mother. But as much as Bill loved his sister, he was not going to tell her daughter that.

In his mind he saw Olivia's golden eyes, like burnished brass. The last time he had seen her, she had been bent over an acoustic guitar, clumsily picking out a tune that sounded familiar but not familiar enough. He had been certain she would get it eventually, though. She was a determined girl.

WILD THINGS

Bill didn't want to think about how long it had been since that day, how long it had been since he had really checked on Olivia, even to see how she was faring. It grieved him to know that he only discovered her plight secondhand. The very thought of it sent shivers of anger and sadness through him, brought the beast that much closer to the surface. If he had run his tongue over his teeth just then, he was sure he would have found them jagged and sharp, and far too many for a man.

With a deep breath he forced the beast down. What else could he do? He could kill. He could hunt. Those things were easy. The hardest thing for him was to do what he was doing now: being patient.

It was more than thirty-five minutes before Lao exited the club. He moved with a grace that belied his size, and perhaps that was something else that bothered Bill about him. Even among his own kind Bill was used to being the most imposing presence in the room, but Lao was simply bigger. His tranquillity combined with his size and that striking tiger tattoo to ominous effect. Lao made people nervous.

The bouncers in front of the Voodoo Lounge did not even glance at Lao as he walked down the stairs and out onto the sidewalk, sniffed the air for Bill's scent, then started toward him. Bill frowned. They had seen him go in, of course, and he would not be as remarkable a sight the second time around. But it seemed odd that they would not even acknowledge his departure. Bill wondered if he was recognized as someone connected to Winter, for that might explain their treatment of Lao.

"You were in there a while," Bill said.

Lao raised his eyebrows, the tiger at his temple rearing back, then he bowed respectfully. "My apologies, Guillaume."

"Did you get any leads on Olivia?"

"No one will confirm that Jasmine is holding her, but there were those within who know the girl. I did not get a sense that anyone thinks her dead."

As he exhaled a chill passed through Bill, as though he were releasing some of his fear, that dark anticipation, along with his breath. But it was hardly over yet, he knew that. It was only beginning. Still, it was something.

"That could mean the word is out that Jasmine has her, but no one wants to talk because of possible repercussions," Bill ventured.

Lao bowed again, but only slightly this time. "That was my thought as well. A direct approach seems most appropriate now. I have arranged for a meeting with a member of Jasmine's pack. Alec Brand. We are to meet him at eleven o'clock."

The beast in Bill Cantwell's heart growled low, wary. "Where?"

Even at eleven o'clock at night midtown Manhattan was abuzz with activity. New York was called the City That Never Sleeps, and Bill had found that to be an accurate appellation. There were parts of Manhattan where people wandered about at all hours, moving from bar to bar to after-hours party, sitting in coffee shops or restaurants when most other people in the time zone had long ago gone to sleep.

But there were other parts of the city that became deserted as the hour grew late. Much progress had been made in the past decade in making New York City safer, in reclaiming blocks and sometimes whole neighbourhoods that had gone to seed. Times Square was a brilliant jewel in the crown of this reclamation.

Walking west from Times Square on Forty-eighth Street, the jewel became tarnished with every block they moved closer to the Hudson River. Bill had seen so many faces on this city over the years, the heights of its greatest glory and the filth of its greatest shame. For better or worse, though, New York was a magnificent place, a city that lived and breathed, alive with the power of imagination and human ambition, yet with a dark pulse of violence and cruelty underneath. The architects of this grandest of cities had built their dreams high, their buildings higher, and Bill thought now as he and Lao walked along Forty-eighth Street that perhaps they had done so in order to draw attention from the streets themselves.

For awful things lurked in the shadows on the street, and beneath it. Abandoned humans, broken children, drug-addled women, the forgotten of their race, all were horrible enough, but there were inhuman things as well. And so there were places in the city that had been overlooked when the wealthy captains of industry decided to give Manhattan the polish it had so badly needed.

PROWLERS

They crossed Tenth Avenue and started for Eleventh, and shortly Bill and Lao came to one of those places. Forty-eighth Street became a bridge there, just for a short span. Perhaps thirty feet below the bridge railroad tracks ran along the bottom of a long, narrow ravine in a bed of gravel. Though it was autumn, weeds still grew up on either side of the tracks where the sun would hit them. To the north the steel rails disappeared into a tunnel beneath Forty-ninth Street that somehow seemed too small for a train to pass through. Chain-link fence had been erected on both ends to keep people from entering the ravine, by accident or by choice.

An aging, filthy, unmarked delivery truck rattled east on Forty-eighth Street. The driver was a swarthy man with a shaved head and a cigarette dangling precariously from his lips. He glared at them as he passed, but Bill knew his obvious rancour was caused not by suspicion, but by a natural response many powerful human males had in the presence of one another, like apes pounding on their chests.

When the truck had rumbled away, Bill and Lao exchanged a glance, took one more cautious look around, and then grabbed hold of the chain-link fence. With speed and agility no human of his size could ever have, Bill scaled the fence in a sliver of an instant, crouched impossibly on the top bar, and then dropped over the edge, plummeting into the ravine and landing on his feet with a grunt and the crunch of gravel. Lao dropped down beside him an instant later, and together they started along the train tracks without a backward glance.

The dim illumination from the lights of the city revealed that the rails had been worn smooth by passing trains. The two Prowlers moved quickly into the tunnel that had been hollowed beneath the city streets. Without the lights of the city Bill felt immediately claustrophobic. He was not so dependent upon nature as many of his kind were—as he himself had once been—but with the stone and metal all around him and the thousands of tons of earth above him, he felt trapped. The air was close and oppressive, rank with the smell of urine and the scents of homeless humans who had made the tunnels their residence.

Scents.

Among the overpowering scents locked in that underground maze was the stench of death, of rotting flesh. The tunnels were deserted, devoid of human presence, save for that smell.

"They're dead," Bill growled.

Lao glanced at him as they followed the tracks. "Yes. I smell it as well. Humans, living down here. Many of them were killed."

"By us," Bill said.

"Not us," Lao said sharply. "Not us."

Bill understood what he meant. Whoever the Prowlers were that had slaughtered the humans who lived down here, Bill and Lao were not like them. Yet Bill could not escape the dread and the guilt that spread through him like poison whenever he discovered another atrocity committed by his kind.

The tracks turned somewhat but stayed on a

northerly course. As Bill and Lao walked Bill tried to gauge how far they had come. At first he had a sense of the distance, but soon that gave way to the darkness of the tunnel, broken only by the occasional lightbulb or by city light streaming down through grates above their heads. After perhaps fifteen minutes the tracks began to hum, and then the screech of brakes, of metal screaming against metal, echoed up the tunnel from behind him. They stood aside to let the northbound train pass, and from the shadows Bill watched the zoetrope flicker of faces, people on their way home from a night out, some laughing, some with their eyes closed, heads leaning against windows. They were travelling across the killing grounds beneath their city and had no idea that there were monsters in the dark.

There was a sense of urgency in the air, and it carried its own scent, like burned rubber. Bill picked up the pace and Lao took his lead. The two of them began to move swiftly now, jumping over pieces of concrete that had fallen away from the tunnel structure, and shopping carts left behind days or years before. Some minutes later the breeze that swept through the tunnel shifted and the air pressure changed noticeably.

They were coming to a station.

Wary now, they slowed as they entered the vast, cavernous place, their lightest footfalls echoing back to them. For the station had clearly been abandoned for decades. Bill knew such structures existed in the vast labyrinth of New York's underground, though some of them had been blocked off. There were, he had been told by those who knew first-hand, entire tunnel systems that had been built in the late nineteenth century and eventually left to rot. This station was not that old, but if it had ever been put to use, its heyday was clearly long in the past.

Bill sprang from the tracks onto the cracked platform. A dim illumination stretched into the shadows of the station from the grates above, and from those few lights on the ceiling of the tunnel that were still working. Arched columns stretched up to the ceiling. Metal gates had been put in place at some time in the past to block off the stairwells on either end of the platform that would have led to the street, but the heavy chains on those gates had been shattered and now hung loose. The stairwells were dark, however, and Bill suspected there was only concrete above. And yet there had to be another entrance, otherwise the chains would still be intact.

Lao sniffed the air and stepped deeper into the station. The air began to thrum again with the thunder of an oncoming train, and a moment later it began to pass through the station, somehow louder now than the other had been when it was right next to him. Lights strobed the dark.

But Bill already had the scent. He did not need Lao to tell him they were not alone.

Prowlers began to emerge from the hidden recesses of the platform, from the stairwells and behind columns. They wore their human faces, but in the flickering illumination from the passing train they began to change. Their bodies stretched, fur tearing up from beneath skin. Their faces elongated into snouts, snapping and gnashing with gleaming razor fangs. The beasts crouched in the dark with their talons curled, and began to close in around them.

The train was gone, leaving only the gloom and the monsters. The tunnel was silent, save for their panting, excited at the prospect of spilled blood.

"So it's to be tooth and claw instead of parley," Bill snarled. His eyes ticked to the right, and he saw the guilty expression on Lao's face. Hatred flared up within him as he tried to decide if Winter had known that Lao would betray him; if Winter had *ordered* it.

With a shudder and a loud growl Bill crouched low and *he* changed as well. He set free the beast within, its fangs and claws slicing the dark, his fur bristling.

"It should be," a gravelly voice said from the pack.

The speaker was a tall, lithe male Prowler with a coat of gleaming fur as black as pitch. He stepped forward, and the others remained where they were.

"Hello, Lao," the black-furred beast said.

"Alec," Lao replied. He bowed low to this newcomer.

Bill growled, kept his back to the tunnel, though even now he caught the scent of others, down there on the tracks, moving in.

"You had to have known, Guillaume," Alec said haughtily. He dropped on all fours and trotted back and forth, capering like a wolf. When he unfolded to his true height again, he cocked his head to one side and slid his tongue along his teeth.

WILD THINGS

"You're Jasmine's mate," Bill said. "You've got her scent on you."

"Good," Alec rasped. "So you know I speak for her."

Silence, save for the distant rumble of trains rushing along tracks elsewhere in that vast underground warren. Fur bristled, eyes of many colours glowed dim in that dead, cavernous place. Bill felt his breath coming short and shallow, possibilities ticking through his mind at a maddening pace. Every few seconds, though, he came back to Olivia. And then to Lao.

Black lips curled back from his fangs. and he snarled as he glared at Lao. The enormous beast would not even meet his gaze, ashamed of himself. *As he should be,* Bill thought. *Coward.*

Alec snapped at the others in a guttural bark and they began to encircle him, yet they kept at least ten feet away. Bill counted heads now, heads and scents, and thought there were at least fifteen of them, including those who had come up now from the tunnel at his back. That didn't count Lao, but Bill was not certain if he ought to be included in that tally or not. No way to know his motivations or alliances now, save that whoever he was loyal to, it wasn't Bill himself.

Muscles tensed, rippling beneath his fur, Bill stood up to his full height and faced Alec directly, ignoring all the others. "You haven't killed me. What is it you want, then?"

"Haven't killed you *yet,*" one of the gathered pack muttered.

Alec leaped across the platform in a single bound and slashed his claws across the face of the Prowler who had spoken. The beast cried out, snarling and hissing in pain, and backed off. After which Alec ignored him, loping easily back toward Bill.

"Got to keep order, you know what I mean?"

Bill nodded slowly.

"It isn't what I want," Alec went on, fangs flashing as he spoke, yellow eyes seeming to sparkle in the semi-dark. "It's what Jasmine wants. And what she *has.*"

Instinct demanded Bill act then. His hackles went up and he bared his teeth further, and every bit of his heart and soul demanded he lunge at Alec, tear his throat out. The beast was talking about Olivia, threatening her without even saying her name. But the only way Bill was going to have any chance of seeing her again was to deny his instincts, to embrace the essence of humanity he had adopted during the years he had spent living as one of them.

Still, he would not step back from Alec. He was not the leader of this pack, but the mate of its Alpha. Jasmine was truly in charge, and Bill would not allow himself to be seen cowed by her lackey.

"What does Jasmine want, then?"

"In exchange for the girl, Olivia?" Alec replied. His tongue snaked out and ran over his teeth suggestively. "A tasty morsel, that girl. Caught her myself."

Bill took two steps forward, towered above Alec, and glared down at the slick, black-furred predator. He breathed in Alec's scent so that he would never forget it, inhaled the other beast's own breath.

"What does Jasmine want?" he asked again, voice little more than a growl now.

Through a grate far above him Bill could hear a police siren wailing. It was nearly midnight in Manhattan, and that cry of sirens acted almost like a bell that tolled the witching hour, when all iniquities were possible and malevolent creatures emerged to stalk the streets.

All iniquities were possible.

Alec contorted slightly, painfully, as the fur withdrew from his flesh and new skin was formed around it. His false human face was darkly handsome and angular, his hair a little too long, his eyes captivating.

"Jasmine will spare Olivia's life, and your own as well. She has no desire to kill her own kind. She would like you to join the pack, but doubts that you will. It will be her great pleasure to let you go on your own way, Guillaume, son of Yves. In exchange, you will linger here long enough to draw the attention of the humans you have befriended. Jack Dwyer. Molly Hatcher. Courtney Dwyer. I suggested that Jasmine have you kill them yourself, but she is merciful. She's content to allow you to be bait."

A blast of warm air washed down the tunnel, the first sign that another train was coming. From deep within that underground maze he heard the squeal of metal on metal again, the scream of the hurtling train, and it echoed with the scream Bill felt welling up within himself. Faces flashed through his mind, images, sensations, holding his little niece in his hands, his only living flesh and blood, Olivia. Olivia as a grown girl, with those penny eyes wide and laughing. Courtney, his love, making him feel that much more human. The way her milky skin felt beneath his caress.

Jack. Molly. His friends.

Then Bill glanced over at Lao, who was staring at him expectantly, a grin on his features. All pretence had been stripped away. The tiger tattoo was buried beneath the fur on his head, but the outline of the mark could be seen in the pattern of the fur. There was a small chuffing noise, and he knew it was Lao laughing. Lao, whom he had known for more than two hundred years, who had been Bill's pack brother for a time when Yves still lived. Lao the warrior. Lao the hunter.

Lao the betrayer.

Olivia.

Courtney.

"I'll do it," Bill snarled, rage and hatred and grief tearing through him. "But first you have to do something for me, to prove you'll keep your end of the bargain."

Alec grunted with satisfaction and shrugged. A human response, now that he wore his human form. "Name it."

Bill pointed to Lao with one long claw. "Kill him."

Lao's eyes went wide.

"It's a deal," Alec replied.

The train screamed past, lights strobing the platform, air pressure thundering against Bill's eardrums, all but blocking out the snarls and screams as the pack fell upon Lao and tore him apart. Blood and fur spattered the crumbling arches.

Bill watched grimly, thinking only of his own blood, of Olivia.

CHAPTER 5

Perfectly innocent, Molly thought. *It's perfectly innocent.*

The phrase sounded prissy and old-fashioned in her head, but the part of her that might have been self-conscious about that was too busy panicking to worry overmuch about being prim. The small hotel was close enough to the small river that ran through Fairbrook that, with the window slightly open, Molly could hear the sound of it burbling over the rocks like gentle laughter. It was still dark outside, but the sky was now a deep blue rather than black, the trees outside the window silhouetted by the predawn. The fresh air that breezed through the window was bracing, but she was snug and warm beneath the thick comforter that lay across the bed.

The single queen-size bed.

As the chilly air washed over her face and she stared out the window, Molly thought that perhaps it was not the comforter keeping her warm, but the heat from Jack's body where he lay curled against her, one leg draped across her hip. He was fast asleep, his breathing slow and even, sweet against the back of her neck. Or perhaps what was truly creating the flush in her cheeks and the warm tingle that rushed through her was the collision of conflicting emotions within her.

Nothing had happened the night before. It had been their misfortune that the hotel did not have any available rooms with more than one bed. Jack had offered to sleep on the floor, but Molly had brazenly waved the suggestion away as ridiculous. They had known each other forever, lived now in the same apartment. Together they were exploring what sort of relationship might come of their mutual love and attraction. Not that Molly wanted to rush things along; deep kisses and soft caresses were exactly what she wanted right now.

But no way was she going to let Jack sleep on the floor.

They had exchanged almost sickeningly shy grins as they slid into bed together, both wearing nothing more than a T-shirt and underwear. It was, after all, the uniform in which they saw each other most mornings these days. Yet Molly had never been quite so aware of how close to naked she was in these two items of clothing, nor how warm Jack's skin was, until he lay beside her under the covers, his leg barely touching hers.

He had kissed her good night, a tender, lingering kiss, and brushed the hair out of her eyes, and then they had turned away from each other. For half an hour or more Molly had lain awake, staring out the window, and though she could not be sure, she thought that perhaps Jack had also had trouble falling asleep.

Then only moments ago she had woken in the darkness, the night a rich indigo as dawn teased the corners of the sky, and felt his body pressed close behind her. He held her, even in his sleep. Somehow during the night they had come together naturally, seeking the comfort of each other's bodies. A delicious shiver ran through Molly as she felt him against her, moulded to the contours of her body, and the flush in her cheeks grew even warmer.

She ought to go back to sleep, she knew. Though they were used to rising early because of the demands of running the pub, here they might easily have stolen another hour or two past sunrise without guilt or hesitation. But a tiny smile turned up the edges of her mouth, and she could not banish it no matter how hard she tried, and she felt totally awake. Aware.

Minutes ticked by and she relished the scent and feel of him. By the tiniest of degrees the room began to brighten, the light taking on a sort of metallic hue, as though everything was made of brass. Almost as though she was some flesh-and-blood marionette, Molly felt herself being tugged, every muscle longing to turn in his arms, to press her forehead against his. To kiss Jack awake and feel his hands on the small of her back, and let the intimacy of this moment blossom into something more.

WILD THINGS

That yearning frightened her. Molly's heart began to race. She pressed her eyes closed and savoured the security and harmony she felt in that moment. Then reluctantly she slipped out from beneath Jack's arm and sat up on the edge of the bed. Disturbed by her movement, he stretched in his sleep and raised his arms over his head, splayed out on the wide bed with the abandon of a child. His mouth was open ever so slightly, and he sighed lightly, still asleep, before curling up again as though she were still there for him to cozy up to.

Molly giggled softly as she watched him. After a minute she rose and went to the window, and stared down at the dark ribbon of river that was only just now becoming visible with the lightening sky. The urge to wake Jack up was strong, but that would not be fair. Just because she could not sleep, that did not mean she should deprive him, but she would be bored out of her mind after ten or fifteen minutes of sitting in the semi-dark staring out the window.

The television was a bad idea. Even with the volume on low it was possible that it would wake Jack. But its dark face called to her, and if she did not find some way to distract herself, she was just going to wake him up anyway, so it was not long before she surrendered. Molly picked up the remote control and perched on the end of the bed. She clicked the set on and turned the volume down instantly, so low she thought it would be barely audible to dogs. The image brought another smile to her face.

The *click* as she changed channels was louder than

the volume, but that could not be helped. *Click*, VH-1. *Click*, PBS. *Click*, Home Shopping Network. *Click*, CNN. *Click*, scrambled pornography. *Click*, Home and Garden. *Click*, the Food Network. *Click*, A&E. *Click*, *click*, *click*, network affiliates too early for network programming. Local news.

A familiar face.

Molly frowned, staring at the nearly mute television set. In that gray morning light, still edging toward dawn, with the feel of Jack's body against her and the warmth of his breath on her neck still fresh in her memory, the room seemed to quiver with a kind of surreal quality, the world in soft focus. Not quite a dream, but not quite life yet either.

A familiar face. What was her name again? Stephanie? No, Suzanne. That was it. Suzanne.

With a frown, Molly turned the volume up just enough to hear clearly.

". . . no evidence that the driver of the truck, Marie Suzanne Robinson, was under the influence of alcohol or drugs at the time of the crash. Although police have offered the theory that the veteran trucker fell asleep at the wheel, other causes have not yet been ruled out. For more on the story, we take you live to Hollingsworth, where . . ."

The image on the screen switched to a live feed that showed a tractor-trailer truck on its side in a tree-lined gulley, jackknifed so that the cab and trailer jutted up at opposite angles. Police and rescue vehicles were parked haphazardly on the soft shoulder, and a group of uniformed men and women stood around together, staring down into the gulley with hands on hips and scratching their heads. Molly sympathized because she knew they had to be thinking exactly what she was thinking. *How the hell are they supposed to get that stupid thing out of the ditch?*

That was a problem, however, because that was not what they should have been thinking at all. What they really ought to have been thinking was, *How many more of these freak accidents have to happen before someone around here's bright enough to start thinking maybe it's not a coincidence? Aren't two in a week enough to give even the rustiest mind a little intuitive oil?*

Molly gazed at the screen, almost numb as the reporter at the scene detailed how fortunate it was that the accident had happened in the wee hours of the morning when there were so few motorists on the road. That another trucker had radioed in the crash but wished to remain anonymous. *I'll bet,* Molly thought. That Marie Suzanne Robinson came from Wheeling, West Virginia, and was a divorced mother of two.

That snapped Molly out of the daze she had been in. Suzanne had been a mother. Two children, both high-school age, according to the news. And hadn't they worked fast to dig up this information on a woman who had been dead only hours?

"Damn it," Molly whispered.

She set the remote control down and moved over to sit just beside Jack. For a few seconds she stared at him, the innocence of his sleeping face in spite of the dark stubble on his chin. She ran her fingers across that rough growth, and then her eyes flicked back to the television. The picture of Suzanne was back, and then it was gone, and a story about pumpkin-carving contests had taken its place.

Something curdled in her stomach.

Molly reached out and shook Jack, whispering his name.

"Hey, Jack, come on. Wake up."

In her dreams Eden Hirsch had hundreds of names, one for each of the lives she had lived over the course of forgotten millennia. Lorenza, Gwendolyn, Astrid, Johannes, Viktor, Collette . . . so many that she could never remember them all. In the landscape of her own sleeping mind her steps took her through time, across the icy fields of thousand-year-old Russian winters and the sparkling spring nights of nineteenth-century Paris, hot summers on the streets of ancient Rome and gentle autumn breezes across the Chesapeake Bay in the Roaring Twenties.

Hundreds of names.

Yet only one face. With each of her lives the face that looked back at her from the mirror had changed, but in the dreamworld that face was always the same. No matter the name, or the memories that spun and traced and molded her dreams like clay on a potter's wheel, she was Eden Hirsch now in body and soul, and that was the form she wore in her subconscious journeys.

This dream took her to an island in Polynesia long

centuries past. Her name was Muani, and each day when her chores were done and the men of the village were fishing, she would take long walks around the island to find a shaded, silent spot where she could sit and listen to the wind and the waves, enjoying the peace of this life and remembering the many others that had come before it.

Muani sat now in her dream—in Eden's dream—beneath the trees atop a small hill that overlooked the cove where the villagers did most of their fishing. She could feel the breeze rustling through her long, dark hair, and she closed her eyes for just a moment, tasting the heat and the salt on the air.

"Beautiful."

Her eyes opened and she glanced beside her. Artie Carroll sat with his back against a tree and his knees drawn up in front of him. He wore blue jeans and a hooded sweatshirt torn at the neck, and his sneakers were untied. The way his unruly blond hair fell nearly to his shoulders reminded her of another time, a Viking warrior she had known in another life, when she had worn another face and name. The warrior was called Ottar, and Artie had the same smile, the same glint of mischief in his eyes. It had occurred to Eden that the two might indeed be one and the same, and Artie never knew. Not all souls returned, and of those that did, few remembered.

When her name had been Roskva, she had loved Ottar.

"It *is* beautiful, isn't it? I never know where my

dreams will take me, and yet somehow I often find myself drifting back here."

Artie grinned. "I'm not surprised. Even when we can't consciously control it, I think our minds are always dragging us back to the things we long for." An expression of surprise appeared upon his face, and then he shrugged. "Not that I want to get all philosophical."

"There's nothing wrong with philosophy, Artie. Each of us spends our lives developing our own. It's how we learn to understand things."

He reached out to her, and her dream shifted just enough so that they might be close enough to touch. Hands brushed close by and there seemed a moment when she grabbed at nothing. Then their fingers intertwined and Eden uttered a tiny gasp. She could feel his skin upon hers. It was only illusion, she knew. In her mind—perhaps in both of their minds—but it felt real.

Artie felt it too, for his eyes widened and then he laughed. "That's new."

"Yes," she agreed, gazing at him. "It must be you. Your focus."

"I'm not doing anything."

"No, but Seth was never able to touch me."

They fell silent then, there on her dream island. Seth had been her spirit guide over the course of many of her lives, a friend from the distant past with whom she had lingered in the Ghostlands, the afterlife, before she had been reborn. Seth had not come back, but he had stayed with her as a spirit, visiting her in her dreams until she died again. And again. And again.

WILD THINGS

Seth was gone now, but almost as though fate had played a role in it, the very night she had lost her old friend, she had met Artie. Somehow her frequent reincarnation had blurred the border between her dreams and the Ghostlands, and spirits could pass back and forth. Artie had begun to visit her in her dreams, and Eden welcomed him. He was sweet and funny and lonely, and he was dead. Without a spirit guide to connect her to the Ghostlands, Eden would have felt lost in the flesh world. Artie kept an eye on those he had loved when he was alive, but now Eden provided him with a vital tether.

The hot breeze blew, and they smiled at each other.

"Eden," he said.

"Muani," she corrected. "It's Muani here."

"Muani. This is pretty cool."

"Yes. It really is."

They found themselves then sitting side by side, backs to the same thick tree. Birdsong filled the air, and the surf crashed on the shore below the hill. Eden felt the warm pressure of his hand in hers and she squeezed. Artie squeezed back.

The phone rang.

Eden woke with a frown knitting her brows. Dawn splashed across the foot of her bed. Outside the window was a golden morning, the sky brightening with each passing moment. The phone rang again and Eden sat up, the tangled mess of her dark curls falling down around her face, across her eyes. With the third ring she stretched and yawned and blinked her eyes, coming fully awake at last. A sadness swept through her, and she glanced around her elegant bedroom.

"Sorry," she whispered to the empty room.

Halfway into the fourth ring she picked up the phone and lay back onto her pillow.

"It is awfully early," she said.

"I know, Eden, and I'm sorry if I woke you up."

She knew the voice right away. "Jack."

"Yeah. Listen, Molly and I are in New York in this little town called Fairbrook. It's off Route Eighty-seven, a little north of—"

"I know where it is," she said, stifling another yawn. "I used to live not far from there."

There was a pause on the other end of the line before Jack went on. "You did? When was that?"

"Turn of the century. It was nice back then. I remember the Wild West show came through in aught-one. That was something else. Truly a marvel, even by today's standards."

"Wow," Jack said, and she could tell by the tone of his voice that he meant it.

Eden smiled. Though she knew Jack's heart belonged to Molly, there were very few people in her life with whom she could speak so freely about her past. It was nice.

"Stories for another time, Jack. I suppose you're calling for Artie."

"Yes. If he's around. We're trying to track down a pack in this area, and we could really use his help."

WILD THINGS

Eden flexed the fingers of her left hand. It still felt warm where Artie's ghost had touched her. The sensation was nice, but also bittersweet, for it was only in her dreams that she could see him, feel his touch, and she had a life to live. Her response to Jack then was tinged with sadness, because if Artie went, she did not know how long he would be gone, how many dreams she would have without him. She would miss him. Still, in life, Jack and Molly had been the people Artie cared about more than anyone else in the world.

"I'll pass it on," she said. "Good luck."

Jack thanked her and they said their good-byes. As Eden hung up the phone she gazed again around the empty room, at the hand-painted Carnival masks and framed pages of 150-year-old fashion magazines that hung on the walls. Antique perfume bottles lined her bureau, and a silk gown hung on the back of her door. Her things. Her place.

With a short, resigned sigh she spoke to that room, to the ghost of a young man she had become quite fond of. His friends needed him, she said, and she explained where he could find them. For a moment her hand tingled with warmth again and she felt a breeze caress her cheek though no window was open.

Then the room seemed even emptier than before.

The Blueberry Diner was a sight to behold. Though only the jutting flagpole of a sign was visible from the highway, the place was a stone's throw from the Hollingsworth exit ramp. With its vast, cracked parking lot lined with trucks and the row of windows along its face, the diner would have been interchangeable with hundreds of others if not for the paint job that gave the Blueberry its name. The entire building had been adorned with several coats of bluish purple paint that gleamed wetly in the sun.

"Wow," Jack said in honest admiration as he pulled the Jeep into the lot. "That's *blue*, all right."

"Oh, yes," Molly agreed. "Sort of purple, too, but all in all, I'm not sure I've ever seen anything so blue."

They both stared at the place in amazement as Jack parked among the handful of cars in front of the Blueberry, a half dozen or so vehicles that were dwarfed by the tractor-trailers, and which Jack suspected were owned by the employees of the diner. Nobody hauled electronic components in Ford station wagons, as far as he knew.

"What was it that guy said yesterday?" Molly asked him as she got out of the Jeep. "The guy with the crew cut?"

"That we should talk to Max, because he knows everyone."

"No, no," Molly said, waving the words away as if they were annoying gnats. "I mean about breakfast. What did he say was good here?"

Surprised, Jack glanced at her. "Where did that girl go? The one who woke me up because she was so freaked about that lady trucker getting killed?"

A hurt look flickered across Molly's features. "Don't do that, even kidding. I know why we're here, Jack, but we also have to eat breakfast."

"Hey," he said softly, slipping an arm around her. "None of this is fun. I was teasing, yeah, but I'm also glad you can think about something else. And it was French toast, I think. The guy with the crew said the French toast was good."

Jack pulled the door open for her. Molly surprised him with a kiss on the cheek, then grabbed his hand and they went into the Blueberry Diner together.

Jack was more than a little relieved to find that whatever mad diner genius had lathered the exterior of the building in gaudy berry colour had been stopped before reaching the interior. Inside, the Blueberry was mundane, a simple arrangement of counter, stools, and booths that had been an unchanged formula for fifty years or more. Four of the dozen or so booths were occupied, as were about half the stools. Normally Jack would have opted for a booth, but aside from breakfast their purpose in coming here was to meet Max, the counterman mentioned by the jarhead the night before.

As they crossed to the counter and slid onto a pair of stools, heads turned. Jack knew that he wasn't the only person who found Molly attractive. Her hair alone, that wild red mane that she could barely control, was enough to draw stares. But the attention they were getting just then was for both of them, not just her, and he supposed it was natural enough for the people in the diner to be curious. He felt as though he was wearing a sign around his neck that said NOT A TRUCK DRIVER.

Once they had settled in at the counter and picked up menus, the truckers all went back to their breakfast and conversation. Jack glanced at Molly and gave her a smile with just the corner of his mouth.

A waitress in blue jeans and a white blouse hustled a tray to one of the booths. She was a thin woman who looked almost too frail to balance such a heavy tray. Over her clothes was draped an apron the same screaming purplish blue as the diner's outer walls, but someone had taken it one step further. On the front of the apron, inside a white border, was a big blueberry with a face and arms and legs and a lunatic's grin. Jack thought it looked like an octopus—like an old cartoon character called Squiddly Diddly, in fact—but he supposed it must be a blueberry.

The waitress slid dishes of eggs Benedict and sausages and pancakes onto the table, along with another plate piled high with an unrecognizable heap of food he suspected must be what the menu identified as the Trash Can Special. She called everyone "hon," as though she had been brought in from Hollywood's central casting to play the gum-snapping, tough-gal local waitress. What ruined that impression was the fact that she was not visibly chewing gum, as well as the light in her eyes and the laugh that seemed about to burst out at any moment, as if she knew all her "hon"s and "sweetie"s were expected of her, and she was in on the joke.

Down along the counter a grizzled-looking, fiftyish guy was pouring coffee for a sad-eyed, dough-faced trucker who didn't look much older than Jack himself. The counterman had a thick head of salt-and-pepper hair and a moustache to match, and he had not bothered to shave for the previous day or so. His apron was white, and Jack had the idea that he would not have worn the maniac octopus-blueberry apron even if someone had held a gun to his head.

Jack caught his eye, and the counterman brightened and strolled over, passing an obscene pleasantry with a coffee-skinned man who clutched a cigarette in his teeth and looked more than a little like the actor Laurence Fishburne. With his laughter still echoing, he zeroed in on them.

"So, what can I get you folks?"

"I'll have French toast," Molly said immediately, "orange juice, hash browns, and bacon."

"Hungry," the counterman said appreciatively. "That's the way we like 'em." He focused on Jack. "What about you?"

"I'll have the French toast too. We heard it was something special."

The counterman scraped a hand across his bristly chin and studied them a bit more closely. "You did, didja? We don't get a lot of tourists in the Blueberry, mostly long-haul folks. I'm glad someone around here appreciates us."

"Actually, it wasn't anybody local," Jack explained. "It was a truck driver. Guy with a crew cut. We met him last night. He was with a few other people, these two brothers, Dave and Hank . . . what was it? Cross, maybe."

"Krause," Molly corrected.

The counterman beamed at her, and Jack knew it was time for him to keep quiet. He figured they had a much better chance of this guy opening up if Molly did the talking.

"Dave!" the man said happily. "Hell of a guy. Then the crew cut had to be John Ford. Ford always gets the French toast. He has it with berries, though, if he didn't mention it. Sort of our specialty."

"Why didn't I guess that?" Molly teased. Then the smile disappeared from her face. "There was a woman with them. Suzanne. We saw on the news this morning . . ."

Her words trailed off as the counterman began to nod sadly. "Saw that myself. A terrible shame. We were all just stunned in here." Then his eyes widened and he pointed at them. "Wait, you know what? The Krause boys were in here last night, and I think they mentioned you two. You're the ones related to the Wilkes boy."

Jack stiffened, a bit taken aback by the man's knowledge of them. But Molly only smiled again.

"You must be Max," she said.

Max's eyebrows went up. "I'm famous now?"

"Your friend John told us you know everyone. I guess he thought maybe you'd heard something that might help us figure out what happened to my cousin." Jack lowered his voice and leaned in a bit. "I've heard about some other things that have happened, about this couple, the Rausches, who were killed, and a trucker just last week, Chester Douglas."

"Yeah, poor Chet. First him and now Suzanne. Been

a hell of a month so far," Max said grimly, real anguish in his eyes. "I wish I could help you folks, I really do. I know the stories, of course. Heard about your young cousin and that married couple, and plenty of others in the years I've been working this counter. Bad things happen on the highway, just a fact of life. World wasn't like this when I was a boy.

"Truth be told, every trucker comes through here has a story or a theory. Serial killers, alien abductions, monsters, hoaxes, Bigfoot . . . you name it. Hell, half of the drivers blame the media for blowing things out of proportion, making things seem worse than they are. Planes and trains and boats and cars, there are always accidents, right? But long-haul truckers, that's a story. Still, you get two in a week like we've got here, makes you think."

Jack nodded, but he was barely paying attention now. Given how secretive, even worried, the jarhead had seemed the night before, he had held out hope that Max would be able to give them a lead, no matter how slim. But the man had nothing. Just rumour, the same way Jack figured the bartender at the roadhouse in Fairbrook would have. This place was a dead end. If he weren't so hungry, he might have simply gotten up and left.

Max scribbled their order on a pad and ripped the sheet off, then turned and slid it through a window to the kitchen, where the cook would grab it. He snatched a plate of sausage and eggs off the shelf and placed it in front of the guy with the Laurence Fishburne intensity.

Then, as though it were an afterthought, Max glanced back at them.

"Kind of surprised you ran into those folks last night, though," he said.

"Why's that?" Jack asked.

Max shrugged. "Well, like I said, most of the drivers that come through here have heard plenty of stories on the road. Some stretches of highway, they're kinda reluctant to spend the night in their rig. This is one of them."

Then he was off down the counter again to refill some coffee cups. Jack stared after him a moment, then glanced at Molly.

At her.

Then past her, to where the ghost of Artie Carroll stood just outside the window staring in, his body a silhouette of translucent mist, barely visible in the bright sun.

Out of the corner of his eye Jack saw Molly staring at him. He turned to her. "Excuse me a second, will you? I left something in the Jeep."

She hesitated just slightly before nodding. "Sure," she said.

But they both knew what was really going on.

Jack got up and walked out of the diner, self-conscious, well aware that many of the people inside were watching him as he left. There were only a few other women in the place, but he was not worried about Molly. It was early in the morning, after all, and despite the rough-and-tumble reputation Hollywood had given truckers, the people in the diner seemed harmless enough.

As Jack pushed out the door Artie sauntered over, his body little more than an after-image, the suggestion of a person, like the shimmer of a rainbow in the spray of water on a summer's day. Jack had thought, early on, that he would never get used to seeing ghosts, these phantom souls transposed against the solid, three-dimensional world, but the truth was, it had become easier for him to deal with. The Ghostlands and the afterlife, the spirit world.

The dead.

But with Artie it was different. The fact of Artie's death still hurt him, the memories they had shared still fresh. How could he be dead, this guy who'd been his best friend since he was old enough to really know what it meant to have a best friend? Taunting their nebbishy algebra teacher in high school; playing one-on-one hoops at a concrete lot behind Artie's grandfather's house in Southie, tough guys at the age of ten; debating the fascism of action films, the dangers of smoking, and whether or not Ghia Frantangelo had really been wearing nothing under her skirt during that assembly in junior year.

Those memories were all laced with a kind of melancholy now, and he imagined that would never go away. On the other hand, though, Artie's appearance did not disturb him as much as it once had. What still unnerved him, however, no matter how often he saw the apparitions of the dead, were their eyes. Artie's eyes. Unlike the rest of him, they seemed solid, not the gossamer texture of spirit forms, which seemed spun of spiders' webs, but black little holes punched through this world into another. Dark rips through which one might see into the Ghostlands for real if one looked hard enough.

Jack had reached the point where he tried not to look.

On top of that, of course, there was still a bit of awkwardness about his feelings for Molly, who had been Artie's girlfriend for years. Still, despite all of that, all Jack had to do was look at the grin on his friend's face, the shaggy blond hair that hung to his neck, the careless way he stood staring at the Blueberry Diner, and he could not help but smile.

Artie stared at the diner and shook his head in astonishment. "*Man,* this place is blue."

Jack laughed, trying to keep his face hidden from the people inside so they wouldn't think he was crazy. "Come on," he muttered as he walked across the parking lot. Once he was inside the Jeep, with the spectre of his best friend—dead half a year now—in the seat beside him, Jack at last spoke.

"Good to see you, man. Thanks for coming."

"Just reach out, partner, and I'll be there."

Jack raised an eyebrow. "Don't sing. Really. That would be bad."

The ghost gave him the finger.

"We could really use your help," Jack told him.

"So I heard," Artie replied, slouched in the seat in an imitation of life. "Another conspiracy. It's good to see you, too, Jack. Always. How are things with Molly?"

Jack swallowed, shifted awkwardly in his seat. "How are things with Eden?"

Artie grinned. "Touché. For what it's worth, I've got my fingers crossed for you two."

"It's worth everything," Jack said solemnly. "You know that."

There was a long moment when neither of them spoke. Then Artie nodded and threw up his hands.

"So, what can I do for you guys?"

Jack gave him the rundown on Jared Wilkes, Doug and Arlene Rausch, Chet Douglas, and Suzanne Robinson. "If you can find any of them in the Ghostlands, or anyone else around here who knows anything about the Prowlers, it would be a huge help."

"Anything," Artie said. "You know that, Jack. Word travels on my side of the fence, bro. If there have been as many attacks around here as you think, it shouldn't be a problem."

"Thanks." For a moment Jack felt the urge to shake Artie's hand or clasp his shoulder, to make contact. It opened a fresh wound in his heart to remind himself that such contact was impossible.

Artie must have seen the pain in Jack's expression, for he gave his friend a knowing look and a gentle nod. "I know. It's getting harder instead of easier, isn't it? Weird."

And that was the truth of it. Jack had just been thinking that he was getting used to seeing the dead, that it was easier now. And that was true, too. But seeing Artie was different. All it did was remind him again and again of what he had lost, what they had *all* lost.

"Weird," Jack agreed.

Artie gazed at him with those eternal eyes. "Give her my love," he said. "I'll be back."

Then he was simply gone, like the flame of a candle that has been snuffed, yet without even a telltale swirl of smoke to mark his departure. Jack stared at the empty seat beside him a moment and then reached out to open his door. As he did the cell phone clipped to the back of his belt began to ring.

CHAPTER 6

The apartment was too quiet.

Courtney was in Jack's room, sitting on the edge of his bed. Her cane was heavy enough to sink deep into the comforter, and this illustration of its weight, its substance, surprised her. Next to the cane was her cellular phone, painfully silent and still, like the apartment. Soon Wendy and Tim would arrive downstairs, and other members of the staff not long after, and then the gears in the mechanism that was Bridget's Irish Rose Pub would start to grind, and they wouldn't wind down until after one in the morning.

Right now, though, the whole building was too quiet. It was all a ghost to her. Not the benevolent spirit of her mother that she often felt looking over her shoulder on the premises of this place that Bridget Dwyer had worked so hard to build. Though Jack insisted he had never seen their mother's ghost,

Courtney secretly felt that the pub would forever be imbued with her soul. But the spectre that haunted her now was something else entirely. It was an emptiness, a loneliness, a dread that filled her with the certainty that awful things were in motion, things that could only lead to grief.

The previous night was the first she had slept alone in the apartment in some time. It had never really bothered her before, but now that she knew her childhood fears were real, that monsters really did lurk in the shadows and closets and under the bed, it was different. More than anything, she needed Jack here, right now.

Right now.

He had been only nine years old when their mother was killed in the same accident that had left Courtney with a permanent limp, and yet Jack had always been her strength. There were other phones in the apartment, but Courtney had come in here to make a call because she needed his confidence to steady her. Even with him absent, just being in his room helped. It held his essence, neat and sparsely decorated. Jack was a kid who had never liked clutter, never needed a lot of things around to distract him from life. They had that in common, Courtney guessed.

And although outsiders might have thought she was the strong one, holding them together despite Jack's age when they were orphaned, building the pub into the successful enterprise it was today, it had really been Jack all along. She could remember with perfect clarity the way he had looked at her the morning after their mother's funeral, when he had walked in to find her crying, wondering aloud how they were going to carry on, to make it work. He had stood there in his Ninja Turtles pajamas, eyes wide and earnest, and insisted that they would be all right if they just stuck together. That they could handle anything together.

Courtney had asked how he could be so sure. His reply was only bittersweet and precious then. Now it gave her chills to remember those words, words she was certain Jack did not recall ever speaking.

"I dreamed about Mommy last night," he had said. "She danced with me to 'Irish Eyes Are Smiling,' and she told me we were gonna be okay, Court. Everything's gonna be okay."

Now, a decade later, Courtney sat on her little brother's bed and picked up his phone from its cradle. She did not dare use her own cellular, for she feared that the moment she tried would be that moment that Bill would try to call. She stared at the lifeless cellular that lay on the bed beside her, cursing it in her head. With Jack's phone in her hand she dialled. On the other end of the line she heard ringing, and then he answered.

"Court?"

At the sound of his voice she fell apart. Her left hand clutched the phone tight enough that it hurt, and her right fluttered up to her face. She sat rigid on the edge of the bed.

"Jack. Have you heard from Bill?"

Pause, as the implications of her question sank in. "No. We haven't. What's the matter, Courtney? It's not even nine in the morning. It's too early to freak out if he hasn't called yet today. I mean, I know—"

"No. That's not it. He *did* call."

Another moment's hesitation. "What happened?"

A sickening flutter began in her stomach. It didn't feel like butterflies, the way they always describe it in books and on television. This felt more like someone had shoved his entire fist into her stomach and was rooting around in there looking for something.

"It rang twice. When I picked it up he was already gone. I checked the caller ID, though, and it came from his phone."

"Twice," Jack repeated.

Courtney knew what he meant. Their signal for an emergency was one ring. Only one ring. If Bill was trying to tell her something, run up a red flag, he would have done a single ring and left it at that.

"Twice," Courtney said again. "But Jack, I tried calling him back, and there was no answer."

"Take a breath, Court," he said. "All right, listen, it's too early to jump to conclusions. Could be he called you from somewhere, then went into a dead zone or something where there was no signal. That would explain it all."

He was right, too. That would explain it all. But the dread that was eating her up inside would not let her believe that was all it was.

"I guess," she replied.

"Chances are he'll call later. If he has a lead on Olivia, he might get pretty sidetracked. Try him every couple of hours. And if he hasn't connected with you by tonight, first thing tomorrow we'll get in the Jeep and drive down to Manhattan. Just try not to panic yet."

Courtney lay back on his bed and closed her eyes. "All right. Okay, little brother. I just hate this, being back here alone. Makes me feel helpless."

"He's probably fine," Jack insisted. "Really. Now, don't you have some work to do?"

A smile spread across Courtney's face. "Jerk."

They both laughed softly, then said their good-byes and hung up. For another few minutes she just sat there, but eventually Courtney picked up her cane and her cell phone, rose, and went out of the room. He might have been teasing her, but Jack was right. She had a great deal of work to do. Work that would help take her mind off Bill, and those two rings.

Two rings, not one.

And yet she could not shake the feeling something had gone very, very wrong.

Deep beneath Manhattan, in a tunnel that lay forgotten by all but a handful of record keepers, on a rail that dead-ended at a stone wall, sat a pair of antique train cars that had not carried passengers in more than seventy years. A cave-in had made the use of that stretch of the line untenable, and only homeless squatters had been aboard since then.

Until now.

The cars had been cleaned inside and out, starting with the scouring of all trace of human presence from the wooden train. The occupants had been dragged onto the tracks first, however. No need to make even more of a mess inside. In a matter of weeks this underground dwelling had been transformed. Alec and several other members of the pack had followed home a trendy Soho couple and slain them in their living room. The very same night a stolen truck had carried drapes, art, carpets, and furniture belonging to the dead pair—Joe and Annie Beldin—to the Forty-eighth Street overpass. A mahogany sleigh bed had been shattered in the process of lowering the booty down to the tracks, but the two train cars were cluttered enough as it was.

Jasmine lay curled upon a bed of goose-down pillows with an ivory comforter over her filled with the same material. She loved the smell of the old wood now that it had been polished, and there was an old beauty to this new lair she had claimed that enchanted her. The Beldins' taste had been superb. The windows were covered with silks, and there were paintings, wood carvings, and handblown glass from Venice.

Though they had tapped power lines in the adjacent tunnel and there were lamps on board, Jasmine much preferred candles. The windows had been repaired and the doors restored, yet there was still a significant draft from the tunnel, and the candlewicks burned with a constant flutter that cast strange shadows on the walls, a strange sort of theatre as dark shapes flowed into one another with each flicker of light.

There were a few spatters of blood on the stereo system, which sat on an antique sideboard at the far end of the car, but Jasmine had not bothered to clean them off. The sultry velvet voice of Billie Holiday lingered in the air with smoke from the candles, along with tinny music recorded in another age. Listening to it was much like going back in time for Jasmine, and she stretched languorously on her downy bed and let herself be swept away by the ache and pain in the voice of a woman long dead.

The music made her think of Tanzer. He had been her lover, the Alpha of her pack, and he had had a great ambition. In long-ago times Tanzer's father had been one of the finest leaders and warriors their race had ever seen, but over time the Prowlers had become little better than vermin. Many of them merely wanted to survive, to live among the human cattle, even to love them. Others, including the remnants of once proud packs, subsisted by hunting only on the fringes of human society, preying upon hunters in the wilderness or the homeless in the inner city.

Tanzer had been a beast with a dream. He wanted to unite all the packs in the world, to repopulate the land with Prowlers, and eventually to rise up and show the humans their place as prey for a superior species.

Jack Dwyer and Molly Hatcher had killed him and engineered the slaughter of most of the pack. Jasmine had escaped alone. She had run away, and the shame of that burned within her.

Now she was the Alpha of a new pack, and with each day that passed they grew stronger and more numerous. Jasmine had loved Tanzer, adored him, but she was not foolish enough to look upon him as perfect. He had made mistakes, that much was clear. If he had not, he would likely still be alive. And so she learned from his mistakes. Tanzer would have been far too proud to embrace this underground lair; he would have considered it cowardly to hide in such a way.

Jasmine considered it simple logic.

From this forgotten place they had access to a warren of tunnels that could take them anywhere in the city. They could hunt wherever they liked, and if they were discovered, there were a thousand possible escapes. Whereas Tanzer would have felt denigrated by living beneath the humans, it gave Jasmine an intoxicating sense of power. She could strike at them whenever and wherever she liked.

First, though, the pack must grow strong. Most of them were unknown to her, and so she must forge a bond with them. Already she had faced half a dozen challenges from the new group, and she had cowed them all in battle, forced them to bare their throats to her. At last they were truly beginning to look upon her as Alpha, as the superior warrior among them.

The music played softly in the candlelit darkness of the train car. Jasmine knew she ought to rise, knew it was midmorning at least, but there was a pleasure in simply lying there, listening to the ache in that human voice. Humans were capable of such beauty, and yet so often they squandered it. It disgusted her. But the pain in that voice made her think of Tanzer, and of how much she missed the wild. At last she sat up and glanced around the car, and she made a silent vow that much as this lair amused her, there would be a time soon when she would take the pack back to the wilderness.

For the truth was, though she had surrounded herself with beautiful, elegant things, and she knew that coming to the city had been necessary, she did not like it here. Humans were the most dangerous prey imaginable, and she would not underestimate them the way that Tanzer had. Down there in the belly of this city she was haunted by the knowledge that humans had the power to destroy them. Jasmine had seen too many of her kind slaughtered by human weapons, human hands.

In the bowels of this city that represented all that humanity was capable of, there was the constant banshee wail of passing trains, their wheels screeching metal upon metal on the tracks. To Jasmine those screams were the death cries of her race.

And that was the true purpose of the music that played constantly inside her strange, beautiful lair. It blocked out the ever present metal whisper of the ghosts.

There was a loud rap on the door at the far end of the car.

"Come," Jasmine called.

The door opened and Alec stepped up into the train. He wore his human face, and, though she had no physical appreciation of humans the way some of her kind did, Jasmine could not deny that his appearance even in that form was pleasing. Alec's skin was a rich bronze, his hair black as tar, and his eyes—his eyes never changed. He was dressed very well, too well for the underground, but their business took him above often. The moment he stepped up into the car, he looked at her and a smile bloomed upon his face as though whatever had been on his mind was gone in a moment, pushed out of his head by the mere sight of her.

Jasmine liked that. That was the way it ought to be.

Alec was followed a moment later by Connor, a recent addition to the pack who had proved himself invaluable in contacting other Prowlers in Manhattan and the outer boroughs of New York City. Where Alec was elegant, Connor was a pit bull, a squat, broad creature whose false human facade made him look like a fortyish ex-boxer. When he entered, Connor's eyes were upon Jasmine, but he dropped his gaze and gave her a respectful nod. He might not be used to life in the pack, but he was learning fast.

"Good morning, love," Alec said sweetly, bright and happy as always.

"I woke and you were gone," she replied, stretching again as she rose to her feet.

Many of the wooden benches that had originally been in the train car were rotten when she discovered it. She had saved the best two and had them restored, while the others had been torn out and disposed of. Now Jasmine sat upon one of the benches and waited for Alec to come to her. He moved to her quickly, slid next to her on the bench, and kissed her temple.

"I went in to visit our guest this morning," he confessed. "I brought him his cell phone and let him make a call back home. He didn't want to actually tell them to come, but who can blame him? He let it ring a couple of times and hung up. I'm headed upstairs now to spread the word to keep an eye and ear out for them. Once they start asking around for him, we'll have them."

Alec seemed as if he had more to say, but instead he laid a hand on her leg and glanced away. Jasmine frowned and studied him. In her peripheral vision she could see Connor shifting awkwardly, watching them in silence.

"There's more?" Jasmine prodded her lover.

"Just wondering," Alec replied. He cleared his throat and sat up straighter, gazed at her again. "Cantwell's playing along. He wants his sister's kid, that's understandable. But everything we know says he cares about this Dwyer woman and her brother. How can you trust him to just go away? He's done his job now, made that call. Why not just kill him and be done with it?"

Jasmine stiffened, felt her hackles rising. Her eyes narrowed and Alec flinched from the look on her face. *As well he should*, she thought. She ran her tongue out over her teeth, and her gaze darted to Connor. He wore jeans and a white shirt, a navy blue jacket over it; dressed to go topside, just like Alec. They had become friends quickly, despite the vast difference in their positions within the hierarchy of the pack. Connor took a step toward the door of the train car as though he desperately wanted to leave, but he dared not go any farther.

With a flourish Jasmine reached out and caressed Alec's face, traced her fingers along the contours of this human masque he wore.

"Let me tell you about our guest in the next car," she said, her voice a rasp, almost a growl. From a nearby tunnel came the scream of a passing train, and a rush of wind blew into the car, snuffing several of the candles and making the illumination cast upon the walls and curtains shudder. On the sound system Billie Holiday moaned out the last notes of the final song, and the speakers went silent.

Alec and Connor stared at Jasmine, waiting.

Jasmine smiled. "I tried to have him killed a couple of months ago. Even before that, if I had been able to, I would have disemboweled him myself. But that was before I knew, before I understood who he was. You already know that he has been living for some time under an alias. This is nothing new. Most of our kind who attempt to blend with the human herd change their name and appearance from time to time, move to new cities, begin new lives.

"His true name, the one he was given at birth, is Guillaume Navarre. Son of Yves Navarre."

The name had the desired effect. Connor perked up, truly interested now, and Jasmine saw in his eyes that he was trying to figure out why he knew that name. Alec's reaction was more pronounced. He blinked and swore under his breath.

Jasmine smiled, glanced at Connor. "You know that Owen Tanzer, who was Alpha of my pack before he was killed earlier this year, was the son of Wade Tanzer, one of the most ferocious leaders our kind ever knew. Before there was ever a United States, Wade Tanzer came to this country and gave the natives here their legends of skinwalkers. Some thought him the trickster spirit of their mythology. Wade was the greatest hunter of his pack, but he was not its Alpha until the death of the beast who was his greatest friend. Yves Navarre."

With a sound almost like a bark Alec swore in a guttural tongue rarely spoken by their kind anymore, the language of the beast.

"Yes," Jasmine agreed. She gazed deeply into his eyes and ducked forward, nuzzling gently, lovingly, at his throat. She licked the salt from his skin. "So now you see."

Once more she lifted her eyes and stared at him. "If I kill Bill Cantwell . . . if I kill Guillaume Navarre . . . I will join the ranks of the most notorious villains in our history. Prowlers the world over would hate me, hunt me, lust for my blood. The wild and the underground alike would despise me. And I cannot have that."

Slowly, deliberately, Jasmine smiled. "However, if this human rabble he cares so much for should discover his betrayal and kill him . . . that would be another thing entirely."

Understanding sparked in Alec's eyes, followed by desire. "You really are incredible," he told her.

Jasmine slashed her claws across his cheek and leaped to her feet. Alec cried out in pain and wonder even as she lunged across the train car at Connor. He froze, too stunned to react, and by the time he had begun to move to defend himself, Jasmine had forced him down on the carpet and torn his throat out with her teeth. Hot blood fountained from his ragged neck and splashed her face, and she licked it greedily from her mouth.

Behind her Alec snarled, and she heard the popping of his bones as he changed. When she spun he was already transformed, his human clothes were too well tailored, and they tore and hung from his sleek black fur in rags.

"What are you doing?" he growled, furious and distraught and afraid.

Jasmine spat a piece of Connor's flesh to the ground and glared at him. "I have done nothing, Alec. You just cost this creature his life. This *friend* of yours. You questioned my judgment, treated me as though I were yours rather than you mine. I will have obedience and I will have respect. Connor saw and heard that conversation, and so one of you had to die. You for speaking that way, or him for having overheard. I chose him. This time.

"You please me, Alec. But if ever you disrespect me again, it will be your blood I wear."

The Jeep was parked in the breakdown lane on Route 87, the passenger-side tires well off the shoulder of the highway in order to give passing cars plenty of room to drift. The hazard lights were on, but Jack hoped that the blinking wouldn't bring the state police by for a visit. Once upon a time, that would have been less likely, but when so many people had cellular phones, chances were there would be one Samaritan in the bunch who would want to help. Of course, once upon a time, people like that would have pulled over and offered their assistance, but everyone was so afraid these days. Who knew what kind of monster might be lying in wait on the side of the road?

The thought made Jack smile, but there was nothing funny about it. On the other hand, he also figured anyone who paid attention to the news in this area would be even less likely to stop, given the rate of strange deaths and disappearances on this stretch of highway.

He slammed his door and dropped his keys into his pocket. Molly was already out of the Jeep, and she took the lead as they scrambled down the embankment to a stand of trees that had been burned out by a fire. The ground was black and charred, and the trees themselves had been scorched before fire crews had managed to put them out. A couple of large evergreens had been brought down at the edge of the wood, but Jack figured that was from the crash of the truck, not from the blaze.

"People are going to think we're pretty ghoulish," Molly said.

She stood to his right, her hands stuffed in her pockets, chin tucked slightly downward, and in that moment she looked to him like a little girl. It was a reminder that she was, after all, just out of high school, not even nineteen yet. Not for another three months. Hell, Jack himself had just turned twenty a few weeks earlier. He was like that blond Hitler Youth kid in *The Sound of Music,* thinking of her as young when he was only a year older. But right then, the way she stood, the sheepish, rather-be-anywhere-but-here look on her face . . . Jack couldn't help it.

"We can go if you want," he offered.

Molly glanced up in surprise. "Huh? No. I was just thinking how any time we're doing this, trying to track Prowlers, it always means we're hanging out in places where people have died horribly. Anyone driving by would think, 'Check out those guys, death-site tourists.'"

Jack laughed, and after a second Molly did too.

"Anyone who sees us down here is likely to think we're either out of gas, needing to pee, or sneaking off into the woods for some cheap thrills. Most of the people going by probably don't have any idea Chet Douglas died here. They'd see what's left of the fire, that's all. Even if they saw it on the news, they might not connect the two."

"I guess you're right," Molly replied.

Then she shrugged, pulled her hands from her pockets, and walked farther toward the place where the ground became charred. Jack thought of stories he had read as a boy, fairy tales about people who had crossed over into magic circles and been transported into fantastical realms. But the thought was gone the moment Molly stepped over that blackened border, the dead embers crumbling silently beneath her tread.

"So, what do you see?" she asked without turning, her attention focused on the burned trees.

And that was the big question, wasn't it? They had already been by the scene of Suzanne Robinson's so-called accident. Police tape was wrapped around trees, and crews were still at work removing the wreckage of her rig. But there had been no ghosts there. Now here, where Chet Douglas and his mysterious passenger had burned in yet another trucking accident, Jack paused a moment before he shifted his perception to look into the Ghostlands, for he knew what he was going to find.

He cleared his mind, took a breath, closed his eyes, and when he opened them again, the world had inverted. A now familiar queasiness hit his stomach as his flesh-and-blood reality became a pale shadow of itself, as though it, too, had been burned to lifeless ash. The Ghostlands, where the lost souls of the dead wandered, was a sea of gray mist that seemed to shimmer and swirl all around him.

Among the trees on the side of the road there were four that he could see perfectly well, in full colour, as though they had grown right there on the Ghostlands. Jack stared at them a moment before he realized what he was seeing. These four trees were dead.

He closed his eyes again and pinched the bridge of his nose. That small pain helped him focus, helped him come back.

"Well?" Molly asked.

He opened his eyes. The sun shone on her lush red hair in odd patterns where it streamed through the limbs of burned dead trees, but she shivered despite its warmth. The October wind was cold this morning. Molly gazed at him hopefully, but Jack was not certain if it was because she hoped he would find something, or because she simply wanted to leave.

"Nothing," he confessed.

Molly shook her head and started out of the trees and up the embankment without him. After a moment, when his stomach still felt a bit unsettled, Jack followed.

"You walk like a girl with a destination in mind," he said. "I was sort of thinking that unless you want to go by the county coroner's office, our best bet is just to wait until Artie comes back, see if he finds anything."

"One more stop," she said as she opened the door and climbed into the Jeep. "I want to go back to that rest stop we were at last night, where they found Jared Wilkes's body."

"There was nothing there," Jack reminded her as he walked around to his side.

"True. But we know Suzanne didn't die in any accident, and that was the last place anybody saw her, with those other three. I'm betting Dave Krause and his obnoxious brother weren't human."

Jack slid into the Jeep and started it up. Molly made complete sense, and he felt a bit foolish for not thinking of it himself. Chances were the Prowlers had watched them go, then waited for that other trucker to leave, the jarhead who'd caught up to them and tried to help. And then they had killed Suzanne.

He turned off the hazards and looked over his shoulder as he pulled out into northbound traffic on Route 87. Beside him Molly was silent and grim.

"You all right?" he asked.

"Just thinking about the kid. And that couple who were so much older when they got married, finally finding the person they thought they were meant to be with. And Suzanne. She was really nice to us, you know?"

"I know." Jack reached out and took Molly's hand.

"I hate this," Molly said. "So how come it means so much to me? It's ugly and sad, painful, never mind the danger we're putting ourselves in. So why can't I just walk away?"

"You've said it yourself," he replied. "We can't *know* about them and not do something to stop them."

Molly only nodded and squeezed his hand a little tighter.

They drove to the next exit and reversed direction, then drove south two exits before reversing again. When they reached their destination, the ghost of Suzanne Robinson was waiting.

And she was not alone.

CHAPTER 7

Jack saw the ghosts as he was pulling into the rest stop.

There were no trucks parked there just now, only a station wagon that he suspected was older than he was. The mom was leaned over the passenger seat trying to entertain a baby in the back, while the dad walked an older child, a boy of perhaps five, to the row of portable toilets.

Twenty or thirty feet along the curb from where the family had parked sat the spectre of Suzanne Robinson. She had her arm around another ghost, a guy about Jack's age. He was hunched over, his face in his hands, and he shuddered with the power of his sobs.

"They're here," Jack told Molly, his voice low.

"You see them already?"

Jack nodded. He knew what she meant. In the city he saw ghosts often enough without even trying. If a spirit was recently dead or simply strong enough, vital enough, it left an echo on the real world, and he could easily see it without looking into the Ghostlands. But along the highway he rarely saw them, save for the occasional hitchhiker, and since he and Molly had arrived, he had not seen even one of those lost souls, forever trying to reach their destination. Not seeing them did not mean they were not there, of course, which had been the whole point of his trying to look, shifting his perceptions so he could see into the Ghostlands.

Now, though, no such effort was required. Jack kept an eye on the two phantoms as he pulled the Jeep up to the curb. "They're over by that family, just sitting there. Suzanne and a young guy. It looks like he's crying."

"You can't talk to her with those people there," Molly said.

Jack had already opened his door, but now he hesitated. "I could. Might get them out of here faster."

A wan smile reached her lips. "Just wait a second."

So he did. They sat there in the Jeep and waited as the dad helped his little boy zip up before walking back to the station wagon together. The boy was skipping happily, singing a little nonsense song, even as the baby in the backseat of the wagon wailed in baby anguish, inconsolable over some unmet desire or another. The mom had gotten out of the car and had a small cooler on the roof, and she was pouring milk or formula from a jar into a bottle.

When Jack glanced back at the ghosts, the baby's

crying made a chilling counterpoint to the silent grief of the dead teenager Suzanne's spirit was trying to comfort. Even when at last the bottle was ready and the baby was quieted, Jack heard an echo of its need in the back of his mind. The family piled back into the wagon, and a moment later the car pulled away.

For just a moment Suzanne glanced up and watched it go. Jack could see the sorrow on her face, and he realised she knew what had happened, knew she was dead. She understood. Conflicting emotions surged up within him. He was sorry for her, and yet he was also relieved. It was better for their purposes if she knew.

He got down out of the Jeep and walked toward the two lost souls there on the curb. As he approached, Suzanne looked up at him curiously. In the shade from the trees she seemed a bit more solid from far away, but as he moved closer the illusion dispersed. Her body was little more than a swirl of vapour given form and dull colour. Through her chest he could see the ragged grass behind her. Through her pelvis, the cracked curb she was sitting on. Sometimes he had to remind himself that no matter how strong their presence, they weren't really there. Suzanne was no longer in this world. Talking to her was really a lot like placing a telephone call to somewhere else. A long-distance call. *Very long distance,* Jack thought.

"Hello, Suzanne," he said.

The ghost blinked her infinite black eyes several times. Then she smiled. "I was just staring at you thinking, 'He can't actually see me, it just seems like he's looking at me. He's probably just going into the woods to relieve himself, just like that boy did.'"

"I can see you."

The other spectre ceased his quiet sobbing and glanced up at Jack. "Allie. Do you know Allie?"

His expression was both desperate and somehow hollow, mystified with everything around him. Jack had seen that same look on the face of Artie's uncle Bob, who had Alzheimer's disease. It occurred to him then that the recently dead must feel an awful lot like those poor souls, unable to recognize anything around them. And yet in some ways once they became acclimated to the truth of their death, they were more the opposite of such people, able to recognise and speak to their loved ones but unable to get any response, as if everyone they had ever known had suddenly come down with Alzheimer's.

"Sorry, no," Jack said gently. "I don't know her."

"There's a monster in her," the spirit said with grave sincerity, gazing up into Jack's eyes. "Not even sure she knows it, but there's a monster in her. Asked her to go camping, and she told me—she *told* me it was a bad idea." He laughed madly and shook his head. "Shoulda listened to 'er, Chuck. Shoulda listened. Thought maybe being all alone in the woods, things might get romantic."

Chuck, if that was indeed his name, started to laugh again, but his voice abruptly choked off and the tears returned. Ghost tears. He was not going to be any help. His murder, the fact of his current state of being, had slipped his mind just slightly off the track, and until he returned to his senses, he'd be useless as a source of information. Jack had seen it before. He shifted awkwardly, looked away from Chuck, and found Suzanne staring at him.

"I know you," she said. "You were here last night." Her gaze went past him. "You and that girl, in the Jeep."

Jack sat down on the pavement right in front of her. There were cracks in the tar, and small sprays of grass had pushed up through them as though trying to reclaim the lot, determined to take back for nature what man had stolen. The thought flashed across his mind unbidden, but upon its heels came another. *Just like the Prowlers*.

"Yes," he said. "That was us."

"And you do see me," she said. "Us, I mean." Suzanne glanced around with a forlorn expression. "That was the third car in here this morning, and I've tried talking to everyone. Nobody knows I'm here. But you can still see me."

Jack nodded again.

"Even though I'm dead?"

There was a desperation in her voice. Everything else had been a statement of fact, but this . . . this was a question. Her plaintive expression was almost more than he could bear, and it was suddenly clear to him that though her mind had clung to logic and order, unlike Chuck's, unlike so many, she still wanted him to lie to her. But Jack could not do that.

"Yes," he said. "I'm sorry."

"Oh, Jesus," the ghost whispered, and she put a hand over her mouth as if to keep from shouting.

Through her hand, through her face, Jack could see the trees beyond, the deep woods where Chuck and who knew how many others had been murdered by the Prowlers. He thought of their meeting with Suzanne the night before, this maverick of a woman driving a big rig across the country, hanging around with lowlifes like Hank Krause—who was probably a Prowler but might just be mean spirited—and yet she had still been kind and courteous.

"How?" Suzanne asked.

Jack closed his eyes a moment, silently cursing with frustration he did not want her to see. *Damn it*, he thought. *Damn it, damn it, damn it!* Whatever had happened to her had been traumatic enough that she was unable, or unwilling, to remember it. At least not yet. He opened his eyes.

"The authorities are saying you fell asleep at the wheel, crashed your truck," he told her.

Anger flared in the black abyss of her eyes. "Bullshit!" Suzanne snapped. She shook her head. "That's crap. I've never so much as nodded off at the wheel. I'm always careful. No way would I . . . but then . . ."

The other spectre, Chuck, recoiled at their exchange and stared at them both in horror. He muttered something else about Allie, finding Allie, warning her about the monster inside, and he got up and walked into the woods, where he disappeared.

Suzanne watched him go, shaking her head. "Poor kid. He's not all there."

Jack wished he could touch her, comfort her somehow. "Suzanne, you remembered me. My name is Jack." He glanced back at the Jeep. "My girlfriend is Molly. You remember us, right?"

The ghost nodded.

"When we met you, there were two other trucks here. Three guys were with you. Hank and Dave Krause, and a guy named John Ford, like the movie director."

Her expression clouded over, and Jack realized he had thrown her off. He loved Westerns, and a man named John Ford had directed a great many of his favourites, but that didn't mean the average person had any clue who he was.

"Never mind that," Jack told her. "These three guys, do you remember being here with them last night? Drinking beer? You had a card table set up and—"

Suzanne nodded quickly. "Yeah, I know those guys. I've known them all for years. You get to know folks that work the same routes you do, though you never see them very often. Any time I ran across the Krause brothers, I always made a point of sitting down with them, maybe camping in a rest stop together for six hours of sleep or so. Not for Hank, mind you. He's harmless but a cranky SOB. But Dave's a good guy. Really loves the job. Ford's another story. Never got much read on him except to say he used to be in the army, or maybe the marines."

"Think hard, Suzanne," Jack said. "Last night, after we left, what happened? Do you remember anything at all strange about the Krause brothers? Was there an argument or anything? Did you see any . . . any animals?"

The last word seemed to freeze her in place. Though the substance that comprised her form now was almost constantly shimmering like the haze of heat off the road on a sweltering summer day, just then it grew very still and calm.

"Animals," she repeated, as though in a trance.

Then her eyes widened with memory and terror, her lips pulled back in a rictus grin, and she ducked and lifted her hands as though defending herself.

"Suzanne," he said softly. "What happened after we left last night?"

She shuddered as she raised her eyes again, but the ghost was no longer looking at Jack. Instead she stared across the cracked pavement of the rest stop as though witnessing from afar the events that had unfolded there the night before.

"You two were asking about that missing boy, your cousin, and it got us talking. Brought up a bunch of other deaths we'd heard of, and some drivers we knew who were always careful. Safe behind the wheel. Started me thinking maybe there's more to all this than meets the eye, sort of what you were saying. Hank and Dave, they thought we oughta bring it up to the staties around here. I figured the cops'd just think we were trying to do a whitewash on the reputation truckers have, trying to fight some of the bad publicity accidents bring. But then I started thinking about the boy again and about the drivers who'd died, and I figured it couldn't hurt to at least talk to the police."

"And then the animals came?" Jack prodded her.

Her expression was confused, searching, and she shook her head. "No, no. Dave and Hank had been sleeping when I got here, and then Ford pulled in not long after. So we were gonna nap a little, but the brothers were on their way. Took off maybe an hour after you left."

Jack stared at her. "They left?"

The ghost nodded. "I climbed up into my truck, got ready for sleep, and then Ford knocked on the door. He wanted to say good night." A tiny laugh escaped her. "I'm not young . . . not pretty, either. . . . He's practically a kid, and in good shape, too. I thought maybe he wanted to do more than say good night. I was gonna tell him good night, that's all."

"So you let him in?"

The lost soul of this kind, sweet woman bit her lip and nodded and suddenly there seemed somehow less of her, as though the essence that coalesced to form her ghostly shape, her *self*, was drifting a little. Her presence was less defined somehow.

"I let him in. To say good night. But it wasn't Ford that came into the truck."

"Yeah," Jack corrected. "Yeah, it was."

Hours later, after a long and fruitless afternoon that took them up and down nearly forty miles of Route 87, Jack and Molly drove back to their little hotel in Fairbrook as evening spread across the land once more.

It was mostly silent in the Jeep, the atmosphere between them heavy with a mutual disappointment that Molly hated. She was angry and frustrated by a feeling of helplessness that she knew Jack must also feel. They had spent the day in bars and diners, convenience stores and gas stations that sold diesel, asking after a trucker by the name of John Ford who looked like he'd just stepped out of boot camp. John Ford, the Prowler who had killed Suzanne Robinson the night before.

They had discovered quickly that Ford was a popular guy with the waitresses at some of these places. It turned Molly's stomach to see the way their faces brightened at the mention of his name. Some of these women were more than a little enamoured of Ford. Apparently he had a few regular runs through the northeast corridor, and so he was quite a familiar face. But none of them had seen him the night before, or today for that matter. And nobody, not even the women who seemed fascinated by him, had an address or phone number for Ford.

As the sky turned dark Molly sat in the passenger seat and gazed out at the trees flashing by on the side of the highway. Jack was preoccupied as well, for though it was past dusk and nearly full-on night by now, he still had not turned on the headlights. Both of them were exhausted by the disappointments of the day. Ford had given them the impression he was heading north to deliver his load. If that part was true, he was long gone by now and they had no way to know when he would be through again. No way to know if he was the only one.

The radio in the Jeep was on very low, so that Molly could barely hear the music, could not even tell what song it was. Her stomach rumbled and she realized how hungry she was. Lunch had consisted of a tuna sandwich and potato chips at one of the diners they had stopped in, and they had not yet eaten dinner. Her stomach growled.

"You want to try that Italian place we passed in Fairbrook this morning?" she asked Jack. "It looked nice."

"All right. Whatever you want is fine." Jack did not so much as glance at her as he spoke, and Molly wondered if he had even paid attention to what he had agreed to.

"It's on Artie now, isn't it?" she asked.

Now Jack's eyes widened a bit and he glanced at her, hands tight on the wheel. After a long moment he nodded. "Pretty much, yeah."

"What if he doesn't find anything?"

This time the pause before he replied was much longer. He gripped the steering wheel and stared past the windshield into the gathering darkness. After a moment he frowned and reached down with his left hand to turn on the headlights.

"I don't know," Jack confessed. The bitter look on his face was unsettling. "Is Ford a solo guy? Where does he live? If all his hunting is done on this stretch of road, that doesn't necessarily mean he lives around here. We might never run into him again. But I can't . . ."

There was an angry set to Jack's jaw as he gritted his

teeth and looked away. He took the exit for Fairbrook.

Molly lowered her window a few inches to let the fresh evening air in. "I know. The idea of going home, of not being able to do anything about it . . . it makes me feel awful. Useless. This is what we came up here for, right? This is our, what? Our crusade now. And there's nothing more we can do."

The quaint hotel loomed ahead, its sign glowing against the deep purple evening sky.

"I guess we just wait," Jack replied, resignation in his voice. "We can wash up, find someplace to get a decent meal for dinner, and wait for Artie to come back. I want to call Courtney, too, see if Bill ever checked in. If not, that's a whole other thing to deal with."

Molly had no interest in following up on that line of thinking, mainly because Jack was right. If anything happened to Bill while he was looking for his niece down in the city, she doubted there was a thing they could do to find him. In a city the size of Manhattan, without any leads or contacts, they would be lost. It was so absurd it made her want to laugh, for it would be yet another fruitless search, like the one they were on now. *Just another shot in the dark.*

"He's probably fine," she told him with a confidence she did not feel. "I have a hard time believing Bill couldn't take care of himself. Still, let's find out if he called in. If not, Courtney's probably going out of her mind right now."

Jack had fallen silent, and as he pulled into the hotel parking lot Molly glanced over at him. Despite his conversation with the ghosts this morning, their day had been wasted. The weight of that knowledge showed on his face, the burden of it turning his expression grim, his eyes dark.

"We can only do what we can do," Molly told him.

Jack actually smiled. "I know that. But don't try to pretend you don't feel exactly the same way I do. This prick, Ford? He told her he wanted to say good night. 'Let me into the cab so we can say good night'. She thought he wanted more. Maybe she was going to turn him down, but it flattered her, I could tell by the tone of her voice. He said he wanted to say good night, and it made her feel good.

"I want to find him and burn him down. Bury him."

Molly reached up to touch the back of Jack's neck, to push her fingers through his hair and stroke his skin there. He pulled the Jeep into a parking spot not far from the side door of the hotel.

"I feel the same way," she told him. "It kills me to say it, but unless Artie comes through, we've got nothing. We were a few feet away from him last night, and he was probably laughing at us the whole time. When there's a pack, maybe we can do something about it. But if there's just one or two, and they don't want to be found, I'm not sure what more we can do."

Jack killed the engine and slipped his keys out. They jangled in his hand as he turned to Molly, bent toward her, and kissed her forehead. "We'll figure something out. Maybe after we have something to eat and a little downtime, we can figure out another approach."

Molly said nothing. She doubted there was going to be another approach, and she figured Jack did too, but he was trying to give them both a chance to talk and think about something else for a few minutes, and so she said nothing.

They climbed out of the Jeep. As Molly slammed her door she saw a dark-skinned guy with a blonde girl who was maybe seventeen get out of a Toyota a few spots down. The two of them were parallel to Molly and Jack as they moved toward the motel, and yet they did not so much as look up. There was something about the man that drew her attention, a sense that he did not want to be noticed, as though he was doing something wrong. It occurred to her that he might be sneaking off for some rendezvous with this young girl, and the thought repulsed Molly.

The girl cast a quick, furtive glance in her direction, then looked away immediately. Molly might have continued to think they were involved in some sort of tryst if not for the grin that spread across the girl's features just then, a mischievous, even sinister, smile that stopped Molly in her tracks.

Molly turned to look at Jack as he was coming around the front of the Jeep, and as she did she caught sight of the two men coming out the side door of the motel. They stared at Jack intently, a dark recognition in their gaze that made it clear he was their objective. A palpable aura of danger emanated from them.

"Jack," Molly muttered, just loud enough for him to hear.

He glanced up, eyes darting from the two at the door to the man and girl coming around the front of the Toyota a few cars down, and then his gaze locked on Molly's. She shivered as a chill went through her, spiders scuttling up her spine, for in his eyes she saw confirmation of her suspicion. Molly cursed silently. She had hoped she was just being paranoid.

"Hang on," Jack said, face expressionless. "I forgot something."

His keys jangled as he went back to the Jeep, quickly opened the door, and climbed in. Molly drifted back toward her door, but even as she did so she heard them begin to snarl. Her head snapped around and she saw the dark-skinned man and the girl changing, fur tearing through skin, even as they leaped up on top of a Saturn sedan. The hood buckled with a metallic *pop*, and the female leaped to the next car's roof, gnashing her teeth, her gleaming, jagged row of teeth lengthening.

"Shit," Molly whispered. She grabbed at the Jeep's passenger door, but it was locked. "Jack!"

The two at the side door of the hotel had transformed as well, but they were going for Jack. One of them raced around to the driver's door as the other leaped on the hood of the Jeep. It ignored Molly, staring through the windshield at Jack. But the other two . . . the female was in the lead, her fur a bright golden yellow, and she landed on the roof of the car in the next parking space and issued an almost sensual growl as she tensed to attack.

Molly heard the *click* of the door unlocking behind her.

wild things

The golden-furred Prowler lunged at her, the other close behind. Molly reached back and grabbed the handle, then swung the door open with all her strength, ducking behind it like a shield. The female hit it with enough impact that the window splintered into a web of thousands of cracks. Molly cried out in pain as her legs were slammed between door and Jeep, but even as she shouted she rammed the door open again, threw herself inside, and slammed it shut.

The automatic locks clicked all around even before the door was completely closed, and the engine roared to life. The beast on the hood kicked at the windshield once, twice, trying to break it, but could not get the right angle or enough strength behind the blows. Out of her splintered window Molly saw the blonde female's mate leaping toward her, the image fractured into a thousand different facets in the cracked glass.

"Go!" she screamed.

"Going!" Jack replied, even as the Jeep shot out of the parking space, tires squealing.

The one on the hood went tumbling off backward onto the pavement. The blonde's mate crashed into the right front quarter and went down hard, and the Jeep jerked as a tyre went over his arm or leg. Jack cut the wheel, the Jeep slewed sideways, and the rear end crunched into a rusty blue Cadillac. The impact snapped Molly's head back, and she wanted badly to put her seat belt on but could not seem to pry her own fingers off the sides of her seat, where she held on for dear life as she stared out the windshield. The beast that had been pounding on Jack's door was running toward the grille of the Jeep. The female stood up as well, shaking off the blow Molly had given her with the door, but she wasn't fast enough.

The other, though, he raced at the front of the Jeep without a trace of hesitation.

Jack popped the shift into drive and floored it. For a moment Molly thought they were going to run him down. She squinted her eyes and tensed in preparation for the bone-crunching impact, but if she had ever needed an illustration of the superior speed of Prowlers compared with humans, this was it. The beast leaped aside at the last possible second, and then the Jeep was thundering out of the parking lot into the street, cutting off a VW Beetle headed in the other direction. Molly glanced back and saw the monsters scrambling for the shadows again, their silhouettes there in the darkened parking lot already shifting back to human. They moved toward the Toyota and Molly swore.

"They're going to come after us," she told Jack as she went to strap herself in.

"Good."

Stunned, she turned to stare at him. Jack gripped the wheel with whitened knuckles and kept the accelerator pinned as they approached the on-ramp for Route 87. Molly reached back to grab her seat belt, and Jack gave her a quick sidelong glance.

"Not yet, Mol. Get the key, climb in back, and get the shotguns. Maybe a couple of nines, too. I want them to catch up to us."

She reached down and grabbed the release catch on the front of her seat, then pushed it backward as far as it would go. Sliding down onto the floor, she reached up under her seat, where a small black box was magnetically attached to the metal springs. Inside the box she found the key to the trunk, but before she crawled between the seats, she turned to Jack again.

"Are you sure this is the best way to do this?"

"No. I'm not. But let's face it, as investigators, we're not Sherlock Holmes. We know what questions to ask, or at least some of them, but we don't have a lot of luck getting answers. Thing is, we ask the questions often enough, and look what happens. We find what we're looking for."

"Or they find us."

"Same thing. 'Cause they always underestimate us, Molly. We're human, so they always think we're nothing but prey."

Molly nodded grimly and pushed into the backseat, then over and into the cargo section of the Jeep. The trunk was covered with a couple of blankets, which she pushed back just enough to get to the lock. Hurriedly she unlocked the chest and with a grunt threw open its top. Blankets slid off and bunched up while she reached in and pulled out two pump shotguns and a pair of nine-millimetre pistols. The irony was not lost on her that Bill had procured the weapons from Prowlers, for them to use against Prowlers. Right now there was something delicious about that.

Molly snapped the lock back on, tossed the key onto

the floor in the backseat, and lay the guns on the rear seat as well before climbing over. She put the nines in the front, then slid up into the passenger seat with her shotgun in hand. Twisted around in the seat to reach for the other shotgun, she glanced out the back windshield and saw the Toyota racing after them. Jack had to be doing eighty, but they were going much faster.

"It's them," she said.

"Good. Strap in."

But just as she began to turn, bright light washed into the Jeep from behind. In the middle lane, right beside the Toyota, an eighteen-wheel rig roared, bearing down on them. The driver of the Toyota, the blonde girl, waved urgently at the truck and pointed to the Jeep.

The sky was split by the deep bellow of the tractor-trailer's horn, and then the rig came on faster.

"No," Molly whispered. She spun around, dropped into her seat, and scrambled to grab at her seat belt. "Faster, Jack. I think that's Ford."

"Yeah?" Jack replied. He shot her a quick glance. "Pick up the shotgun."

"Jack!" Molly warned as the horn blared again. The lights seemed brighter, blinding as the truck bore down on them, sliding into the fast lane just behind them. There were plenty of other cars on the road, but the lane ahead of them was clear, the nearest car a hundred yards up and going even faster than they were. Other motorists honked or swerved to be sure they were out of the way, but Molly knew that even if one of them phoned the police on a cellular, time would have run out before anyone could help them.

"The shotgun, Molly, come on!" he snapped. "I can't outrun them, not now."

Heart drumrolling in her chest, she grabbed the shotgun and pumped a shell into the chamber. "What are you going to do?"

Jack stiff-armed the wheel with his right hand and reached with his left to hit the button that rolled her window down. The second it started to be drawn down inside the door, the splintered glass gave way and shattered, cascading down inside and outside the speeding Jeep like a shower of rock candy.

"Hang on," he yelled.

The sound of the truck's engine filled the Jeep now, so close was it behind them. Molly saw the driver of a minivan shoot them the finger as they passed. Jack cut to the right, and the Jeep swayed and slid all the way across to the slow lane. They had a couple of hundred yards of straightaway with no other vehicles in that lane, but Molly could see red tail lights far ahead. A lot of them.

"The exit's coming up for Hollingsworth," she told him anxiously. "Just get off, Jack."

"Come on, come on!" Jack muttered to himself, ignoring her as he stared in the rear-view mirror and then at the lanes ahead.

Molly glanced back and saw the truck make the same insane cut across the highway. Horns blared, cars swerved, and a station wagon actually slewed off the road and onto the shoulder, nearly careening into the forest on that side. Then, again, the truck was gaining. Beyond that she saw the Toyota, and it began to accelerate as well.

"Sit tight, Molly, and get ready."

Her throat was dry, her hands damp on the shotgun as they raced along the slow lane. Again she glanced over her shoulder and saw the truck roaring up behind them. Ahead, to the left, there was a Chevy in the middle lane going far too slow, but beyond that the lane was clear. Jack punched the accelerator a second before the big rig would have slammed into the back of the Jeep. They shot forward, past the faded red Chevrolet. The wind coming through the broken window blew Molly's hair in her face, and she pushed it away.

"Now!" he snapped.

Jack cut the wheel to the left, the Jeep darted into the middle lane, and then he hit the brakes, pinning the steering wheel with both hands. The driver of the Chevy laid on his horn, but Jack wasn't stopping, just slowing down. A lot. The engine of the Jeep groaned, and the driver of the tractor-trailer started to brake as well, but at eighty-five miles per hour there was little he could do without jackknifing his rig. The truck ploughed along in the slow lane, moving past them.

"Do it. Shoot him!" Jack snapped.

They had dropped back almost the entire length of the truck, but now Jack began to accelerate again. The Jeep crept up beside the enormous, roaring gray dinosaur of a truck, and Molly turned in her seat. The shotgun's barrel poked out her window and she aimed at the cab of the rig. The second she could see the silhouette of the driver, she pulled the trigger.

The shotgun roared and glass blew out of the driver's window; divots of metal were torn from the door as well. The driver ducked, but Molly could see he was bleeding. The rig wavered as he righted it, trying to avoid driving off the shoulder, crashing the same way it had been made to appear that Suzanne Robinson and Chet Douglas had crashed.

Molly pumped another shell into the chamber. Even as Jack raced up next to the truck again, the driver turned to glare down at them.

It was John Ford, all right, lips peeled back in a grimace of such fury that though he still wore a human face, he looked as savage as any Prowler. Molly pulled the trigger, but even as she did so Ford swerved the truck into their lane. Metal shrieked and tore, her shot went wide. The rear tyre of the truck dug into the side of the Jeep, and for a moment they were up on two wheels. She dropped the gun and screamed, eyes wide as the horizon tilted, and Molly was certain she was going to die.

Then the Jeep's tyres touched ground again.

But Jack had lost control. He jerked at the wheel and he slammed on the brakes to try to keep the Jeep from spinning. It swerved; the station wagon coming up behind them jerked left and crashed into the Chevy.

The Jeep started to skid sideways.

Molly held her breath, afraid her heart would burst from the terror that spiked through her.

PROWLERS

The Jeep skidded off the highway, onto the soft shoulder, and then they were rolling, glass was shattering, air bags exploded into their faces as the Jeep turned over once, and then again, and came to rest at the bottom of the gulley along the side of the highway.

CHAPTER 8

The crash seemed to happen in some kind of drag time, not slow motion, but a surreal version of time where Jack could mark each passing second. He felt the seat belt constrict across his chest as the windshield shattered and glass fragments made tiny, sharp cuts on his face and hands. The air bag slammed him back against the seat, held him there even when the Jeep came to rest upside down. He heard Molly scream, and he prayed it was fear, not pain, that made her cry out that way.

Then they were just upside down and the engine cut out and all Jack could hear were the wheels of the Jeep spinning and screeching tyres and car horns and shouts up on the highway. Time seemed to skip the way he remembered vinyl records doing on his mother's turntable when he was very small. Images and sounds seemed to fade in and out, lurching forward as though seconds of his life were being snatched away in ragged handfuls. It took Jack nearly a full minute to realize that he had been fading in and out of consciousness, yet at the moment that understanding dawned on him, his awareness seemed to come back to him fully.

"Molly," he rasped.

He hung there, upside down, trying desperately to orient himself. The air bag held him firmly against his seat, but he could feel a little give in it. With great effort he craned his neck to get a look at Molly. Her hair hung beneath her, and her face was dotted with tiny cuts, but from what little he could see of her past the white of her air bag, she seemed unharmed. Molly's arms hung limply, dangling toward the roof of the inverted Jeep, and her eyes were closed. Unconscious. Which meant she might have sustained more damage than he thought.

"Molly," he said again. "Hey, Mol! Wake up."

She did not stir, and the spark of hope that had bloomed in him when he saw no obvious injuries was snuffed. Jack cursed silently as he began to wriggle behind the air bag. He had known the Jeep had them, of course, but he had never fully appreciated the miracle of air bags, or even given any thought to their presence when he bought the vehicle. They were just another item on the list of things that came with the car, like the tow bar on the back that he had never used. At the moment, though, he regretted that lack of appreciation. Indeed, he felt like dancing a little jig and singing a hymn of praise to the divine air bag. And he might actually do that, just as soon as he was certain Molly was all right.

The blood rushed to his head, and his skull started to ache, but he ignored that pain and glanced down at the ceiling of the Jeep. One of the nine millimetres and both shotguns lay there. That was bad. Cops and EMTs would be along in a few minutes. Also bad was that the guns were in the midst of a sea of shattered glass, the dome light peeking out from among the tiny square shards. That was safety glass. It broke like that, into a million little pieces, so nobody got impaled by huge chunks of windshield. But those tiny pieces were still sharp, could still cut, as his face and hands had found out. Small cuts, yes, but they stung. The idea of dropping down onto that broken glass had absolutely no appeal whatsoever, but the alternatives were equally unpleasant. If something was wrong with Molly and he just hung there waiting for EMTs to arrive, that could be bad for her, never mind their going to jail for the guns.

Then there were the Prowlers. He had no way of knowing if the monsters would come back to see if they were still alive.

"Screw it," Jack muttered.

He had a light jacket on, thick enough to protect him as long as he didn't stick his hands into that pool of broken glass. With effort he reached out and grabbed the door latch, tried to push the door open, and found it jammed. The frame of the Jeep had protected them, but it had buckled enough to wedge the doors tight.

Grunting with effort, he worked his body against the air bag and managed to slip his right hand up beside his hip to the catch of his seat belt. He braced his knees on the air bag, thinking it might help hold him up, then stretched his left arm out to hold on to the armrest control panel that jutted from his door.

After a deep breath to steady himself Jack released the belt, and then he was falling, shoving, sliding, hanging on to the door as best he could. He poked his head out the shattered driver's-side window just as his back slumped down onto the ceiling full of broken glass. The impact jarred him and a spike of pain shot up from his right knee. He glanced down at his jeans, but there didn't seem to be any blood. *Must have hit the dashboard,* he thought, hoping that it was only bruised or twisted. *A shattered kneecap would be very bad.*

But when he hauled himself out onto the prickly brush in the roadside gulley, the pain in his knee had reduced to a dull throb. Up in the breakdown lane three cars were pulled over, and it looked like more traffic had started to slow down and rubberneck for a glimpse of the carnage. Jack's memory of the minutes before the crash were only flickering images in his head, but he thought he remembered a couple of other cars getting into a fender bender as well. The good news was there was no sign of Ford's truck or the Toyota with the other Prowlers in it.

Guess we were asking the right questions, he thought.

One of the people up in the breakdown lane started down the incline toward the overturned Jeep. Jack's mind flashed to the guns and he waved the guy back.

"Just stay there!" he shouted. "I think I smell gasoline. Somebody up there have a cell phone?"

A woman in a business suit held hers up and pointed at it to indicate that she was already on the phone, then she resumed speaking into it. Jack was relieved, but also panicked. He would have to hurry. The guy who had begun the descent was still partially down the hill into the gulley, and Jack waved him back again.

"Stay back. I'm just gonna check on my girlfriend," he said, hoping they would all listen. Then inspiration struck him. "And for God's sake, nobody smoke!" he cried with an air of melodrama that sounded false to him but seemed to have the desired effect, as the Samaritan scampered back up to the supposed safety of the pavement.

That taken care of, Jack started around to the other side of the Jeep, beyond which there was nothing but forest. His knee felt swollen, and he figured he had torn something but nothing was broken. Still, he was forced to limp as he hurried to Molly's door, and instead of kneeling he sat down beside her. There were a lot of tiny cuts on her face, and safety glass in her hair and on her clothes. One of the cuts, right on her cheek, had bled enough that a tiny tear of blood ran from it down along her temple and into her hair. Though Jack tried not to think, tried to push away his fear for her, the sight of Molly hanging unconscious like that tore into him. His breathing became shallow and he felt as though his whole body were made of glass. And not safety glass, either, but the kind that really made some music when you broke it, long, delicate razor shards of ice.

"Molly," Jack said, and his own voice sounded far away.

He reached for her, and the moment he touched her dangling arm, it was as though a spell was broken. He slid closer on the brush, reached down to touch her throat with one hand even as he felt for her pulse with the other.

A pulse.

"Molly!" he snapped.

She moaned and shifted slightly, her arms pulling up toward her body, toward the air bag. Her eyes began to flutter open.

In the distance police sirens wailed, echoing across the highway and into the trees. Jack wanted to get Molly out of that car, but first things first. He had no idea where the other nine millimetre was, but he reached in through the shattered back window and withdrew the one on the ceiling, along with the two shotguns. If he stood up, despite the darkness, the people up on the road might see him toss them. Even now they were shouting down to him, telling him that the police and ambulances were on the way, that if there was no gasoline leakage, he should just leave her there, that it was going to be all right.

The trees were very close. Jack scuttled toward them on his knees, with one hand on the ground and the other cradling the guns. The throbbing in his knee increased to a spike of pain that lanced through him again with every foot, but in a few seconds he was slipping between trees and into the underbrush.

The sirens came closer. He thought that he might even have seen blue lights against the night sky. One by one he threw the guns as far into the woods as he could without drawing attention to himself. Then he scrambled back toward the Jeep. He had not responded, and so now the voices from up on the highway were calling even louder, asking if he was all right. Any second now, if the police didn't arrive, that Samaritan whose instinct had tried to get him down here in the first place was likely to come running to the Jeep, thinking he was in trouble.

It was all right now, though. He hoped that the other gun had been thrown from the Jeep when it rolled, and that the cops wouldn't open the trunk. With a grunt he sat down beside Molly, who moaned again as she heard him, and her eyes fluttered open.

"We're not dead?" she asked.

"Not dead. Are you all right? Anything broken?"

"Not that I can tell. . . . I think I hit my head, though. Maybe on the door frame. . . . I don't know. Got a big bump."

"If that's all you've got, it's a double miracle. Let's sing the praises of the god of air bags," he said with a grin. Then he reached out to touch her arm. "I was pretty afraid," he confessed.

"Me too," Molly replied. "Of your driving. Get me out of this."

Jack nodded. The cops would be there in seconds, but Molly wanted out and he did not blame her.

"Can you release your seat belt?"

"I think so." She pushed against the air bag and shoved her hand down to find the catch.

Jack reached into her broken window and got ahold of her shoulders. "Lift your head when you undo the belt. Just keep your hands and your head from hitting the glass."

"Ready?" Molly asked.

"Go," Jack told her.

Suddenly she collapsed into his hands, and he hauled her upper body through the broken window. A second later and Molly was helping, scrambling out from under the air bag. They lay on the rough brush, breathing heavily, staring up at the stars that were scattered across the October evening sky.

Something snapped in the woods.

Jack turned just as the Prowlers lunged from the trees, keeping low and out of sight of the road, just as Jack had done. He started to get up, Molly cried out, and then the beasts were upon them. One of them struck him a hard backhand across the face that dazed him, then the monster hit him a second and a third time, and Jack slumped to the ground, blackness enveloping him.

As he lost consciousness he could hear the sirens growing closer, tyres screeching as emergency vehicles arrived. And one other sound, even as he felt himself dragged into the woods. The sound was completely incongruous, made no sense at all.

Back in the wreckage of the Jeep his cell phone rang.

Courtney sat in her bedroom with the phone cradled against her ear and listened to the hollow ringing on the other end. All day long she had tried to occupy her mind with thoughts of anything other than Bill, and yet the world had seemed unwilling to cooperate. Business was slow that day, and the staff was more than capable of handling the flow. The passing seconds, minutes, hours, had seemed empty and endless to her without crises to fill them. Each time the phone rang, her ears perked up, her eyes ticked toward the sound, and she uttered a small, expectant noise no one else could hear.

Bill had never called. Time and again, as the day passed, she assured herself it was only that Bill was in the midst of his search, that some lead or another had distracted him from checking in. Excruciatingly, the lunch hour passed and the long afternoon dragged on and the dinner crowd appeared. Some of the regulars at the bar asked after Bill. With each tick of the clock her reassurances began to seem less and less plausible.

Panic had threatened so many times and she had beaten it back, denied it as childishness. Bill was more than capable of taking care of himself. Courtney was a grown woman, responsible and secure, and not given to indulging in mercurial emotion.

But Bill's words the day before had been "Talk to you in the morning."

Talk to you in the morning.

And the dinner crowd was already thinning.

Talk to you in the morning.

So even though she did not want her brother to think she was overreacting, she had left the pub and come up to the apartment to sit at the desk in her bedroom and call Jack on his cell phone.

Talk to you in the morning.

It was ringing. The room was scented with a citrus aroma from Courtney's hand lotion, and beneath it a masculine odour that was Bill's *smell*. Hanging over the edge of the bed was a New England Patriots sweatshirt with a few paint stains on it that she had borrowed from him when she redecorated her room. It had been cleaned many times, but she could still feel him in it.

Her gaze was roaming about the room, darting from one spot to another. The closet, the carefully made bed, the bulletin boards, the computer, the news stories taped to the walls. Mutilation murders, child disappearances, urban myths, and though for the most part they did not mention Prowlers, still to her eyes each piece of paper said, *Prowlers, Prowlers, Prowlers.*

Lost in thought, she barely listened to the phone ring. And ring. And ring. It was several moments before it struck her how empty and hollow it sounded. Third ring. Fourth ring.

The dread that had spread out inside her throughout the day blossomed in full then. Normally that apartment was abuzz. Even empty it echoed with the lives of the people she loved. Now the place felt enormous and hideous around her, far too big and lonesome, a cruel irony considering the dozens of people dining, drinking, and working downstairs. And yet who might she call upon? The newly promoted managers? No.

She was alone.

Talk to you in the morning.

Jack had told her not to worry yet, to wait.

But Jack was not answering his cell phone.

Again her gaze flashed across the news stories and urban legends pinned and taped to the walls. She hung up the phone and sat alone in the silence, and though she tried to convince herself she would not jump to conclusions, in her heart she knew that her fears had substance.

The phone seemed sinister to her now.

Something had to be done.

Talk to you in the morning. But no Bill.

And now no Molly and no Jack. Jack, her little brother who had nearly always done his homework the moment he got off the bus. Who had been so serious and dedicated about working at the pub, even by the age of eleven. Jack, who was all the blood she had in the world.

The last time Courtney had felt so helpless was the night her mother died and left them with only each other. It filled her with terror to think that now she might not have even that.

Molly fought. In the dark wood the Prowler ran, carrying her under its arm, its free hand clamped over her mouth. Its fur pressed against her lips. Despite the burden she presented, it moved swift and stealthy along unbroken paths. Her eyes were wide as she searched the night for some sign they were being followed, but she saw nothing, only the other beast, who led the way with Jack thrown over its shoulder, unconscious, the side of his face bloody.

And so she fought.

From some reservoir beneath her fear Molly brought up a burst of adrenaline and she bucked in the Prowler's grasp. In her mind was an image of the police and other emergency vehicles back at the sight of the crash, cops milling about, puzzled by the absence of victims in the Jeep, maybe shining flashlights into the woods. So she bucked, and she tried to turn in the thing's clutches, and she twisted around to swing her feet at its legs. Their limbs tangled, the Prowler grunted, and then they were falling. The momentum of its gait threw them into an arced tumble. Molly struck the ground hard, roots and small stones underneath her, but she was still moving, trying to extricate herself. In her mind she could still see confused police faces, flashlights in the woods, and she opened her mouth to scream.

The Prowler leaped on her, one clawed hand squeezing her throat. It drove her down hard and fell upon her chest, and all the air went from her lungs in a pained gasp. The scream never came.

"Did you not see your boyfriend?" the thing growled. "Coulda knocked you down and out like him.

Might be brain damaged, even. Count your blessings, Red."

He choked her, leaning on her chest, depriving her of any air at all. The edges of her vision blurred and began to go dark. Molly's eyes bulged and she tried weakly to fight him. Then suddenly he let up pressure on her chest and took his hand away from her throat. His feral eyes gleamed in the darkness of the wood and he stared at her, fur bristling. She understood that he was waiting for her to try to scream again, but Molly realized now in this moment of stalemate between them that the police would never reach her in time. The Prowler could tear out her throat in an instant and be gone before the cops had moved five feet.

Slowly she sat up and nodded to the beast crouched in front of her.

"Count your blessings," he growled again.

Then he changed. The fur began to diminish, almost to wither, as pale flesh grew upon it in a sort of gelatinous sheen that settled in an eye blink to become new skin. The snout retracted, the ears shrank, and yet because of the radical nature of the change, it took Molly several seconds to realize that she had seen this face before.

"You . . . you're . . ." She searched her mind for his name. "Max. You're Max."

He smiled then, but it was not the kindly expression of the man who had served them breakfast that morning at the Blueberry Diner. This was the smile of the predator.

"Flattered you remember. If you behave, I'll let you walk."

Again Molly only nodded in silence. She did not want to risk more noise, but more than that, she was afraid if she opened her mouth, she might ask the question that was foremost on her mind. Not *What are you going to do to us?* Rather *Why haven't you killed us yet?* To ask such a question seemed too much like an invitation.

"Walk," Max said, nodding in the direction the other beast had taken Jack.

Molly walked.

"Stay with me," Artie said, reaching out his hand.

The boy smiled and took it. He had died a teenager, but with the flip of blond hair that fell across his eyes and the wide grin he had worn ever since Artie had found him and *known his name*, Jared Wilkes looked like a child.

Jared turned then and took the hand of the other one with them, the other ghost, though Artie had discovered the kid didn't like that word. The other *soul*, then, belonged to a big, broad shouldered man with thick, dark hair and a moustache,and a round potbelly that might or might not have been beer related.

"Come on, Chet," the kid said to the ghost of the truck driver. "Hang on to Artie so we don't get lost."

"Lost?" Chet replied dreamily. Then a look of alarm crossed his face. "Lost! We're lost!"

"Chill out, Chet," Artie said. "Turn it down a notch, hombre. We are not lost. I've got it covered."

WILD THINGS

That seemed to pacify the ghost. Chet's gaze drifted, as it so often did. He went in and out. Artie was fascinated by the dead trucker because most spirits he had met were either painfully clear about their circumstances or little better than lunatics, shell-shocked by death into a kind of drooling vegetative state. Chet might be completely lucid one moment and nearly catatonic the next.

Almost as if the thought were a command, Chet snapped his head around to gaze at Artie. "You know where we're going, Artie?"

"I know exactly where, Chet."

The big man's eyes narrowed. "I guess I can stop worrying about getting those electronics parts to Albany on time, huh?" There was a twitch at the corners of his mouth that might have been the beginning of a smile.

"Pretty sure they're gonna be late," Artie agreed.

Chet's gaze drifted off again, eyes riveted on the shifting greys and muted colours of the Ghostlands, the forever paths that swirled away around them, the dark, flat mirror of the old world that moved swiftly past as they traveled through it, a flash of people and architecture, like some nightmare cinema.

"Late," Chet repeated. He laughed softly. "Gonna be late."

He was gone again.

"Hold on to him," Artie told Jared.

"I will. You're sure you can find your friends?"

"Oh, yeah." Artie nodded. He could always feel Jack

and Molly inside him, just as he could his mother and father. They were like tiny flames burning inside him that tugged at him, drew him toward them. "Don't worry, kiddo. I've got a pilot light."

Jared frowned, not understanding, but Artie chuckled softly to himself. *Pilot light*. He liked that one. And even as he thought it, he let his heart go to Molly, the little piece of his soul that would always be with her, calling out to him. He focused on her, seeing her face before him, as if she were the spectre and he the human, the dreamer. With Jared's hand held tightly in his, Artie *went* to Molly, felt the Ghostlands bend and rush and sweep around him.

Artie arrived in the woods trailing the kid and the trucker behind him, as though he were Peter Pan and they the Darling children. He hovered there among the trees, feeling the Ghostlands around him but not the earth beneath his feet; never again, that. A smile crossed his features when he saw Molly emerge from the trees, walking toward him at a good clip. But his smile disappeared when he saw the blood on her forehead, the myriad small cuts on her face and hands, the glass in her hair.

Then the other figure emerged from the wood behind her. It wore a human face, but Artie could see its true shape. Artie was about to shout a warning— though he knew she would not hear it—when the monster spoke.

"Faster, Red. Move."

Molly picked up her pace, jogged right past where

Artie and his companions stood. He felt Jared squeeze his hand more tightly as he glanced at them.

Chet was whimpering, cowering back away, afraid of the monster but even more afraid, apparently, of letting go of Jared's other hand. Artie's heart went out to both of them, but he had no choice.

"Come on," he said, and hauled them after him as he followed Molly and the Prowler.

A short while later, though Artie could not really tell how long—time blurred in the Ghostlands—Molly and the Prowler emerged into a parking lot behind a dark building. The bulkhead doors in the back of the building stood open, and the ghosts were just in time to see another beast descend into the basement through those doors with Jack on his shoulder, unconscious.

Artie whispered his friend's name.

"Wait, that's Jack? The one you said could help? The one you said would kill them?" The disgust in Jared's voice was clear. He wanted blood from the Prowlers, wanted to know the monsters would be destroyed.

"He *will* help," Artie replied, staring down at the kid. "But first it looks like we're going to have to help *him*."

Chet snorted with laughter, suddenly focused again. "We're dead, Artie. How are we supposed to help?"

"I think I know a way, but you two are going to have to wait here. Watch them, and call for me if anything else happens."

Artie let go of Jared's hand, and once more the Ghostlands bent and rushed around him, but this time he was alone. As he moved through the afterworld he could hear Chet crying out in alarm, the fear in his voice echoing along the paths travelled by the lost souls of the dead.

Somewhere nearby a door slammed.

With a long, rumbling groan Jack came awake. His fingers crept spiderlike up his face and over his head, wincing at the tiny cuts he found there. Still, despite those small injuries, he was surprised and relieved to find that although the pain told him otherwise, there was not an enormous crack in his skull. He might even have been elated, if not for the driving, cutting pain that went along with that suspicion. It was as though a blade had been driven through his temple and as he opened his eyes and tried to sit up someone twisted the knife.

Jack hissed, and mouthed quiet obscenities.

"Hey." A soft voice. Molly.

He opened his eyes despite the pain and found her kneeling by him, a tender, worried expression on her face, her hand hovering near him as though she wanted to touch him, to soothe him, but was afraid she might only make it worse. There was still a streak of blood on her face where blood had run up into her hair as she had hung upside down, but the rest looked more like chicken pox than anything else.

"Hi," he replied, risking a tentative smile, then allowing it to bloom once it proved not to increase the pain in his head.

Gingerly he began to sit up, and she helped him.

"How's the head?" she asked.

"Amazingly intact."

"Just as hard as Courtney always said it was."

Molly slid her hands into his, and they sat facing each other on the cold concrete floor. There was a single light in the room, at the bottom of a set of stairs that led up to a steel door. In that meagre illumination Molly's green eyes gleamed.

Jack smiled again, but then all traces of good humour drained from within him. "Why are we still alive?"

"I've been wondering the same thing."

A whisper of motion from the shadows, silk and cotton, and a figure shifted and walked toward them. Pain knifed through Jack's head again, and he stared in astonishment. Though the far side of the room was pitch dark, neither of them had sensed that they were not alone.

"If you're alive, it means she *wants* you for something," the figure said.

"'She'?" Molly demanded of their fellow prisoner. "Who the hell is '*she*'?"

From silhouette the figure stepped farther into the light. She was easily six feet tall, beating Jack by a couple of inches, slim at the waist but with hips that gave form to her blue jeans. Her black hair was straight and hung as a curtain down upon the shoulders of her deep red V-necked top. When she spoke, it was without humour or warmth. She regarded them gravely.

"Jasmine, of course."

The girl flipped her hair back from her face and crouched by them, resting her elbows on her knees.

"My name is Olivia Navarre," she said. "Talk to me."

CHAPTER 9

A caged animal would slink back and forth across its enclosure, pacing out the limits of it, troubled by captivity and searching for some opening, some opportunity for escape.

Bill Cantwell wanted out, no question, and the urge to stride back and forth across the antique train car in which he had been imprisoned was great. Instead, he eschewed even the chair and bedding that the pack had provided for him and he lay at the centre of the car with his arms under his head, staring at the ceiling. He was aware of his surroundings, of course, and he did seek an opportunity for escape. But he would not pace like an animal.

He waited, and he said not a word. In his mind he held an image of Olivia, the last time he had seen her. Thoughts and images of Courtney and Jack and Molly made their way into his head from time to time, and he pushed them out again as best he could. He was not always successful. It was impossible for him not to wonder where they were now, what his betrayal had set in motion. But Olivia was his only blood in the world.

When he thought of his sister's death, Bill wanted to cry. But he would not do that. Not here.

The smell of the old wood of that train and the ghost-shriek of the subway tunnels not far away enveloped him and the hours went past. He ate what they brought him, but otherwise he lay there on his back and stared at the ceiling. By the time the door opened and Jasmine stepped in, elegant and sensual in leather, Bill had lost track completely of the hour, the day. It might have been afternoon or early morning, but if he had to guess, he would have said it was night.

Night-time was when Jasmine seemed most alive, and she burned with life now as she leaned against the wall of the car, arching her back and crossing her arms to stare at him with those unearthly orange eyes. Bill knew she was waiting for him to speak, to ask what she was doing there, and so he said nothing.

At length she sighed. It was almost theatrical. "You asked for proof."

Bill sprang to his feet and stood glaring at her. "You've brought Olivia here?"

Jasmine laughed, and it was a throaty, dusky sound. "Am I a fool? No. You will not see Olivia until Jack Dwyer is dead. The others, well, I want them, but I'm not unreasonable. As long as I have my hands on them, that's fine. But I want to see Jack Dwyer die before I'll bring Olivia to you."

For a moment Bill only stared at her. Then he turned and strode to the other end of the car, keeping his back to her.

"You said you had proof."

"Do you really need it?" Jasmine purred. "Tell me you don't believe I have her."

"Oh, I believe you." He turned. "I suspected as much before I came down here. That's why I'm here. You know that. But I have my doubts. And if you can't offer me proof, they're going to grow a lot stronger."

Jasmine stared at him then, her head hung almost sadly. In the dim light of the candles inside the train car her hair cast deep shadows across her face, so that all he could make out in that moment was her mouth, those perfect lips. When she smiled, her teeth were too long, too sharp. He wondered if she had shown her fangs on purpose, or if she simply had that little control of her emotions. It was the smile of a gleeful killer.

"Very well," she said.

She pushed open the door and beckoned to someone outside. A moment later a Prowler came in, a skinny little beast who was one of his guards. He carried a TV set in his hands, but it was a combination thing that had a VCR built in. Its cord was plugged into a long, thick orange extension cable, duct-taped together. It snaked out the door behind him as the guard set the TV down on the floor.

"Go," Jasmine told him.

The guard frowned, glanced at Bill worriedly.

Jasmine snarled quietly and the guard fled.

"The tape's already in it," Jasmine said. Then she took up her former position against the wall, cruel and alluring all at once.

Something twisted in Bill's gut, but he forced himself to approach the machine and turn it on. Then he pressed PLAY. The screen flickered white at first and then the picture resolved. It was a dank concrete room, probably a basement from the looks of it. A man—or a Prowler, he could not tell the difference from video-tape—placed a tray of food down on the concrete.

"Come and get it, honey," he said, taunting the darkness deeper in the basement.

And the darkness erupted. A girl with long black hair lunged across the room at the man who had brought the tray. Her face was pale and she was much older than the last time Bill had seen her, but he would have recognised her anywhere. Especially when she began to change, her fur bristling as she tussled with the male, clawing at him. He started to transform as well, and then others entered the view of the camera, two dark figures who kicked at her, grabbed her arms, drove her backward so that the bearer of the tray could retreat.

The numbers in the bottom right-hand corner of the screen indicated that the video had been made only a few days before.

The screen went dark and then bright white.

Bill closed his eyes and breathed evenly, needing now more than ever to control the beast within. He heard a *click* and looked up to see that Jasmine had shut off the television. She seemed to float across the candelit train car to him and stood only inches away.

"It doesn't have to be like this, Guillaume," she whispered, gazing up at him with those strange, beautiful eyes.

"Explain."

A smile played at the edges of her lips. "They were in awe of Tanzer, you know? Part of that was his own charisma, but part of it was his heritage. His father was among the greatest warriors in our history, a legend. All Tanzer wanted was to unite our race, to take back the freedom and primacy that was once ours. Is that so terrible a dream?"

Bill studied her carefully. Jasmine breathed deeply, edged even closer to him. He could almost feel her pressed against him, and yet there was still the slightest of distances separating them.

"That depends on the means used to achieve it. And the cost."

"Does it?" she asked. "Isn't it worth any price?"

He could see in her pout, hear in the rasp of her voice, that she meant it. That this dream truly was hers now as well. Bill did not respond.

"I don't have the legacy that Tanzer did. The packs and the prodigals are starting to come around out of curiosity, some out of fear. I am Alpha, but there will be challenges. I know there will," she said sadly. Then that smile returned, sharp and deadly. "Tanzer's father was a great warrior, Guillaume, but your father was the most respected leader we have ever had. You have that in your blood. You could be that. You could *have* that."

A shudder went through him as she reached up to run a finger along his face.

"How do you figure?"

"I am Alpha. If you were my mate, we could truly unify the packs. We could have it all." Jasmine gazed up at him expectantly.

Her proximity was too much for Bill. He turned and walked again to the other side of the train car. When he faced her again, he saw that Jasmine had not moved.

"I just want Olivia. When she's free, I'm gone."

Into the lion's den.

The taxi dropped Courtney off a few doors down from the entrance to the Lotus Club, and as she stood on the sidewalk and watched the cab pull away, she wondered how difficult it was going to be to find one later to take her home. After another moment's hesitation she glanced up the street at the sign for the Lotus and straightened up, steeling herself. There was nothing she could do to hide her infirmity, no way to ditch the cane. Instead she used it, drew from it a certain dignity and strength, and she started toward the club, relying as little on the stick as possible.

At the door she paused to take a breath, to set her features, to calm the flutter of trepidation in her belly so that her face revealed nothing. This was not her element. It was rare for her to take time off from the pub, rarer still for her to dress for anything but comfort or business. Though she supposed this was a kind of business. Yet the memory still existed in her of what it had been like to float through a dance club, wrapped in leather and tight cotton, and to feel the spotlight upon her. Before her mother's death, though underage, Courtney had done her share of clubbing.

With the lion's head of her cane she rapped hard on the door.

By the count of three it swung open.

The music that poured from inside was an incessant, repetitive techno beat that thumped her chest with the sheer force of its sound. Courtney did not flinch. She could not afford to, not under the gaze of the doorman, who peered at her from within. He was tall, his hair neatly trimmed, and he was handsome in a grimly serious way. He appeared to be Chinese, but she knew that was only the masque, the illusion the Prowler wore.

Her heartbeat tripled, now matching the rhythmic backbeat of the electric drums in the techno jam that pounded from the open door. Only months earlier her abdomen had been torn open by one of these things and she had nearly bled to death. Her body remembered those wounds, remembered the searing pain of it, even better than her mind did. The skin on her belly where doctors still needed to repair some of the scar tissue stung now, and she hissed through her teeth as she offered the doorman a coquettish smile. Cane or not, though she rarely had opportunity to think about it, Courtney knew she could still grab the spotlight if she wanted to.

WILD THINGS

The doorman had a toothpick jutting from the corner of his mouth, and for a moment he only glared at her. Then an enormous, clowning smile blossomed on his face, as though he wanted her to know he had only been joking with her.

"I think you came to the wrong place, sweet one."

Courtney lifted her chin, used the leverage on the cane to arch her back a little. "I don't think so. I'm here to see Winter."

She stared at him and let him do the same. His eyes roved over her body, the caramel pants she had zipped herself into, the cream top and the soft, stylish leather jacket whose cut flattered her so well.

In the end he stood back with a playful, courtly flourish to let her pass. "His booth is at the back on the left." But as she moved by him, forcing her bad leg to obey, steadying her gait with the cane, the grinning doorman slid up next to her with inhuman speed. His fingers clutched tightly to her bicep and he whispered, not unkindly, into her ear.

"I hope you know what you're getting yourself into."

Though the urge to flee tugged at her and she found it difficult to catch her breath, she swivelled her head to gaze steadily into his eyes. "I don't have a choice."

The grin vanished and his eyes narrowed. His lips parted, so that she could see the toothpick pinched in his teeth. "Watch yourself, then, sweet. Just because our clientele wants to blend, wants to get by, doesn't mean there aren't some who cheat once in a while. It's like a diet, you see? There are vegetarians who aren't averse to sneaking a little red meat now and again."

He released her, and Courtney walked through the inner door into the club. It was clear to her that he truly wanted her to be cautious, but his warning shook her. As if it had not been difficult enough to disguise her fear. She emerged into the club proper, the unrelenting rhythm hurting her ears, the lights painting a nightmare of reds and greens that drained all other colours from the spectrum. And on the dance floor, where dozens of bodies twisted to that primal beat, those nearest to her paused and glanced over at her, some of them smirking as though they *knew*.

And of course they did.

They could smell it.

The hell with you, Courtney thought, her anger burning off some of her fear. She glared back at those who had looked at her, and one by one they turned away, swept back into the rhythm on the dance floor. Not until the last had averted his eyes did she continue on across the club, skirting the bar and cutting through the lounge area to the far left corner, to a booth where a lone figure sat, a scarecrow-thin man with skin as dark as his hair. A streak like bleach in his hair reflected back the flashing multicoloured lights in the club.

This was Winter. Bill had not told her much about him, save that he was a kind of mediator, that he was old and powerful and had kept peace with the underground as well as those Prowlers still wild. Courtney hated him for that. Winter might not be a killer, a monster like Tanzer and Jasmine, but he apparently had no objection to their predations.

Trepidation mingled with indignation, but she would not be stalled. As she strode across the floor, at great pains to keep from appearing to rely too much on her cane, his gaze never touched her. The thin creature sipped from his drink and watched the club as though she were invisible, a ghost to him.

Courtney blocked his light, throwing a shadow across this venerated beast. At last he looked up at her, but there was neither warmth nor hostility, nor even curiosity, in his features. He spoke before she could open her mouth.

"It's your fault, you know."

Thrown off guard, she faltered. "What?"

Winter glanced away a second, annoyed and impatient. "Sit."

She wanted to argue, but who else could she have gone to? If she wanted to find Bill, figure out what had happened to him, Winter was her only choice. Courtney slid into the booth.

"Can I get you a drink?"

"No, thank you."

He smiled at her manners and swirled the ice around in his whiskey glass before sipping from it. "We disappear," he told her, studying her face. "That's what you have to understand. Most of my people who go underground—an ironic turn of phrase, isn't it? I mean, in many ways by living among your people, they're going above ground, aren't they?" He mused on that a moment before focusing on her again. "Look out at the dance floor."

Courtney did as she was asked. Smiles and laughter, knowing looks between partners, it might have been any dance club in the world.

"Nearly all of them have disappeared. They have joined the world of humans, become part of it. Lawyers, waiters, accountants, even actors. But they remember what they are. They may not wish to be wild now, but they still love their wild brothers."

Ah, she thought, *I see where this is going.* "But Bill doesn't."

Winter nodded. "Guillaume allied himself with your people against his own."

Courtney bristled. "What, are you all dense?"

The thin Prowler sat up straighter, mouth twisted into a snarl.

She leaned forward and fixed him with a withering look. "I'm serious. Go ahead, attack. Tear me up. Wouldn't be the first time. Or maybe you should think about it for a second. If Bill hadn't helped us kill Tanzer, he would have kept going, kept drawing attention until the public figured out what was going on. And then what? A witch hunt, my friend. Villagers with torches. Paranoia ensues and everyone's looking at one another differently, trying to figure out who's human. And when they realize you're not, do you think they'll care about your diet? About how long it's been since you bellied up to the buffet table? By helping to take Tanzer down, Bill might just have saved you all."

The snarl dissolved into a contemplative, faraway look, and then Winter sat back in the booth and sipped his drink again. He watched the dancers, ignoring the way Courtney glared at him. Her words had been propelled by righteous anger and by fear, but not fear of Winter or of the others. Bill had gone off the map, incommunicado. Jack and Molly weren't answering their cell phones. That might be because they were out of range or the batteries needed a charge. It could be anything.

But it could be bad. It could mean the worst. At the moment Courtney had no way to track her brother, but Winter could find Bill. She had to pray that Jack and Molly were just out of reach at the moment. But if they weren't, once she found Bill, he would be able to track them.

She didn't know what else to do.

"How did you know who I was? Why I was here?" she asked, much of the fire gone from her tone.

Winter still did not look at her. "The one I sent with Guillaume, Lao, has disappeared. None of my contacts know what has happened to them, but I suspect that some know and will not say because they fear Jasmine."

"She's the same, you know? She'll be the death of all of you eventually."

"Perhaps," he replied thoughtfully. Then he glanced at her as though he had forgotten she was there. "I will find him. Not because you love him, or because you have come here, but out of respect for a friend long dead. Yves Navarre was the finest student I ever had."

"You were a teacher?" Courtney asked, eyebrows raised.

Winter seemed almost hurt. "Why should that surprise you?"

She said nothing. Any reply she might have given would only have alienated him further. Winter seemed not to notice.

"It isn't only Guillaume. Jasmine likely has Olivia as well. After what he did, the underground might have stood by and let Guillaume be killed, no matter how much respect his father's memory holds, but the girl has done nothing. Once word gets out what Jasmine's done, things are going to get bloody. It's going to cost me a lot. I can't be neutral anymore. But if they're still alive, I will find Guillaume and his niece."

Winter chuckled as though the idea of the chaos he referred to amused him.

Courtney hesitated a moment before going on. "I can't reach my brother, either."

The Prowler stared at her, brow knitted in consternation. "What a pity. But what's that got to do with me? Either he's all right or he isn't. Maybe he's tracked the wrong prey, that brother of yours. You see us as killers. You want to stop the ones who still hunt humans. But that's what we are, Miss Dwyer. We're predators. And so, by the way, are you. That's why I have no feelings about your brother one way or the other. I understand what he and that redheaded girl hope to accomplish. Good for them. Hunting the hunters.

"May the best monster win."

He tilted his glass back, polished off the rest of the whiskey, and stood, unfolding his long, thin frame from the booth.

"I'm coming with you," Courtney said.

Winter smiled, offered a curt little bow. "I had no doubt that you would."

"You're not going to try to stop me?"

The beast feigned a hurt expression. "Who am I to stand in the way of love?"

He turned and walked off, and Courtney had to hurry to keep up, unmindful now of relying on her cane. Winter paused and looked back at her, eyes glancing from her face to her walking stick, then roving over her body, the stylish clothing she had worn.

"We'll stop so you can pack a bag and change into something more suitable for travel," he said, a grave expression on his face. Then he spun and marched off again. When he spoke to her with his back turned like that, she could only just make out the words over the blaring techno beat.

"Come on," Winter said. "Let's go start a war."

Eden nearly always knew she was dreaming. Aware of that, she could often change the course of a dream, guide it and shape it so that it became a kind of exploration. Often she dreamed of days gone by, lives lived, passions and fears that had once existed in her heart. Sometimes these journeys were nightmares, but as visits to the past, they held no lasting terror for her. In dreams she might choose to face them, or turn away. Wake up.

But not always.

On the battlefield with a rifle in her hands. Smoke from cannon fire swirls in the air and night is coming on. Caleb is her name here, but still she wears her own face, her now face. Her uniform was grey once but is so matted with dirt and blood that it is nearly black.

From across the field the blue coats advance, the Union soldiers with rifle and cannon, tired horses carrying men with swords drawn. The Union flag flies, and it strikes her that the flag looks clean and new, and how can that be?

Now she is retreating, Caleb's legs moving beneath her, Caleb's hands raising the rifle to her shoulder and firing; reloading as she walks backward, raising the gun and firing again. The constant barrage has deafened her. Backward and backward and farther still, long strides and careful steps, and the gap between North and South, between Union and Confederate soldiers, is closing tighter.

One glance back, only one, and she sees that they are near the trees, and she knows that they have lost this bit of ground, that she has bled for it, that all around her friends are dying for it. Elijah Samuels goes down with a scream and a spurt of blood from his chest. Will Kent is erased in a cannonade and his leg lands nearby, foot still in its boot. There is a small hole worn through the sole of the boot.

Backward, backward, tears streaming down her face, she raises the rifle and fires, steps back and reloads and retreats some more. Trees, where are the trees? Her heel catches on something and Caleb falls, Eden falls, and the rifle flies from her grasp. As she scrambles to rise she realizes that she has fallen over the broken remains of a grey-uniformed soldier, a member of her battalion, but she cannot tell whose corpse it is because there is no face. Only shattered skull and bits of gelatinous brain and a flap of blond-haired scalp. There is no cap over it, but they all have lost their caps by now.

She cries out and pulls away, and only then does she glance around to see that the retreat is over. The battle is over. She is the last. And the Yanks march toward her, one last rebel on a field of blood, and they are still firing.

And she wakes.

Breathing hard, eyes wild as she peers around her room. Voices in the hall, and how can that be? Eden rises from bed, heart still beating too fast, relieved, oh so relieved to be awake, away from the nightmare. But whose voices are these? Wary but also angry at the intrusion, she throws open the door.

The hall is full of Prowlers. They crouch on the banister at the top of the steps and lounge on the grand staircase. One of them, a male whose golden fur reminds her of the one that tried to kill her, pisses on the carpet, and the stink is acrid and nauseating.

He looks up at her. "Our territory now. There's no waking up."

Short of breath, pulse racing enough to nurture a blossom of pain in her chest, she slams the door, puts her back against it. And she knows she is still asleep. She raises her hands and stares at them, remembering that you're not supposed to be able to see your hands in a dream. That's how you know you're dreaming.

PROWLERS

A sharp rap on the door. "Little pigs, little pigs . . .," a voice begins.

She snaps awake in her bed. It is still night outside and the window is open, a soft breeze flowing in. "Oh, my God," she whispers in the dark, and she wants to cry. A shiver goes through her as she begins to calm. Eden rises from bed, unnerved by her dreams, and goes to peek into the hallway.

When she opens the door, it is empty.

As she turns she hears the rustle of bedclothes behind her. In her bed is a sleek female monster, a Prowler with jaws open, slavering, her copper fur shedding on the bedclothes and beginning to reveal a face underneath.

"The better to eat you with," she says.

Eden closes her eyes, yearning to wake up, pleading in silence to all the ghosts of those she has loved in her brief eternity in the flesh world. It isn't supposed to be like this, and she wonders, with mounting terror, what will happen if she can never wake up.

Again she wakes. Cautious now, she slips from bed, afraid that this is still not real, trying to feel the floor beneath her bare feet, the cool breeze through her cotton nightshirt. She manages to hope.

She opens her bedroom door. A dark silhouette blocks the light in the hall, and she screams.

Artie looks at her with heartbreakingly blue eyes and reaches out to take her hands. She feels the rough texture of his hands, warm in hers, and Eden pushes herself into his embrace, muttering words she cannot remember even as she speaks them. His arms slip behind her and he hushes her.

"It's all right now. It's only a nightmare."

WILD THINGS

"I can't wake up," she says, the horror of those four words making her chest tight, the panic in her growing, despite his comforting presence.

"You can. You will in a moment. You'll have to. We need you."

And he whispers to her, and slowly she wakes.

But the memory of her nightmare stays, and his words only heighten the awful dread that still grows and lingers within her.

Eden was curled in a tight ball when she awoke. Her eyes flickered open and she stared into the darkness of her bedroom. The texture of the sheets beneath her, the caress of cool air from the partially open window, the tick of the clock on the wall, all of it seemed a temptation, a seduction, meant to convince her that she was awake now. That the world had returned. That the nightmare was over.

Her eyes burned and felt heavy with the burden of sleep, its allure almost too powerful. Fear forced her eyes open again and again, and she knew she ought to throw her legs out of bed, to sit up, to take time before going back to sleep, for fear the nightmare would be there waiting to claim her.

At last her mind began to clear and her body to obey her commands. The surreal quality of the air changed, no longer made malleable by the remnants of her dreaming mind, her altered perceptions.

Awake. She had escaped the nightmare, a dream unlike any she recalled having ever had, in all her lives.

Then she remembered. Artie's embrace, his comforting voice. His words. *We need you.* And she remembered, too, what he had told her. With a whispered curse Eden sat up in bed and clicked on the light on her nightstand and stared at the clock: 11:37. She had been asleep less than half an hour.

The phone was a white, cheap plastic thing that had cost her fourteen dollars. When she picked it up, the keypad glowed a dull green. From memory she dialled the phone number for the apartment above Bridget's Irish Rose Pub, but after half a dozen rings the answering machine picked up. Eden swore softly, urgency drumming in her chest.

"Courtney, hi, it's Eden Hirsch. When you get this message, call me back. It's . . . it's hard to explain on a machine, but it's important."

She rattled off her number and hung up, then quickly dialled the number for the pub itself. The phone was answered on the second ring, but the girl who picked up said that Courtney was out of town for a couple of days. Questions burned through Eden's mind: Where had Courtney gone? Did she already know that Jack and Molly were in trouble? She left a message with the woman at the pub and hung up, then sat on the edge of the bed and stared at the hard, gleaming plastic surface of the phone. The remnants of her nightmare, that seemingly inescapable dark dream, lingered like cobwebs not only in her mind, but in her vision, like mirages lurking in the shadows of the room.

Her gaze went back to the phone. Artie had given

her the impression that the situation was dire. If so, Jack and Molly didn't have time to wait for Courtney to call in for messages. Eden mentally calculated how long it would take her to drive to upstate New York by herself, but even if she went, what could she possibly do for them on her own? What they needed was a cadre of armed warriors on horseback, Attila and his Huns, the proverbial cavalry. Though she had been a soldier more than once in her eternal life, she was not capable of that now.

Silent, the drumming in her chest increasing in tempo and urgency, she sat on the edge of her bed and grew angry with herself. Artie had come to her because she was the only person he could communicate with. But what could she do?

The phone was so still it was almost an insult.

Cavalry. The cavalry.

Eden's eyebrows shot up. Hope rising in her, she picked up the phone.

Jace Castillo hated domestic-abuse cases. In the time he had spent as a detective with the homicide division of the Boston Police Department, he had seen far too many women end up dead at the hands of boyfriends or husbands. There were more-horrifying murders, bloodier and more-savage killings. Certainly the domestic cases were usually a lot simpler to solve. Half the time they had the perp in custody within forty-eight hours, often far less. But inevitably, while putting together the paperwork on a case, he would have to wade through the history of a relationship, the times the victim had been abused, maybe even pressed charges. A lot of them had those worthless pieces of paper called restraining orders, which were supposed to keep the abuser away.

It twisted him up inside to read those sad, pitiful histories, to see how lost people could become within their own lives. It was going on midnight now, and he rubbed tiredly at the corners of his eyes and typed the last bit of his report before saving it and shutting down the computer.

The circumstances of his current case were so familiar; there was no secret to it, no mystery. It depressed him to know that in a situation like this there was nothing he could do to make it better. He had put the abuser in jail, but the deed had been done. All Castillo could do now was add his victim to the catalogue of those who stood as a horrid warning to others, a warning that seemed universally ignored.

With a sigh he slipped on his leather jacket, slid the chair in tight against his desk, then gave a halfhearted wave to Detective Pepper on the other side of the room and wished her good night. Castillo started for the door.

On his desk the phone rang.

With a roll of his eyes he turned and glared balefully at it.

"Want me to get it?" Amy Pepper asked.

"Would you?" Castillo hated how pleading his voice sounded, but he just wanted to go home.

Detective Pepper picked up his line. She spoke briefly, then clutched the phone against her chest with her brows knitted in consternation. "Some girl named Eden Hirsch. Says you've met through the Dwyers. Said to tell you Jack's in trouble."

Castillo forgot all about the case that was haunting him. He strode over, nodded his thanks to Pepper, and took the phone from her.

"This is Detective Castillo," he said.

He listened to Eden Hirsch's voice, tight with panic, and he dropped his chin to his chest and massaged the bridge of his nose, rubbing at his tired eyes again.

"Jesus," he rasped. "When will this kid stop sticking his head into the lion's mouth?" Castillo got the details from her, jotted them down on a pad, then tore off the sheet and folded it once, slipping it into his pocket.

"I'll get back to you tomorrow with an update," he told Eden.

When he hung up, Pepper was watching him.

"So?" she asked.

"Just someone who expects me to play nursemaid."

Pepper smiled, but there were questions there. "Dwyer. That's the brother and sister who own that pub near Quincy Market, right? One of these days, Jace, you're going to have to tell me how you got so involved with them."

"But not tonight," Castillo replied. "Tonight there's sleep."

He waved casually and strode from the room as though he had already forgotten the entire thing. But the moment he stepped off the elevator on the ground floor and started toward the front door, Castillo had his cell phone out and was dialing. He and a handful of his fellow officers were fighting a kind of shadow war, out of the public eye, against a race of monsters that lived and bred among them, a race of killers. But most people, even most cops, had no idea they existed, and Castillo had orders to keep it that way.

Jack and Courtney Dwyer and their friends were part of that war as well, fighting on the side of the angels. Their paths had crossed a number of times, but as deep as he got himself into things, it seemed like the Dwyer kid always managed to get himself out. From the sound of things, though, he'd really stepped in it this time. Castillo had worked with them in the past, but this was the first time Jack and his girlfriend, Molly Hatcher, had really needed to be bailed out.

The problem was, of course, that they were hundreds of miles away.

On the sidewalk in front of the division headquarters he held the cell phone to his ear and strode quickly away from the building. The line crackled with static, but after a few rings it was answered abruptly.

"What?" a scratchy voice barked. It belonged to Delaney Orton, a captain at the state police barracks in Buffalo, New York. Once upon a time, they'd worked together, but Orton's wife had wanted to move home to be near her family.

"Del? Jace Castillo."

"I'm sleeping, Jace Castillo," Del rumbled. "Go 'way."

"Wake up, Del. I've got a situation in a town called Hollingsworth, a ways south of Albany on Route Eighty-seven. I need your help."

"Ever look at a map, Jace? I'm in Buffalo. Buff-a-lo. Look it up."

"It's an animal control problem," Castillo replied, glancing around the street to make sure he was not being overheard.

When Orton spoke again, he sounded very awake.

"Talk to me."

Talk to me.

Those had been Olivia Navarre's words to Jack and Molly, and in the ensuing hours that was just about all any of them had done. Jack sat with his back against the concrete, his gaze ticking back and forth between Olivia and Molly. It was still difficult for him to accept this girl as Bill's niece when he had not even known Bill had family until a few months ago. And yet how much more difficult than the many other discoveries he had made since the spring?

Only recently had Jack learned that his friend, this being who was his sister's lover, had never even told them his true name. Bill was a variation on Guillaume. But only in this conversation with Olivia did they come to the startling realization that Cantwell was a completely manufactured surname, that their friend's family name was *Navarre*.

Olivia also explained to them the significance of the Navarre family to the history of the packs, and the relationship of her grandfather Yves Navarre to Owen Tanzer's father, Wade. That particular bombshell had left both Jack and Molly both wide eyed and shaking their heads that Bill had conveniently neglected to mention any of that to them in the past.

But Jack did not blame him. When they first discovered what Bill was, it would likely have been even more difficult for them to accept his true nature if they'd known that his lineage was so linked to Tanzer's. Still, it made Jack wonder what else they did not know.

For her part, Olivia had seemed even more surprised to learn about her uncle's current situation than they had been to discover his history. When Molly explained that Bill was in a relationship with Jack's sister, the astonishment and quiet revulsion on her face had been plain, and instructive.

"With a human?" Olivia had asked, wrinkling her nose, her features shaded by the straight black hair that framed her face.

Jack tried not to take offence. Though he had known Bill for years and had come to terms with his sister's relationship, the same sort of repugnance, though in reverse, had still been his first response.

Olivia knew about her uncle's wish to live among humanity, to merge with human civilization. She knew he had played professional football, and had confessed that her own interest in writing and performing music would likely not have been nurtured in her if not for the example he had set. But he had his own life, and she hers, and since her mother died a few years before, she had almost entirely lost touch with her uncle. By the standards of the previous six months Olivia's story seemed almost normal. In the wake of her mother's death she had done a great deal of soul-searching and focused more than ever on her love of music. With her absentee father never available, she had returned to her mother's pack, her distant relatives, for a while. At seventeen she had set herself up in New York City with the help of other Prowlers in the underground and begun to work the music scene with some small success, spending a lot of time busking—playing out in public for tips—in places like Washington Square Park and South Street Seaport. There had been some attention from A&R execs at more than one recording label.

Jasmine had violently interrupted that process.

Now the stories had largely been told, and Jack and Molly sat beside each other in the basement, leaning against the wall, with the delicious scents of coffee and bacon and other greasy food wafting down to them and making Jack's mouth water. As the girls talked he was only half listening, far more interested in the basement, in the concrete walls and the two doors off the wide, nearly empty room. The rear door, up to a bulkhead in the back of the parking lot—the door they'd been brought in—was steel, and so was the one that led up into the Blueberry Diner.

We need to get out of here, he thought for the thousandth time. Neither one of them had life-threatening injuries, but both he and Molly had dozens of cuts that ought to be disinfected. A ridiculous thing to think about, considering that at any moment Prowlers might come down and rip their throats out, but nevertheless, his mind went there. Even if Olivia was right and the Prowlers were going to hold on to them until Jasmine arrived to witness their execution, there was no way to know exactly how long that was going to take. At first the conversation had seemed important and necessary, but as it began to wind down now, he started to think the get-to-know-you session had been a mistake.

"You know what?" he said suddenly, interrupting the two girls. "Maybe we can continue this later. I don't want to be here when Jasmine comes. I have a feeling she won't be interested in keepin' us alive if she has you, Olivia."

The Prowler girl nodded and flipped her hair back away from her face. She stood, and once again Jack was struck by how tall she was. "I'm all for leaving. But I've been down here awhile, and it isn't like I haven't tried. No offence, but I can't see how a human can get through one of these doors if I can't."

Jack bristled. However progressive Bill was in dealing with humanity, his niece needed a few lessons in interspecies diplomacy. Jack had the idea that in political terms she might be what Prowlers would consider middle-of-the-road. In other words, she might not eat small children, but she wasn't likely to have much objection if her friends wanted to indulge. It was a lesson to him: Don't trust the girl just because of who her uncle is. After all, Olivia's father, Dallas, had tried to kill them back in August, and they had ended up punching his ticket instead. Not that Jack was prepared to tell Olivia that.

"I'm not so sure we need to go through the door," he told her.

Olivia frowned, but Molly interrupted before she could respond.

"Wait a second, you two," Molly said, leaning forward. "There's a part of this I need to understand that isn't making any sense to me."

Her eyes fixed on Olivia, and Jack sensed a kind of understanding between them. He realised with no small interest or surprise that while his mind had been wandering, between the lines of their conversation these two had been forming a sort of alliance. They had connected.

Good for them, he thought. But it gave him no feeling of warmth or comfort toward Olivia. No matter how striking her outward appearance, he knew there was a monster underneath.

Jack and Olivia gazed at Molly expectantly.

"Well," Molly continued, "if Jasmine didn't know Bill—our Bill—was the same person as Guillaume Navarre, why did she take you in the first place? You've been her prisoner for months and you're still alive. I don't get any of that."

Olivia nodded, her heavy-lidded gaze moving back and forth between Jack and Molly. "I see your point. It was a hell of a game she was playing, dangerous to her and to her plans. See, at first she came to me to recruit me."

When she grinned, Olivia's teeth looked cruel and sharp.

"Jasmine has grand plans, I'll give her that. Tanzer

must have been a charismatic son of a bitch to convince her so completely of his dream. She's shrewd and cunning, but even the smartest cur can be blinded by zealotry."

Cur, Jack thought, and shivered. Months ago, with Artie's death, he had discovered an entirely new world existing beneath what he had known. But since he stepped into the Lotus Club a few days earlier, he had begun a descent into that world that chilled him. It was a world with its own politics, customs, and jargon, none of it very pleasant.

"Your music," Molly said softly, knees pulled up under her chin. "She knew you were a musician, how much that meant to you, and she still thought you'd go along with her?"

Olivia chuckled. "Amazing, huh? I understand the predatory impulse, believe me. Maybe that's an area we shouldn't get into. But hell, who'd want to live in a world without people like B. B. King and Bonnie Raitt in it? Jasmine was a fool to think I'd join her."

Jack raised an eyebrow. "Maybe not."

"I'm sorry?" Olivia replied edgily.

"You're a Navarre. Think what that would have meant for her, long-term. It was a risk she was willing to take. When you didn't go along with her, she snatched you up, but she didn't dare kill you yet. She'd keep you around in case she needed you. Once she figured out that Bill and Guillaume Navarre were one and the same, she planned to use you against him. He's down in Manhattan looking for you even as we speak."

There was more to this thought process, but it

involved the death of her father, and Jack wasn't ready to have that conversation with Olivia yet.

"That makes sense," Olivia said then, understanding dawning upon her features. "She had me down in the city for a long time. Then they must have heard he was in town, because all of a sudden, in the middle of the night, they moved me up here."

"It's probably the nearest large concentration of Prowlers outside the city," Molly reasoned. "The better to hide you. Not to mention what brought *us* here in the first place."

"Right," Jack said. "Now, can we get the hell out of here?"

Olivia only stared at him as though he were mad, but Molly smiled sweetly and slipped her hand into his.

"What've you got in mind?"

It was Jack's turn to smile, and he flattered himself by thinking that this particular grin might be just as dangerous looking as Olivia's. "Well, they want to keep us alive until Jasmine gets here, but they probably wouldn't bother to stop Olivia from killing us." His gaze ticked toward Olivia and his smile disappeared. "On the other hand, if they thought we might kill you, the granddaughter of Yves Navarre, they'd have to step in, wouldn't they?"

The Prowler girl actually snorted in derisive laughter. "You two? Kill me?"

Molly let her legs slide down and she leaned back against the concrete again. Her expression was deadly earnest. "We killed Owen Tanzer, Olivia. We destroyed the sanctuary in Vermont. As far as they're concerned, we're capable of just about anything."

A wistful look crossed Olivia's face. "The sanctuary. That's a shame, it truly is. The fight goes on." Then she nodded. "All right, then. Let's try it your way. But if they come down, you better make it look good. If you're supposed to be trying to kill me, they have to buy it completely."

Jack nodded. "No problem."

CHAPTER 10

Jack tried to imagine what was going on upstairs in the Blueberry Diner. It was late enough at night that there was little chance of a random tourist happening through, but the odds were high that at least some of those upstairs were actual human truckers just in for a sandwich and a cup of coffee to break up the monotony of the road. It was Jack's hope that what he was about to do would not get any of them killed.

Ten or twelve feet from the bottom of the steps he stood facing Olivia, his fists clenched at his sides. This was not only crazy, it was stupid. He knew what his reputation was among the Prowlers, but even so, how could they believe even for a moment that he was capable of killing one of them with his bare hands? Not that it mattered anymore. This was the plan, and they didn't have a better one. It had to work.

Of course, they'd stacked the deck in their favour a bit.

"Molly," he said, voice low. "The second we're at it, you start screaming. Only a few seconds."

Though she made no verbal response and Jack did not turn to look at her, he could almost feel her assent. They were in this spot together—a crappy plan was better than no plan at all. However, it was hard for him to be so casual about it when he thought about exactly what he was about to do. Olivia stood before him, apparently completely at ease, and stared at Jack as though she were waiting for him to ask her to dance.

"What are you waiting for?" she demanded.

Jack flushed and felt stupid. He knew what she was, but in spite of that, he looked at this tall, lithe girl and that's what he saw. Olivia studied him a moment, a deep frown creasing her forehead, and then she got it.

"Oh, hell, you're kidding me!"

With a shudder she changed, fur sprouting all over her flesh, joints popping and stretching, changing the shape of her body beneath her clothes. From beneath the striking, commanding appearance of this human girl a monster erupted. Her fur was as black as her hair. Her snout snapped and gnashed, and her razor teeth gleamed as she took a step toward him.

"Is this better? You need me to start something?"

Jack grimaced. "Oh, yeah. That's *much* better."

He felt keenly the emptiness of his hands. Whoever Olivia was, she was a Prowler, and you just did not fight one without a weapon. Even as that thought went through his mind Jack put his hands together, fingers twined, and brought both fists around in a sweeping arc. The Prowler did not even try to defend herself or dodge, but took the blow full on. It knocked her, staggering, several feet back. And it was the best shot Jack had in him.

Olivia snarled, loud and ominous.

"Jack, no don't!" Molly screamed, back by the stairs. "She'll kill you! God, Jack, no!"

Her fear for him sounded a little too real for comfort.

Olivia lunged at Jack, fangs gnashing, and drove him down to the concrete hard enough to knock the wind out of him. Trying to catch his breath, he glared up into those feral eyes and saw not a trace of the girl with whom he had hatched this plan. Olivia growled and raised a talon above him.

Jack drove his right fist up into her throat. The Prowler reared back, clutching at her neck, and he sat up and drove punches into her abdomen, once, twice, three times, like working a heavy bag at the gym. Jack was a little bit more than average height, but he had been carrying cases of beer and alcohol around the bar his entire life, and there was power in his arms and shoulders, enough to really hurt this beast.

He hesitated.

A massive Prowler hand flashed down, a single claw tore the skin on his right cheek. Jack hissed in pain and glared up at her.

"Don't hold back," Olivia whispered, the words raw and guttural from her bestial throat.

"Fine," Jack snapped. He hammered her in the side of the head with a powerful blow, behind which he put all his weight. It drove the Prowler back again, and this time Jack followed up on it. His legs were free and he swept them under her. Olivia tumbled to the concrete, and then Jack was up, kicking her in the side, feeling the sting of the slash on his feet and the blood trickling down over his chin. Tasting the copper of his own blood on his lips.

In the back of his mind was a picture of this girl and a knowledge of their alliance. She was Bill's niece, and that counted for something. It wasn't that he disliked her, though there was a kind of animal swagger to her that made him uncomfortable. But that cut on his face had galvanized all his fear and hatred for the Prowlers, and so even though she barely struggled, he kicked her one more time before falling down upon her.

Molly screamed again, a short cry of alarm that he was not certain was feigned. Jack grabbed Olivia by the throat and slammed her head into the concrete.

At the top of the stairs the door banged open. Jack had his back to the Prowlers who rushed through the basement door, their feet pounding the landing at the top of the steps. He gripped Olivia's throat tighter and slammed her head against the concrete, maybe a little too hard, for she snarled loudly and bucked against him. Jack did not dare to turn around, but he listened closely to the sounds behind him and he prayed that there were no more than two of them. Certainly it would have been overkill to put more than two guards on the steel door at the top of the stairs.

He struggled with Olivia, afraid to bang her skull

again. Their eyes met, hers flaring with a bestial light that made him glad there was someone else here for her to punish for the pain she had just endured.

"Ah, shit, he's gonna kill her!" a voice snapped, and Jack recognized it at once. John Ford, the Prowler who had driven them off the road.

Heavy footsteps slammed into the wooden stairs yet still he did not turn. The last thing he wanted to do was alert them that their arrival was far from unexpected. Or have them notice that Molly was nowhere in sight, that the lightbulb near the stairs was shattered, the stairs themselves cast in darkness. It would not do to have them realize that Olivia had used her prodigious strength to tear up one of the wooden treads, nails and all.

A stair was missing.

With a grunt of surprise the Prowler in the lead put his entire weight down on the spot where the next step ought to have been. Jack spun just in time to see it happen. John Ford's foot passed through open space, his entire leg shot through the hole in the stairs, and he roared as something snapped inside him. His chest hit the next stair, and one of his legs twisted up at an odd angle. Ford cried out again in agony and snarled, changing even as he tried to claw free.

The one behind him saw instantly what had happened. Even in the darkness of that corner where they had shattered the bulb, Jack could see the very moment when he got it, when he looked up from Ford's painful writhing and put it together. Jack didn't recognise the human face on it, but clearly this one was smarter than the average Prowler. Old cartoon voices drifted like ghosts through Jack's mind and were instantly dispelled as the thing leaped over the broken and grunting Ford and landed in a crouch on the basement floor.

He was changing even as he rose from that crouch.

Molly stepped from the shadows and swung the heavy wooden plank that had once been the missing step. Nails still jutted from it, and when she slammed it into the Prowler's face, it tore flesh.

The thing screamed in a voice that sounded all too human and rounded on Molly, but by then Olivia was up. She bounded across the concrete at it and slammed into the beast, and her claws began to rise and fall in powerful sledgehammer blows, pummelling and slashing the guard simultaneously. Its blood flew, spattering the clothes Olivia still wore. The other had the weight advantage, but Olivia had momentum and surprise in her favour. She was brutal, even savage, and Jack watched in horrified fascination as she beat the other Prowler down. In those few moments as she was killing the guard, he found he could not even bring the picture of her human face into his mind. Or he did not want to.

She was beautiful, even like this. The way a jaguar or a tiger is beautiful. And he realised that that beauty, the lithe, confident menace of a jungle cat, was the same thing that made her human countenance captivating. No matter how buried she became beneath a human facade, he knew he would never be able to separate the two in her again because Olivia could not hide the truth of her nature. The truth was, she reminded him of Jasmine, and Jack did not like that thought at all.

Then, still trying to pull his broken body from the hole in the stairs, the mangled Prowler, Ford, began to call out in alarm for the others. "Down here!" he shouted angrily. "Move it, they're trying to get out! Jasmine will kill us all! Down here, you idiots!"

Molly ran to the bottom of the steps and hit him again with the board, bloody nails tearing his fur and flesh. Ford grunted with the first blow and tried to reach her, but the second thump of the wooden plank dazed him, and the third left him barely conscious. When she stepped back, there was a tuft of fur and a hank of something that might have been flesh on one of the nails. One of Molly's strikes had taken out Ford's left eye, and the empty orbit leaked blood and clear fluid.

"Move it!" Olivia snarled at Jack when she spotted him just standing there staring. She kicked the dead Prowler at her feet once. "Show's over. There's gonna be more—"

As if on cue, shouts came from above and Jack looked up to see several thick-bodied figures blocking the light from the kitchen of the diner at the top of the stairs. Carefully the one in front started down. *No element of surprise left*, Jack thought.

Olivia fished a set of keys out of the pocket of the guard she had killed. They jangled in her hand and she tossed them to Molly, who started for the back door and handed the plank to Jack. He tried not to notice how frightened and hollow her eyes seemed. Instead, he stood shoulder to shoulder with this beast that was his ally, this girl who was his friend's flesh and blood. He and Olivia would fight side by side.

Or they would have.

From upstairs in the kitchen, beyond the threatening figures who were beginning to descend the steps, they heard shouts and a brief blare of a police siren that cut off after just a few seconds. Then a voice on a bullhorn.

"Attention! This is the New York State Police. You are holding hostages within the building against their will. You will turn them over to our custody now and surrender yourselves for questioning. You have ten seconds to comply."

Jack stared up the stairs in disbelief. He figured the expression on his face mirrored that on the faces of the Prowlers who had been about to attack them. Instead of coming farther down, however, they quickly retreated back up the stairs, and the steel door was slammed shut and locked from above.

At his side Olivia turned to stare at him. "What the hell is going on?" she asked.

Feeling foolish, he shrugged. "Not a clue. Not that I'm complaining."

From the other side of the basement Molly hissed at them in a low voice, "Let's go!"

Upstairs gunfire erupted. Through the concrete and steel they could hear muffled shouting and gunshots, glass shattering. Jack had no idea what extraordinary coincidence had led to the police arriving at that moment, but he dared not even question their fortune. It might have been possible for them to escape without that intervention, but it was even more likely that they would have been killed. Even if they had gotten away, they would have been hunted immediately.

This, though . . . this was like the greatest birthday present he had ever gotten, and it wasn't even his birthday.

"Can we go?" Molly called to them, a bit louder. Olivia was already loping across the basement toward her, and as Jack went to follow, Molly fixed their Prowler companion with a grave stare. "You might want to change back now, so just in case the police see you, they won't *shoot you dead*."

Olivia actually laughed at that as she transformed once more, her true visage retreating beneath a human mask. She paused at the bottom of the steps and shuddered as her face restructured itself, her jaws and lips retracting as new skin stretched to cover them. Molly was only a few feet from her, and she turned away from the sight. Jack wasn't certain if Molly had averted her eyes to give the other girl privacy or out of revulsion, but he had an idea it was more the latter. For his part, he stared in fascination during the change, stunned by the feeling of intimacy that came over him as he watched the process. It lasted only a few seconds, and when it was through, Olivia glanced over at Jack as though she had caught him watching her undress.

"Time to go," Olivia said, her face cast into deep shadow by the long, straight tresses that framed it. She looked like a human again, but Jack thought he could still see the echo of the beast in her features.

Olivia was the first one up the stairs. Molly dropped the keys on the floor and followed, and Jack took one last look at the Prowlers in the basement—one dead and one unconscious—and went after the girls. He ran up the stairs and out the open bulkhead doors, and nearly crashed into Molly, who had stopped short in the broken, overgrown lot at the rear of the diner with her hands up. Slowly Olivia also raised her hands.

Both girls were silhouetted in the headlights of a pair of police cars. Their blue lights began to flash. Behind the open doors of the cars uniformed officers stood with guns levelled at them. Jack swore under his breath. How stupid had they been to think the cops might actually forget to cover the rear? More gunfire erupted around the front of the diner, and he wondered if there was a standoff up there now.

"Police!" called a plainclothes officer who stood between the two cars. "Hands where we can see them."

Jack raised his with great reluctance. "Look," he said loudly, "this isn't what you think. We were prisoners down there." He sighed as he realized how lame that sounded. Both he and Molly had little scratches all over their arms and faces, and the gash Olivia had cut on his cheek might need stitches. Olivia had blood on her clothes.

The plainclothes cop kept his sidearm steady as he advanced upon them, staring at each of them in turn, appraising their appearance, brows knitted in consternation.

"You," he said to Jack. "What's your name?"

Not the question Jack had expected. Then again, he had not expected any questions at all, just handcuffs. "Jack Dwyer."

"Got any identification on you?"

Confused, Jack slowly reached around to his back pocket and was pleased to find his wallet still there. He pulled it out and handed it to the cop, keeping his right hand up. The plainclothes officer holstered his weapon and took a step back as he opened up the wallet and pulled out Jack's licence. He glanced once at the picture, then up at Jack, before closing the wallet and tossing it back through the air. Jack caught it.

The cop raised a hand and waved at the others, and they lowered their weapons. Olivia dropped her arms, and after a moment Molly did the same, though more slowly. The plainclothes cop had thick eyebrows shot through with gray, and he raised them now as a smile flickered across his grizzled face. He held his hand out to Jack.

"Del Orton. Jace Castillo sends his best."

Dumbfounded, Jack glanced at Molly, who looked just as bewildered as he felt. *How the hell did Castillo know we were in trouble?* Jack shook Orton's hand and was about to ask that very question when the state police detective—or Jack assumed he was a detective—went on.

"Your Jeep is totalled, I'm afraid," Orton said. Then his voice lowered. "The weapons you were carrying are gone and so are the ones you dropped at the site. According to Castillo, we're on the same side in this, but we couldn't just give them back to you. Maybe that makes you an easier target, and if so, I'm sorry. At least you won't have to worry about any of the mutts from this place catching up to you."

As if to punctuate that sentiment, more gunfire could be heard around the front, along with shattering glass.

"Kind of at a loss for words," Jack told him, still stunned.

Molly stepped up beside him. "Thank you, Del. You might just have saved our lives."

"Might?" Orton said with a chuckle. "Yeah, I guess you kids are tougher than you look. At least from what I've heard. Let me get you a ride back to your hotel. I can have an officer run to the pharmacy for you too, get yourselves cleaned up. Have a rest. Tomorrow morning call your auto insurance company, get a rental car, and get the hell out of Dodge. That's all the thanks I want."

Orton pulled a business card from his pocket and handed it to Molly. "And next time you've got a pest problem in New York State, you can just let me know instead of travelling."

He turned and walked back toward the cars, laughing softly and muttering, "*Might* have saved their lives." A uniformed officer stepped forward from the car on the right and beckoned for them to get into the vehicle. Olivia hesitated for a moment until Molly whispered something to her that Jack couldn't hear. Then the three of them got into the back of the police car, separated from the cops by a cage between the seats that made Jack feel like a criminal. He didn't mind, though.

At least they weren't being arrested for real. Once again they had been saved by a conspiracy of silence among law enforcement agencies keeping the truth from the public. He understood the need for that conspiracy, but it made him bitter nevertheless.

Still, the biggest question looming in his mind was how Castillo had known they needed help, never mind where to find them. It was impossible, and yet it couldn't be coincidence.

As they pulled from the parking lot he stared at the front of the obscenely blue diner. All of the windows had been shattered. Several Prowler corpses could be seen on the pavement in front, where a semicircle of police vehicles acted as a barrier for the armed officers who had cordoned off the building. Silence had fallen and nothing moved within. It was not over, but it was close.

Then, just before he lost sight of the diner, Jack saw several figures standing in the parking lot, their backs to the carnage. Ghosts. The phantoms stared after the police car as it rolled away, and Jack stared back. One of them had shaggy blond hair and wore a torn sweatshirt; the ghost of Artie Carroll raised one arm and waved.

Jack understood then. Somehow Artie had gotten word to Castillo. Somehow. He smiled and waved back.

"What the hell are you waving at?" Olivia asked in a harsh whisper.

"The cavalry."

The taxi cruised north on Amsterdam, and Roger Martelle slumped against the seat, completely ignoring the tinkling bells of the music that played soft and low on the sound system and the smell of incense that barely covered the driver's body odour. He was too tired even to crack the window for fresh air, and was a little bit drunk as well. Scotch on the rocks had been his drink of choice tonight, and he had lost count of them.

His eardrums still thrummed with the music that had been playing at the Club Clandestine earlier, and everything sounded muffled to him, like he had cotton stuffed in his ears. Which might have explained why he did not ask the driver to turn down the Scheherazade bump-and-grind that was coming out of the taxi's speakers. His mind was still back in the club, grooving to the true funk of the L.A.-based quintet whose showcase he had gone down to see. The band was called Nevermore, and the singer was a long-limbed, exotic goddess by the name of Katya Raven.

Martelle smiled to himself. *"Quoth the Raven, 'Nevermore.'"* That poem by Edgar Allan Poe. More than likely where they'd gotten the name, and he felt like an idiot for not having picked up on it earlier. They were a hell of a band, too. Nevermore played a kind of moody groove music that was part Billie Holiday, part funk 'n' roll, and part hard-core blues. It wasn't like anything else Martelle had ever heard. From the moment he walked out of the Club Clandestine he had been determined to sign them to his label. It wasn't going to be an easy sell to his own superiors, but Martelle didn't care if Nevermore wasn't a smashing success. They were good, and that had to count for something.

WILD THINGS

The taxi came to a stop in front of his building, and Martelle paid the driver, probably too much, but what the hell—it was only money. With the music of Nevermore still rolling through his head like the echo of distant thunder, and the singer's sultry voice laid over it with the lilt of a lullaby, he dug out the keys to his townhouse. Despite the scotch, Martelle was sober enough to wait until the outer door had closed and the lock had engaged before unlocking the inner door.

He hummed to himself as he shut the door behind him and began to unbutton his shirt. As he walked from the foyer into the living room he frowned and sniffed at the air in the dark room. Alarmed, he reached for the light switch.

"Leave it dark," said a female voice.

A growl rose up in Martelle's throat, and his teeth began to elongate and sharpen, but he fought back the change. Again he reached for the light. Powerful hands grabbed him from behind, laden with a familiar scent that terrified him enough that he nearly lost control of his bladder. Martelle was lifted off the floor and thrown across the room. He crashed down upon the glass coffee table and it shattered, cutting him, drops of his blood sliding on glass shards down to stain the carpet.

He looked up into the face of a Prowler whose fur was so dark it might have been the night itself, save for the white streak across his head.

"Winter," Martelle murmured, frightened. "Why . . . ?"

Lips curled back from Winter's fangs. "The lady said to leave it dark."

Martelle sucked in long breaths, trying to hide his fear. But this was Winter. Even if he could have defeated the creature in one-on-one combat—which he doubted—Martelle would not have dared to raise a hand to him.

"She's a human," Martelle whined. "Why would you bring her here?"

The woman stood up then, with the aid of a cane. She was young and petite, and in the light from outside he could see that she was naturally pretty. Her dark blonde hair was pulled back into a ponytail, and a cascade of freckles fell across her face. Those things ought to have made her look cute, but her expression was severe and unforgiving. With the cane at her side, she hobbled toward him and stood over him.

"Mr. Martelle. Sometime in the last couple of days you talked to a man named Bill Cantwell. Maybe you know him as Guillaume Navarre. He was with an associate of Winter's called Lao. Winter himself told them to seek you out, so we know they came to you. The question is, what did you tell them? Where did you send them? Who else did they see?"

His hearing was still muffled, but the music in Martelle's mind had ceased. Now all that was in his head was a kind of birdlike trilling, a constant tingle of fear. It made him want to throw up, made him want to tear out this woman's throat. He had never been afraid of a woman before, but her tone and the ominous presence of Winter shook him. Desperately he tried to figure out what answer would keep him alive.

"I know who Guillaume Navarre is," he said quickly. Martelle could taste the scotch in his mouth, but its effects had burned off. "But I've never met him. I don't know what you're talking about."

For a moment he thought the woman would cry. The corners of her eyes crinkled with emotion and her lips pursed together as though she was trying to hold in a whimper. Then her countenance changed completely. Her lips pulled back into a rictus grin, and in that moment he thought that she looked for all the world like a Prowler.

"Lying son of a bitch," she snapped. Then she brought the silver lion's-head tip of her cane down across his skull.

Pain shot through his head, and Martelle recoiled, snarled, and began to rise from the shattered glass of the coffee table. The change started to come upon him again, and his hands curled into talons, claws jutting from the tips of his fingers as he lunged for her.

Winter slammed him to the carpeted floor and stood staring down at him. Fury nearly overwhelmed reason, but after a moment Martelle lay still. The human woman tapped him with her cane, and he growled but did not move.

"Where did you send them?" she demanded.

Martelle laughed, mostly in disbelief, but also in surrender. "Fine. You want to know? I didn't send them anywhere, really. They came to me and I told them to go down to the Voodoo Lounge, that that was where Jasmine had been recruiting. Navarre's niece had wanted to play music there and I put the two of them together. Jasmine and Olivia Navarre. I had no idea what Jasmine would do, but I'm not going to stand in her way, either.

"But Lao was playing along," Martelle said, sneering the words at Winter. "Your boy was playing both sides against the middle. Maybe he learned that from the best, eh? He told me to let Jasmine know they were coming."

The woman gripped the head of her cane more tightly and Martelle winced. Winter knelt down beside him then, and all thoughts of the human were gone as he gazed up into the face of this ancient warrior, this seasoned diplomat.

"And you told her," Winter said. It was not a question.

"I told her," Martelle confirmed.

Winter's eyes narrowed and he bared his glistening, needle fangs. "You should not have acted against the Navarres."

"At least I picked a side."

"So have I," Winter snarled. "At long last, so have I."

Martelle stiffened as Winter tore out his throat. His last sight was of the human woman with the cane, staring down at him. She winced but did not look away.

CHAPTER 11

My car, Bill Cantwell thought. *The bastards are using my car.*

He sat in the backseat of his Oldsmobile, pressed between a pair of Prowlers who had also guarded the old subway train he'd been imprisoned within in that subterranean lair Jasmine had established. They were both light-skinned males, one blond and one with a stubble of red hair, and they wore dark sunglasses even though they were in the backseat of a car rolling through Manhattan at going on three in the morning. *Men in black,* Bill thought. *You look like a couple of idiots.*

And they did. Their arrogance was so completely absurd it was tempting to treat them like the fools they seemed to be. But like their human appearance, he suspected this ridiculous affectation was merely that, a facade. In the time they had been guarding him, Bill had not even learned their names. Mr. Blond had spiky hair and wore small steel hoops in each ear. Mr. Red allowed several days' stubble on his chin and had a symbol comprised of interlocking circles that looked vaguely Celtic tattooed on his forearm.

The driver was a tall Prowler with dark skin and a goatee. He wore no sunglasses, but his eyes were glazed and dead. In the front passenger seat was a female whose raven black hair was stylish and short. Everything about her spoke of power, but a human sort of power. She was a Prowler, no doubt of that, but from the jut of her chin and the cut of her suit it was clear she was a professional in every sense. Bill guessed that in her human guise she was a lawyer. There was just something about the way she carried herself.

They were silent as the car moved south. Bill had a feeling he knew where they were going, but he said nothing to disturb the quiet. Rather, he stared out the window at the darkened streets of Manhattan, at the storefronts flashing by. *The City That Never Sleeps,* he thought. And it was true; there was activity even this late, after-hours parties and all-night delis. But by 3 A.M., it seemed, the witching hour had finally come to Manhattan. The city might never sleep, but Bill guessed it nodded off now and again.

He shifted his weight and felt Mr. Blond and Mr. Red stiffen in alarm on either side of him. Bill ignored them. He wished desperately for a shower. Not that he smelled particularly bad, but after the time he had spent locked in that ancient subway car, he felt filthy. The only saving grace was that in a painfully transparent pretence of goodwill Jasmine had sent one of her pack to fetch his suitcase, so he had clean clothes to wear. Of course, that was probably the same time they had decided to use his car.

My car, he thought again, jaw tight with the urge to hurt them. But he would do nothing to put Olivia's life in further jeopardy. The weight of his situation was heavy upon his shoulders, and he knew there would be no clean way out of it. The time he had spent in that hole in the ground had been filled with regret and fear and rage as he tried to figure a better way to resolve this mess, a way that would leave everyone he loved alive, even if it cost his own life.

Bill scratched at his beard and Mr. Red twitched. From the front seat the lawyer slid sideways to regard him more closely. There was a kind of sparkle in her eyes, as though the entire scene amused her, and it only added to the fire of his rage. The driver remained completely impassive, behaving as though he were alone in the car.

As Bill had guessed, the Oldsmobile pulled up at the curb in front of the Voodoo Lounge. The lawyer and Mr. Blond stepped out onto the street and stood waiting for Bill. He hesitated a moment, and Mr. Red lashed out, grabbed a handful of Bill's hair, and slammed his forehead into the door frame. Bill felt the other Prowler's breath, hot and fetid with the stench of raw meat, on the back of his neck.

"We're not supposed to kill you. Doesn't mean we can't hurt you. Jasmine picked us for this 'cause she knows we don't give a shit who your daddy was. Get out of the car."

Bill felt a ripple of tension pass all through him, his muscles tightening beneath the dark green wool sweater he wore. But he kept the beast quiet within him, kept stillborn the growl that threatened to rise in his throat. With a single grunt he stepped out of the car, crossed his arms, and simply stood there, breathing in the cold, fresh air of that October night.

"This way," the lawyer said, her tone as sharp as the creases in her suit.

The driver stayed in the car as Bill followed the lawyer up the steps, flanked by Mr. Blond and Mr. Red. The doors opened before they reached them, and it was clear someone had been watching for them. Once they were inside, the doors closed again, and Bill was nearly overwhelmed by the smell of Jasmine's pack and of many other Prowlers. Down in the subway lair the wind had passed through so much that the scent had not been as powerful. But here, in this enclosed space dedicated to music and dancing and sweating, the musk of his kind seemed to hang heavy around them like the dampness of the air before a thunderstorm. It spoke to the wild in him, and Bill felt something shift in his mind, as though he were suddenly looking back at himself from the opposite side of the mirror.

This time he could not stop the growl low in his throat. He crouched slightly and padded into the club with his guards on either side of him. The Voodoo Lounge was a wide-open space with a bar at each end and a low stage on the far wall, opposite the doors. Support beams jutted up from the centre of the room to the high, arched ceilings, giving the place an almost churchlike feel. Around the beams were cushioned benches that matched those along the walls, but there were no tables or chairs in the rest of the club. That was not what the club was for.

Above his head were rows of heavy spots and coloured lights aimed at the stage. They creaked on cables that hung from the ceiling, and swayed though there was no breeze inside. There was a rustle in the balcony behind him, and Bill did not have to turn to know there were Prowlers there. He had their scent. Four of them, and others in the stairwells off to the side. Others were in the process of cleaning the floor and the bar areas, but they paused as he came in.

His hackles rose and he hesitated. Mr. Red prodded him on, and it was all Bill could do to restrain himself from tearing the Prowler's hand off.

They crossed the enormous room, and the lawyer nodded to Mr. Blond and Mr. Red before disappearing through a door to one side of the stage. Bill kept his gaze resolutely forward and refused to look at any of them. They were beneath his contempt and he wanted them to know it.

Then that stage door opened again, but it was not the lawyer returning. It was Jasmine. She wore black leather pants and a silk shirt the colour of cinnamon, the colour of her skin. Her auburn hair was a calculated mess, and her orange eyes were as remarkable as ever.

A kind of invisible aura emanated from her, so that her presence was palpable; it might have been called charisma if not for the darkness in it.

She smiled when she saw him. "Hello, Guillaume. Happy to be free again?"

He narrowed his eyes. "Free?"

Jasmine gave a carefree toss of her head. "You saw the sky. It's something, after all. Not to worry, though. It won't be long before you and your Olivia can be reunited, the last of the Navarre line together at last."

A chill passed through him, but Bill did not flinch. "Good."

A mischievous grin flickered across her features. "Oooh, you're so unflappable. And so quiet. You don't want to know what's happened? Why you've been brought here?"

Bill stared gravely at her.

Mr. Blond slapped the back of his head. "Answer her!"

He exploded then into a single moment of violence so swift none of them had time to react. Bill rounded on Mr. Blond and struck him with one huge fist. The force of the impact cracked the bone in Mr. Blond's cheek and drove him to the floor. There was an uproar as Mr. Red and several of the other Prowlers nearby changed and lunged for him.

"Stop!" Jasmine shouted.

The beasts halted at her command. Only Jasmine herself had not changed, her cinnamon skin still unblemished. In a room full of animals she and Bill faced each

WILD THINGS

other. No claws, no fangs, no fur. Bill met her gaze, then turned and spat at the Prowler on the ground.

"I don't like to be pushed."

"Noted," Jasmine purred. "But don't think you'll survive much more of that sort of behaviour."

"Noted," he replied.

As if they were old friends, Jasmine turned and began to wander around him in a kind of circle. "You really think I don't know what's going on in that head of yours, Guillaume? Don't be coy with me, and I'll afford you the same respect. You're still hoping everyone's going to come out of this alive. But I promise you, that's not going to happen."

She had made it nearly all the way around him when she stopped and looked up, all trace of amusement gone from her features. "You thought you would alarm your human pet, the woman from the bar, and she would alert her brother. You counted on Jack and Molly to come down, guns blazing, like in some old Western, creating enough of a disturbance that you might free yourself and kill me. Then you could find Olivia. And, credit where credit is due, the Dwyer boy has proved hard to kill time and again. But not anymore."

At her words Bill felt his chest tighten and a glacial cold spread through him. "What have you done?"

The smile returned, and he was certain her teeth had lengthened, sharpened. Even without knowing it, she was letting the beast out. Jasmine strutted as though she was in complete control, but she could not even cage her own wild soul.

"Not what I've done, Guillaume, though I'd like to claim responsibility. It's what they did. Stuck their noses in where they didn't belong. Upstate, they tried to prey on some friends of mine but got their own legs stuck in the trap. We've got them."

Then, they're alive, Bill thought.

Jasmine must have seen his reaction in his face, for she frowned. "I'm on my way up there now. They killed Tanzer. I plan to tear out their throats myself. He would have done no less for me."

Thoughts raced through his mind as he tried desperately to put together some response, either in word or action, that would save the lives of these young people who had become his family. Nothing he thought of would end without their death, or Olivia's, and he simply could not make that choice.

Satisfied by his inaction, Jasmine turned her back on him and began walking across the club toward the doors. His guards closed in again on either side of him, not bothering with human masques now. Mr. Blond was bleeding from his snout, and some of the blood streaked his teeth; they gleamed pink. The injured Prowler seethed with menace, but Bill ignored him. His mind was on his friends, and on Courtney. If Jack and Molly had also disappeared on her, he could hardly imagine how panicked she must be.

Jasmine paused at one of the support columns and turned to him again. "I'll be back late this afternoon. By then, of course, your lover may also be dead, in which case I'll be more than happy to release you and Olivia."

Her orange eyes went wide in feigned surprise. "Oh, that's right. I neglected to tell you that she's here. The Dwyer woman, I mean. Right here in the city. Looks like when she couldn't reach Baby Brother, she decided to come after you herself. Adorable, isn't it?"

Bill stood stiffly, frozen inside now, and simply stared at her. All the rage he felt growing up inside him, the beast that scented others of its kind and wanted to run wild, showed only in the flare of his nostrils and the clench of his jaw.

Then the doors of the Voodoo Lounge flew open and Jasmine's mate, Alec, strode in. His face was etched with panic, and when he saw Jasmine, he looked for a moment as though he might bolt. *What's this?* Bill thought, but already he knew it was something he was going to like. Alec hesitated a moment and then crossed to Jasmine. He kept his head bowed as he whispered to her. Jasmine snarled a curse, but there was more. As if confessing to cleanse his soul, Alec leaned in farther, whispered something else.

Jasmine spun away from him, furious, and advanced on Bill. After a second he realized her focus was not on him, but on Mr. Blond and Mr. Red.

"We're going to keep him here now. Put him in the back, find a room without windows. There's a storeroom or something there. Make sure he doesn't get out."

"Change of plans?" Bill asked lightly, certain to keep his face without expression.

Her lips curled back but she said nothing. After a

moment she turned to Alec again. "Put out the word. I want them all dead, and their heads as proof."

Bill felt practically giddy. Jasmine wasn't going anywhere. That meant that Jack and Molly were no longer prisoners, if they had ever been.

"What about Tanzer?" he reminded her. "Aren't you supposed to do it yourself? In his memory?"

All the attention in the room had been on Jasmine's tirade, but now with his question it *shifted*. The gathered Prowlers wanted an answer to that question as well. Jack Dwyer seemed almost like a demon to them now, unkillable, waiting for them in the shadows, when they were the ones who were supposed to be lurking there. Was Jasmine now afraid of him?

She stiffened, obviously aware of the impact of the question, and glared at Bill. "I'll be hunting them myself. But I grow impatient enough that I'm not so picky anymore." Then she glanced at Alec again. "Spread the word. Kill them, or draw them here. I want all of them dead."

"But Jasmine," Alec began tentatively. "What about Winter? You can't really mean for us to—"

"Stop," she said, her voice soft but carrying all through the cavernous room, thanks to its acoustics. Jasmine looked suddenly tired, and she shook her head. "Don't tell me what I mean, Alec. There's a dream in the balance here. I want the wild back, don't you?" She looked around at the others gathered there. "Don't all of you? I don't want a chain or a collar or a yoke. I want to be wild."

There was a collective grunt of assent and some attendant growling. Both Mr. Blond and Mr. Red seemed to have forgotten Bill for the moment, captivated by the leader of their pack. Her command over them was frightening.

"If Winter has thrown in with the Dwyer woman, he stands against the dream. We have no choice but to kill him."

With that, Jasmine at last left the floor of the club, back through the door to the right of the stage. Bill stared after her, taking it all in. Jack and Molly were free and on their way, from the sound of things. Courtney was already here in the city. And Winter was with her. Winter had chosen sides.

The creature that had once been called Guillaume Navarre smiled. Jasmine had asked him to act as bait, never imagining that she might become the prey. Now if only he could discover where Olivia was being held, Bill thought things might work out after all. Not without bloodshed, of course, but that was all right. He kept the beast within him in check, but that did not mean he did not feel its savagery. After what Jasmine had done, she could not be allowed to survive.

In the end he would have her blood.

When grey dawn filtered down into the canyons of Manhattan, Courtney rose from bed and limped to the windows without her cane. The curtains in the tiny Fitzgerald Hotel were just as dingy as the rest of the place, but she needed to see the morning, and so she parted them, then wiped her hands on her nightshirt.

Though the clock on the night table did not work, she gauged that she had slept only a few hours the previous night, and fitful hours at that. Roger Martelle had been an animal, a Prowler, and a traitorous beast besides. He had conspired with Jasmine and with Lao, and might well have sent Bill to his death. For all of that, the memory of the night before sickened her. Not merely Winter's murder of the other monster, but the satisfaction she had felt when she struck Martelle with her cane. The sight of his blood had pleased her, and she had spent the night nauseous and feverish over that pleasure. It was one thing to kill the animals to stay alive or to keep them from killing others, but what Winter had done was murder.

If she could allow her fear for Bill and her hatred of these things to take her so firmly in its grasp, to overwhelm her so completely, then what separated her from the Prowlers? It was a question that had haunted her throughout the night, along with her fear for Bill. Now, as she stared out at the city, already alive with delivery trucks, taxis, shops and restaurants opening up, and a scattering of people on their way in to start work early, those questions dogged her again.

How do you define a monster?

Aren't humans also animals?

"Jesus," she whispered to herself, a hint of her mother's Irish brogue in her voice. "Stop thinkin' of yourself, Courtney."

Her gaze ticked to the night table, where her cell

phone lay on its side, long charge cord plugged into the wall. Its face was lit and it had to be fully charged now, but it had not rung. Not all night. No matter how much she had hoped it would, or had stared at it in frustration.

Now Courtney turned her back on the dawn, went to the edge of the bed, and picked up the phone. It was too early for Tim or Wendy to be at the pub, assistant managers or not, so she dialled the number of her own apartment. When the machine picked up, she pressed the "9" key twice.

"You have two messages," an electronic voice told her. "Message one . . ." There was a beep, and then another voice broke in, a girl's voice. "Courtney, hi, it's Eden Hirsch. When you get this message, call me back. It's . . . it's hard to explain on a machine, but it's important."

Courtney was troubled by the urgency in the girl's voice but had no plans to call Eden back right away. Whatever was happening at home, finding Bill took precedence. That, and figuring out why Jack and Molly had never checked in. She held her breath as the machine told her it was about to play her second message.

Beep.

"Hey, it's me."

Courtney let out her breath. Jack. Her relief was almost painful, and only now did she realize how worried she had been for him and Molly.

"Listen. . . . We had some trouble up here. We're

okay, now. Headed down to Manhattan. I tried calling your cell phone, but I can't remember the number. It was preprogrammed, but our cells are trashed. Gone. I'll explain later. And I had it written down on a piece of paper in the Jeep, but . . . Look, I'll tell you all this when I talk to you, but I'm gonna have to call you back. The important thing is this: If Bill checks in, tell him we've got Olivia. She's with us. We're going down to the city first thing in the morning to try to find him and maybe settle things with Jasmine once and for all."

There was a long pause as her brother tried to figure out if he had anything more to say. It was the way he ended every phone message he had ever left her.

"I'll . . . I guess I'll talk to you later—soon as I know where you can reach us. Watch yourself up there, all right?"

There came another beep, and the machine announced that there were no more messages.

Watch yourself up there.

Something had happened to Jack and Molly in upstate New York. From the sound of his voice, and what he *didn't* say, Courtney figured it had been pretty bad. But they were all right. Safe, for the moment. More than that, they had found Olivia somehow, which meant that if she and Winter could find Bill, that would be the end of it.

The end of it, she thought, and smiled to herself.

But the smile was fleeting. It wouldn't really be the end as long as Jasmine was still alive. Her stomach churned at the flash of images from the night before that returned to her mind then. Winter was an animal, little better than Jasmine, for all his airs. But how much different was she, truly, when despite her horror at Winter's murder of Martelle, she was prepared to do the same to Jasmine with her own hands if she had to?

Courtney considered calling back and leaving a message for Jack with her cell number, but since he had no idea she had left Boston, it would never occur to him to actually listen to the messages. She only wished she knew how to change the main message, the one callers heard, from here. But she did not. Courtney had no choice but to keep checking in until he left her a contact number.

Meanwhile, though, she would talk to Winter. After leaving Martelle's townhouse the previous night, Winter had told her that this morning they would begin to reach out to members of the Prowler underground who were likely to know where Jasmine's lair was. Courtney thought that might be walking right into trouble, but she had little choice other than to follow Winter's lead. Whatever the beast had once been, no matter how much diplomacy he had engaged in once upon a time, she believed now that he would do anything necessary to keep Bill alive.

They had that much in common. Courtney hoped that was the only thing they shared.

It was already past noon when Jack followed Olivia and Molly along a narrow Greenwich Village street. He had lost all track of where, exactly, they were, instead merely following Olivia's lead. It had been a long and terrible night, and the morning had seemed to go on forever. A sort of relief washed over him when he glanced at his watch and realized the morning was over. Hollingsworth, and all that had happened there, was behind them. Jack tried not to think about what lay ahead.

The night before, the state troopers had dropped them at their hotel and then actually brought in a first aid kit. None of his or Molly's injuries from the car accident were severe, though Jack found now that he had a pain in his lower back that he could not get rid of. But if some antiseptic and gauze were all they needed to deal with everything else, he figured they ought to be grateful for small miracles. There had been a small debate about whether or not he needed stitches for the long scratch Olivia had given him on his left cheek, but once it had been cleaned it didn't seem quite as deep. He would have a scar, no question, but probably not a bad one.

All in all, they had been lucky. Too lucky, in fact. Jack had a feeling they had used up all their luck for the year. Maybe for life. On the other hand, it wasn't all luck. Artie had not appeared since Jack saw him in the parking lot the night before, but he hoped the ghost would soon return so Jack could properly thank him and find out exactly what had happened. They had not spoken since he asked Artie for help in locating the spirits of local Prowler victims, but clearly his friend's ghost had been up to more than that.

Before going to sleep—he and Molly had offered to let Olivia take his place in the bed, but the Prowler girl had demurred, insisting that she was used to the floor— Jack had called the apartment. Though it was the middle of the night, Courtney had not answered the phone. He could only think that she was exhausted and had not heard it ring, so he had left a long message, promising to call back as soon as they figured out where they could be reached.

This morning he had tried her once more, again with no luck. He assumed she was at the market, and left no message because they had yet to stop anywhere long enough for her to call him back. Now, as the day began to slide into afternoon, he felt more than ever a need to touch base with his sister, to reassure her that he was all right, and satisfy himself that *she* was.

Of course, if he told her he was all right, he would be lying.

The state troopers had driven them over to a car rental agency just after eight o'clock that morning. Olivia had apparently slept quite soundly, but she was the only one. Jack and Molly had shifted anxiously all night, consumed by their own apprehension and sensitive to each other's. The drive down to Manhattan had been peppered with small talk, stories from one another's lives, and they had gotten to know Olivia a little better. Such trivialities passed the time and helped them avoid discussing the matters at hand. Upon arriving in the city Olivia had helped navigate them to an outdoor parking lot in Greenwich Village, and they had left both the car and their bags there.

As Jack followed the girls he glanced around nervously. It was lunchtime in Manhattan, and people milled around all over. Up ahead he saw the massive marble arch of Washington Square Park, pigeons spying on the crowd below, waiting for bits of sandwich to be dropped by people enjoying the perfect October day.

And it was a perfect day. The sun shone with an autumn glow, the sky was blue and clear, and a cool breeze rustled fallen leaves in the park. Jack figured it was in the mid-fifties, but with the sun so bright, he felt warm in the hooded sweatshirt he wore.

They crossed the street and went into the busy park. A couple of kids sat on a bench with their skateboards across their laps and with sullen expressions on their faces. Now that the lunch crowd had hit, there wasn't room in the park for them to board. Not far away a dreadlocked, thirtyish woman strummed an acoustic guitar and accompanied herself with a harmonica set into a funky neck brace.

Olivia stood at the edge of the park and gazed out over this sea of New York culture. On the far side of the park there was more going on. A juggler in clown makeup rode a six-foot unicycle. There was more music coming from over there as well. A saxophonist played Dave Brubeck's "Take Five."

The Prowler girl turned toward them, focusing on Jack and Molly for what felt like the first time since they

WILD THINGS

had parked the car. She wore a pair of Molly's pants and a light green cotton top with spaghetti straps. *Too cold for that outfit,* Jack thought, *but then, she probably doesn't feel it the way we do.*

"This way," she said, and then Olivia was off through the crowd.

As Jack tried to follow he glanced around at the crowd, picking out individual faces, frowning at anyone who seemed to be looking at him. He passed under the arch, and when he emerged on the other side, he watched the trees on the other side of the park, just to be sure no one was in them.

"Hey." Molly poked him in the side as she fell into step beside him.

Jack started. Then smiled. He reached down to take her hand in his, and they walked like that, as if this were a date instead of . . . whatever it was.

"What's going on with you?" she asked, her voice just loud enough for him to hear. "You look like a mouse in cat territory."

Something twisted in his stomach. "Kinda what we are, isn't it?" he asked, and finally met her gaze full on. "Sorry. I just feel like, without our cell phones, without any weapons, we're walking into the lion's den here. Or Jasmine's den, at least. Makes me nervous. I don't know what I'm expecting to see, maybe snipers on every rooftop."

Molly's expression was grave as she reached up to slide her hand across the back of his neck. She pulled

241

him to her and kissed him softly on the mouth.

"We're all right," she said. "We've gotten this far, Jack. Once we track Bill down, we can make a plan. But we're going to be all right."

"I know," he replied, and the truth of it was that he did believe that. But he felt keenly that they were targets out here, and he would feel better if he had something to fight back with.

He glanced around again, fighting his paranoia, and then leaned in to whisper to Molly, "This thing is getting bigger every time we turn around. With Olivia and Bill and this underground, with Jasmine and her new pack and the rest of the Prowlers that are still wild. All along we were just trying to do the right thing, take these monsters down, but I'm starting to think if we stir things up enough, maybe we won't have to do it alone. The Prowlers who just want to disappear into the human race, they're in danger of discovery every day, thanks to the wild ones. Jasmine's a threat to their existence. They may not like us, but we're doing them a favour."

"Yeah, but I hope we can get them to see it that way," Molly replied. "We're going to need their help."

Jack squeezed her hand. "Yeah. But whatever happens now, there's no going back."

With that, they both turned to glance around for Olivia. She had left them in the crowd, but after a moment Jack spotted her standing by the saxophone player, who was finishing up a tune, nodding his head to people who strolled by and dropped bills and change into his open instrument case.

"Come on," Jack said, and he led Molly through the throng to where Olivia stood.

They reached her just as the saxophone player finished his song. He was a thin guy with a goatee, dressed in a white T-shirt and black jeans. There was no way to tell his age from his appearance, but Jack guessed anywhere between twenty-five and thirty-five. As he began to adjust the knobs on his horn Olivia crouched at his side, one hand on his arm.

"Bowden."

The sax player gaped at her in happy astonishment and stood up so fast the horn banged against his hip and then swung by its strap down at his side. He ignored it, pulling Olivia up into a hug.

"You had us so worried," Bowden told her, squeezing Olivia even harder. "When you didn't come back, we all figured you'd just hit the road, playing clubs and bars or whatever. But then after a while we heard whispers. I didn't know what to think."

"It's good to see you, too," Olivia told Bowden. "You still have my spare guitar, or did you hock it already?"

"Still in its case," he promised. "Probably still in tune."

He held her at arm's length and grinned broadly. Olivia grinned as well. Uncertain what to do or say, Jack shifted awkwardly and felt Molly doing the same beside him. His attention apparently drawn by their discomfort, Bowden finally looked their way. The saxophone player's eyebrows went up.

"Who are your friends?" he asked Olivia.

And then he sniffed the air.

Prowler, Jack thought. *Of course.* And yet somehow he was surprised. This guy was just too happy and too nice to be a Prowler. But that's what he was.

Olivia moved slightly away from Bowden, creating with her own physical presence a kind of connection among them.

"Molly, Jack, this is Bowden," she said. "Bowden, meet Molly Hatcher and Jack Dwyer. They're friends of my uncle's."

The sax player seemed amiable enough and was reaching out his hand to shake Molly's when the smile evaporated from his face, the light in his eyes dimming. He dropped his hand and turned to Olivia again.

"Oh, hell, Olivia. Your uncle . . ."

Bowden glanced down, shook his head.

Bill's dead, Jack thought instantly. *Oh, my God, Bill's dead.*

Around them the lunch crowd nattered on. Pigeons flapped down to pick up crumbs. The juggler shouted as he fell off his unicycle, but he landed on his feet. Across the park the woman with the guitar sang, "I'm your ice cream man, baby, stop me when I'm passin' by."

Olivia stared at Bowden. "What? What about my uncle?"

Bowden shook his head again. "It's just rumours, O. I don't know if they're true."

"What rumours?" Jack asked, voice clipped. At his side Molly gripped his hand tight enough that it hurt.

Bowden glanced at them both, and then his gaze went back to Olivia. "Well, word on the street is he's joined Jasmine. Guillaume Navarre is part of her pack now."

CHAPTER 12

It couldn't be, of course. Molly was certain of that. No way in hell had Bill Cantwell thrown in with Jasmine. But even the rumour seemed to have shell-shocked both Jack and Olivia. For the rumours were absolutely certain of one thing: Guillaume Navarre, the man they knew as Bill Cantwell, was keeping company with Jasmine. And if he hadn't joined her by choice, there was only one possible explanation. *He* was now her prisoner.

As Bowden led them along Saint Mark's Place toward his apartment, Jack and Olivia hung back and spoke quietly but emphatically, trying to determine what to do next.

Guess I should be jealous, Molly thought. But the idea amused her. Maybe his older sister had fallen in love with Bill, but no way would Jack ever be attracted to a Prowler.

WILD THINGS

They walked along the cracked sidewalk amid the avant-garde Village population. Molly watched the faces as they passed. Clothing purposefully ragged and studiously torn; brows and lips and noses and even chins pierced and festooned with bright bits of metal; hair teased up and dyed a rainbow of unnatural colours. Many of them seemed to wear their outward appearance as a costume, a facade not unlike that of the Prowlers themselves. Yet among these students and artists who strove to be different were also those more comfortable in the role, individuals and couples whose faded casualness was worn as a genuine expression of who they were inside. Molly found herself able to tell the difference with very little difficulty. She wondered if that ability came from months of watching people's eyes and body language, second-guessing their intentions, even their humanity.

"So, you and Jack been together long?" Bowden inquired.

Shaken from her reverie, Molly glanced over at the lanky man who walked beside her with his sax case slung from his shoulder by a leather strap. Here he was, then, the perfect example of what she had been thinking about. Bowden wore blue jeans frayed to tatters at the cuffs and sandals that were not just broken in but nearly broken *through*. He had a saunter to his walk, as though he could hear the music even when he wasn't playing it. Some people referred to the artistic community in Greenwich Village as bohemians. If so, Bowden was a true bohemian.

But he was also a Prowler. *So much for my powers of observation,* Molly thought. If she had not seen him sniffing the air earlier, if she did not know Olivia was a Prowler, she would never have guessed Bowden wasn't human. But maybe that was a testament to this man's— *There I go again, this creature's*—ability to blend. Just as Bill did. Which made her wonder just how many of them there were, doing that. Blending.

"I'm sorry," Molly said with a self-deprecating smile. "I'm drifting. What did you say?"

Bowden tilted his head to indicate the pair walking behind them. "You and Jack. Just wondering how long you've been together."

"Not long, actually."

"Really?" The Prowler's eyebrows went up. "I wouldn't have guessed that."

"Why not?"

He shrugged. "Couples who've been together a long time, they've got this kind of telepathy down. Don't need to talk to each other a lot about what their next move is. Shared intuition or whatever. You two are pretty young, but seems to me like you've got the beginnings of that."

Molly felt herself blushing and was surprised. She wasn't a girl who blushed; never had been. But she was blushing, nevertheless. It was ironic that only moments before she'd thought about how she could read people, and now here was Bowden, who wasn't even human, doing a better job of it than she ever could have.

"We were . . . friends for a long time before we got

involved," she explained, not wanting to say more, to talk about Artie. Some people might think it weird for her and Jack to be involved after what had happened to Artie. Odd as it was, she found that she suddenly cared what Bowden thought.

"There you go!" Bowden said, happy to have his observations proved.

"You're sort of a romantic, aren't you?" Molly asked.

His smile went away. "I guess I am. Hard to believe for you, I guess. The monster with stars in his eyes. I'm like that elf in *Rudolph*. I don't wanna make toys, I wanna be a dentist."

Molly got the reference but did not laugh. There was a gravity to his tone that undermined any humour. *The monster with stars in his eyes,* she thought as she shoved her hands into the pockets of the battered brown leather jacket she had borrowed from Jack, feeling suddenly cold.

"How did you know we knew? What you are, I mean?"

Bowden laughed. "You kidding? I know who *you* are." He cocked a thumb back at Jack and Olivia. "I know who he is. Maybe the Prowlers in Peoria haven't heard about Jack the Giant-Killer yet, but this is New York City, honey. The heartbeat of America."

Now he did smile again, and it was infectious. But Molly's mind was awhirl with the implications of that. Theirs was intended to be a quiet little crusade. Watch the skies, so to speak, keep their eyes on the news, go out hunting now and again. But if what they were doing was going to make them celebrities among the very monsters they were hunting, it wouldn't be long before they dared not set foot out the door of the pub, for fear of repercussions.

She'd have to put some thought into that.

"It's just up here," Bowden said, gesturing toward a building on the left just ahead of them.

Molly didn't know anything about architecture, but the apartment house impressed her. The building itself was made of light brown stone, but around the windows the stone was a different colour, a brick red that was rounded into arches above each window. Around the small set of steps in the front there was some garbage and broken glass, but the building looked as though it had been renovated in the last few years.

"Nice place," she said. "Guess playing sax in the park is more lucrative than I would've thought." Even as she spoke the words Molly covered her mouth. "Sorry. That didn't come out right. I wasn't trying to say—"

Bowden chuckled softly. "It's all right. I do okay, I guess. But the truth is, I live in a tiny apartment with two roommates. Mags is an illustrator and Julian a freelance writer. Whoever has the money pays the rent. Sometimes we have other people crashing, and they kick in to the kitty as well. Somehow it all works out."

A kind of unorthodox family, Molly thought. But she knew all about that, living with Courtney and Jack, and half the time with Bill as well.

Bowden unlocked the door and held it open as Olivia and Jack caught up to them. The Prowler girl caught her eye and smiled as though she had only just remembered Molly was there at all. Molly surprised herself by smiling back at this beast dressed in her borrowed clothes.

"We've got a plan," Olivia said.

The way she held her head in that moment, chin raised, eyes steady and brooking no argument, reminded Molly powerfully of the girl's uncle.

"Why am I not surprised?" she replied, her gaze ticking toward Jack.

He reached for her hand, and she relished the warmth of his touch. His hair had dried crazy that morning and was spiky and ruffled, and he needed a shave, but there was something alive in his eyes now. A strength she had only rarely seen there before. It was as though, despite how heroic he had behaved in the past, he was only slowly becoming alive to the truth of it, awake to the knowledge that he was now a vital player in an ancient war. All along, what he had been doing was noble and courageous, but Jack had been sort of a reluctant hero. He did what he did to get back to the pub, to his regular life.

Not anymore, Molly thought. *This is regular life now. We're a part of this.*

"It's not a really good plan," Jack confessed. "In fact, there's a wicked high level of risk. And we're gonna need reinforcements. But I can't exactly go home and tell my sister I left her boyfriend to . . ."

His face went slack and his gaze went past her, his attention drawn by something or someone beyond

Molly on the sidewalk. *Ghosts,* Molly thought. Olivia and Bowden were already in the foyer of the building, and both of them focused on Jack with some alarm.

"Jack?" Olivia ventured.

A fond expression blossomed on Jack's face, and he glanced at Molly. "I'll be up in a minute, all right?"

Not just any ghosts. "Take your time. Give him my love."

He squeezed her hand and Molly went into the building. Behind her she heard Jack start to speak in a low voice. Fortunately, people talking to the air at one thirty in the afternoon was considered only passing strange in a city like New York.

"Uh, it's the third floor. Apartment C," Bowden told him.

Then the door swung shut, leaving Jack on the sidewalk, seemingly alone.

When Molly turned to start up the stairs, she nearly ran into Olivia. The much taller girl was staring down at her, face cast into shadow by the long hair that framed her features.

"I have to ask. Who the hell is he talking to?"

"My ex," Molly replied. "It's a long story."

"Once again I owe you," Jack said, keeping his voice low. He sat on the bottom step of Bowden's apartment building.

The ghost of Artie Carroll floated over and sat beside him. Though Jack tried not to pay too much attention, there was a kind of liquid flow to the motion.

The phantom seemed more to settle upon the stoop than to sit there, and it took Jack a moment to figure out what it was that seemed so alien about the way he moved. Then he had it. Gravity. For a long time after his death Artie had mimicked the effects of gravity, whether consciously or unconsciously. Now, though, he had either abandoned the pretence or forgotten how to do it. How to pretend.

Jack noticed something else, too. Artie's clothes had changed. They were still the same. The same sweat-shirt, torn at the throat. The same high-top sneakers, unlaced. But once upon a time, that sweatshirt had had pockets in the front. They were gone. And the sneakers—Jack didn't remember what colour they had been the first time the ghost appeared to him, but he was sure they hadn't been red. They were red now. He wondered if Artie was having trouble visualizing himself now, what he'd looked like when he was alive.

The ghost was changing.

It chilled him.

"You don't owe me anything, Jack," Artie replied. The words buzzed in Jack's ears as though they came as much from inside as from outside. "Not after all you've had to sacrifice to take up this fight for me."

Jack nodded slowly, then stopped and gazed away, along the street. A trendy-looking vegetarian restaurant with a small patio dining area was doing booming business. Even the patio was full, despite the time of year. "It isn't just for you."

"Not anymore," Artie agreed. "But it started with me."

"What happened upstate, anyway?" Jack asked.

"I found a couple of the souls you sent me searching for. That trucker, Chet Douglas. He was sort of a wreck, actually. And the boy, Jared. I was bringing them back to talk to you and saw the . . . saw the animals taking you and Molly down into that basement."

The spectre's voice had changed. Jack glanced over at Artie and saw that his features were pinched with emotion. Then Artie actually laughed, breaking the moment.

"Stupid, isn't it? I mean, I'm already dead. I know what's in store. And I still get all torn up when I think of anything happening to you guys."

Jack didn't know what to say to that. He loved Artie, somehow missed him more every time he saw this ghost. But there was an awkwardness growing between them now that had nothing to do with Molly, and rather more to do with their mutual awareness that they were holding on to strings maybe better left to fray.

"Anyway," Artie went on, a bit uncomfortably. "I got word to Eden, figuring she'd call Courtney. I had no idea she'd called Castillo until all those cops showed up. Smart girl, our Eden."

"No doubt about that," Jack replied, pleased to hear the fondness in Artie's voice when he talked of Eden. She needed a dream companion, a spirit guide, and he needed a link to the world of the living that they all knew Jack and Molly could no longer be. It hurt too much. And Jack knew Artie had never wanted to haunt them.

Again Jack glanced away. A woman in leather pants and designer sunglasses pushed a stroller past them. The infant rode along happily, a Yankees baseball cap on its bald head. A car rolled down the street slowly, carefully navigating around a delivery truck double-parked in front of a small bodega.

"So, what now?" he asked.

"Jared's still with Chet," Artie said, speaking of the other lost souls as though they were old friends. "The kid's ready to move on. And he's going to, I think. But Chet needs some time to come to terms with things, and I don't wanna leave him alone to do it. I'm gonna try to keep an eye on him, maybe coach him through it."

The ghost did not so much stand then as he did simply float up off the stoop. Artie scratched at the back of his head idly, forgetting apparently that any itch he felt was just as much a phantom as he was. He floated above the sidewalk a good half a foot, his shoelaces dangling down. He would not meet Jack's eyes.

"If you need me, y'know, for anything, you can call Eden again like you did. I'm going to be hanging with her for a while."

Jack stood. He felt the urge to touch Artie, even to throw his arms around his friend. But that was the pain of it all, that was the part that really sucked the most. Artie wasn't even really there. He would never be there again. Not ever. Jack had never wanted to grab him, to hug him, more than he did right then, probably because he felt that this really was good-bye. A good-bye they'd both been putting off for far too long.

But Artie was dead.

"Be good," Jack told him, and he hated how light and fragile the words sounded.

"Never," Artie replied. "You take care of yourself, Jack."

The ghost turned away and began to drift off. His gossamer form was translucent, of course, but now it became even more diaphanous, shimmering, dissipating like ice on a car windshield once the defroster's been running.

Jack began to turn.

"Hey," Artie called.

Surprised, Jack faced him again. Artie was pointing at a Toyota parked a few cars away, a blonde woman with a ponytail behind the wheel. "That honey there? Not human."

Anxiety twisted in his gut, and Jack stared at the woman who was not a woman. She glanced around, looking bored, studiously avoiding looking at him. *Trouble,* Jack thought. *Bowden's place is being watched.*

"Guess Jasmine didn't take kindly to Olivia getting away," Artie noted. "You want me to stay?"

Jack thought about that one, but really, what could Artie do? "No, you go ahead. We'll come by Eden's when we get back to Boston. Hope things go all right with that truck driver."

"Chet," Artie reminded him. "Yeah, me too. Take care, amigo."

"See ya," Jack replied.

His mind was racing, working out how the crappy

plan he'd made with Olivia would be affected by Jasmine finding out where they were. *Go upstairs,* he thought. *Get Olivia and Bowden, maybe a weapon. Come down and take out the female in the Toyota.* Then he shook his head. *Yeah, in broad daylight.*

But he could not just let her drive away and tell Jasmine where they were. Jack started up the steps, then took another look at the Toyota. The driver was not looking at him. Instead, she had glanced over at a well-dressed white guy who was exiting the vegetarian restaurant up the street. The guy was staring at something far above Jack's head, and then suddenly he looked right at Jack. Their eyes met, and the guy quickly glanced away.

Clearly, though, that look was not coincidence. *Two of them, then.* Jack replayed the moment in his head as he started to open the outer door, and stiffened when he saw again the way the well-dressed guy had been looking up. Above him.

Jack tilted his head back and shielded his eyes just in time to see the head and shoulders of a powerfully built black man withdrawing from the edge of the roof, where he had been staring down. Swearing under his breath, his heart pounding, Jack rushed into the foyer and stared at the rows of buttons with names written beside them. The one for 3C had no name label. He pressed the buzzer, shaking with tension and fear.

"Come on, come on," he muttered.

Upstairs. They're already upstairs. Molly was upstairs.

The door lock beeped loud and long. Jack was startled.

He had expected Bowden to talk to him on the intercom first, giving him a chance to warn them. He considered buzzing again, but instead reached out and yanked the inner door open just before it stopped beeping.

Pulse beating in his temples, entire body prickling with fear, Jack ran for the stairs. His right hand slid along the banister as he launched himself upward, taking the steps two at a time. As he ran he stared up, trying to get a glimpse of the third-floor landing.

What the hell were we thinking? Coming down into the city, into Jasmine's territory, without any weapons. All right, Olivia and Bowden are Prowlers, but what're two of them against an entire pack?

Jesus, Molly.

The stairs were narrow and steep. As he reached the second floor Jack's foot slipped and he fell forward, rapping his shin painfully on the wooden step. He grunted, ground his teeth together, and ignored the sting of it. With a low curse he grabbed the newel post and pulled himself up, then hustled along the second-floor landing, neck still craned back, trying to get a glimpse up at the third floor.

Footfalls on wooden stairs. And they weren't his. Somewhere above him someone was rushing down. Not just someone, though. Jack knew it had to be the Prowler he had seen on the rooftop. Horrifying thoughts and images began flashing through his mind. If there were two of them on the street and one on the roof, who was to say that there weren't more inside already?

Jasmine's pack could have been waiting in Bowden's apartment. Hell, they had to have figured Olivia would hook up with this guy when she escaped, if he was as good a friend as she'd told Jack and Molly he was.

Damn it, Jack thought, cursing himself for being so stupid, for not being more cautious.

He ran alongside the railing that overlooked the stairs he had just come up, and tried to get a better view of the floor above. His boots sounded loud on the steps, clumsy and truncated as he took them two at a time once more. Bile burned, rising in the back of his throat, and his mouth was dry.

As Jack rushed up the steps he glanced to his right, and through the bars of the third-floor railing he could see the Prowler striding toward the door to 3C. With no weapon Jack knew he had no chance against one of them. He might get one good blow in, and then the thing would rip his head off. But Jack didn't want him getting inside that apartment, either.

"Hey!" he snapped as he hit the third-floor landing.

The Prowler he had seen on the roof turned to look at him, frowning. Twenty feet away, if that. Jack didn't slow down. He strode quickly toward the tall creature, whose false skin was smooth and dark, handsome if it hadn't been a facade.

As Jack approached, the Prowler's expression grew angry yet also uncertain.

"What's your problem?" the beast growled.

"Me?" Jack asked, putting on a wild grin. He spread

his arms wide and high, drawing the monster's attention to his hands. "No problem."

Then he shot his foot up and swung a brutal kick right between the Prowler's legs. The beast roared in agony and doubled over. Even as he did he snarled and glared at Jack in fury, lips curling back from suddenly longer teeth that were sharp and gleaming. Fur shot up through that smooth skin, tearing through it, and his face began to stretch. Jack could hear the click of bones restructuring themselves.

But he wasn't listening. He followed through instantly on his first attack. The Prowler was crouched over in pain, changing out of both shock and anger. In a second the thing would tear into him, but Jack wasn't willing to give him that second. With a shout he lunged at the beast. The Prowler lashed out with one hand, but only halfheartedly, still momentarily crippled by the pain between his legs.

Jack didn't hit him. Instead he ducked beneath his wavering arm, grabbed his wool coat in both hands, and twisted the monster. Jack used the beast's own momentum to drive it right through the third-floor railing. The balusters snapped and gave way, and the Prowler shouted in surprise as he landed painfully on the stairs below, then tumbled, limbs flailing, to the second-floor landing.

The Prowler groaned and began to rise, fully changed now. He sprang for the stairs, limping slightly.

"What's the ruckus, Jack?"

In the heat of the moment Jack had not heard the

apartment door open. When he turned, Bowden stood inside the open door, staring at him with a dubious expression on his face.

"Get inside! We've got company!" Jack rushed at him, pushed through the door, and started to slam it closed.

A large hand slapped against the door, forcing it open again. The Prowler stood framed in the doorway, but he had transformed again, resuming his false human appearance.

"I am done playing games with you, boy," the beast warned through clenched teeth.

"Oh, back off, Knox," Bowden said tiredly. "You're not going to do a damn thing."

Jack gaped at them, feeling stupid as he tried to bend the scenario into some semblance of logic in his head. Bowden sighed and ushered Knox in, shutting the door behind him. Jack and Knox stared at each other, violence thick in the air. The moment was broken by a voice from deeper within the apartment.

"Why do I think you boys got off on the wrong foot?"

Even as Jack edged backward down the narrow hallway he realized that he knew that voice. He stepped into the living room and his suspicion was confirmed. Winter sat next to Molly on a dark plaid sofa. The thin, elegant Prowler held a cup of tea in one hand and smiled pleasantly as Jack froze on the other side of the room.

"Winter," Jack muttered.

"Good to see you again, Jack. Sorry it has to be under such difficult circumstances."

"Maybe you should sit down?" Molly suggested.

But Jack still couldn't move, and he was certainly not ready to sit down. Winter's gaze suddenly went beyond him, and Jack flinched as he realized Knox and Bowden had come into the room behind him. He spun, keeping his back to the wall and his eyes on Knox.

"I saw some others out front, watching the building. I figured they were with Jasmine," he said slowly.

"Ah, now I see. Of course you would," Winter said. Then he glanced at Knox. "You can't exactly blame him."

The big Prowler grumbled, but nodded once and wandered toward the windows, sliding down into a torn leather chair.

"They're with Winter," Molly explained. "They were waiting for us when we got up here. There are more on the way, including Bowden's roommates. The word is getting out. Looks like we may get those reinforcements we need."

Jack relaxed slightly, letting some of the tension go at last. But Bowden was staring at him.

"How'd you know? That they weren't human?"

Back in the hallway Jack saw movement out of the corner of his eye. He turned to see Olivia emerge from the small kitchen just down the corridor. But she wasn't alone. Behind her, cane in one hand and a can of soda in the other, was his sister, Courtney.

"He sees things other people don't," she said with a fond smile. "Don't you, little brother?"

"Court?" Jack rushed across the room, threw his arms around her, and squeezed. He kissed her on the top of her head and then stood back to stare at her in amazement. "What the hell are you doing here?"

All the pleasure went out of her face, and Courtney glanced at Olivia before focusing again on Jack.

"Talking to Olivia about her uncle," she replied. "And how we're going to keep him alive."

Out in the streets of the city the word spread.

In the bars and restaurants, to deli owners and taxi drivers, to lawyers and accountants, to club kids who'd stolen or accumulated wealth over the years in order to avoid real work—all through the underground the word went out. Guillaume Navarre was a prisoner and his niece intended to free him.

But the whispers spread far and wide, and among those who heard them were some who dreamed of a return to the old ways, to a wild time when they roamed the land and their human prey cowered in fear. There were some who believed that Jasmine could bring them that dream.

Throughout the city the atmosphere changed. It became charged with the certainty of imminent bloodshed. Beasts on both sides abandoned their human lives that afternoon, unsure if they would ever reclaim them.

They were wild.

The hunt was on.

chapter 13

Clouds had rolled in late in the day, and by dusk a cold rain had begun to fall lightly across the city. Jasmine ignored the icy chill of the precipitation as she strode quickly along the sidewalk, delicious anticipation rising within her as she came in sight of the Voodoo Lounge. Several feet behind her walked a trio of bodyguards, members of her pack. Though none of them had dared to say so, she knew they all thought she was insane to relish the coming conflict.

Jasmine cared not at all. Once she learned that Olivia and the humans had escaped, she knew it would only be a matter of time before she clashed with them. If it was to come, she thought, better it be on her terms. She was certainly not going to run away. Instead she would bait the trap and let them come to her, the more public the better.

There was something marvellous about it all. She

knew they would come. They knew she knew. Yet what would they be willing to risk? That was the true question in this game of predator and prey.

The line in front of the Voodoo Lounge was down the steps, along the sidewalk, and around the corner, and most of the young revellers hoping to make it inside were human. The bouncers at the door were Prowlers, of course, as were most of the staff and a lot of the club's regulars. Yet in spite of her growing power, it was *not* Jasmine's place. Neutral ground, supposedly. But that was a joke. The owners of the club were part of her pack now; they had exposed their throats to her, taken a subservient position in the hierarchy. It was only a matter of time before she controlled all of the wild Prowlers in New York City. Even now, those who did not call her Alpha still bent to her will.

As Jasmine made her way toward the front of the club, heads turned in line and voices hushed. They didn't know who she was, most of them, but they knew she was *somebody*. They stared and she let them, these human cattle. Jasmine wore a black leather duster that blew in the cold October breeze, billowing slightly behind her. Beneath it she was dressed entirely in crimson, her copper skin set off by the deep red.

She swept up the steps, past the club kids waiting in line. Some voiced complaint but were quickly silenced either by their friends or by the glare of Jasmine's bodyguards. At the top of the steps the bouncers inclined their heads and did not meet her eyes as she passed them. The buffoons were so cowed they did not even remember to get the door for her. Jasmine grabbed the handle herself and pulled it open. Her bodyguards followed her as she went inside.

It was after nine o'clock when she entered the Voodoo Lounge. The sound system played an elegant song by Sting, the music low and yet pervasive. Up on the stage the crew was testing out the drum kit and tuning guitars for Thornbush, the band that would provide the evening's entertainment. At least until the real entertainment began.

The crowd was already thick, massing at the bars on either side of the club. Despite the law, smoke curled and wafted on the air. As she moved among them Jasmine marvelled at the mixed crowd Thornbush had brought in. More female than male, more human than Prowler, but even so, the audience was a true mélange of creatures, of skin colours and lifestyles. Pierced and painted, or straight and well-coiffed, the crowd reflected the growing popularity of the all-girl band.

But how popular would they be if the humans in this place knew that at least a few of the members were Prowlers? Jasmine wondered.

When all was said and done, in the aftermath of whatever happened here tonight, she planned to speak to the Prowlers in the band. It had occurred to her even when she was Tanzer's mate and not herself the Alpha that if members of their species had reached positions of power and visibility in the human world, they could be instrumental in wooing other Prowlers to the cause.

Her bodyguards caught up to her, formed a kind of

wedge in front of her, and shoved human and Prowler alike out of her path. Some of the humans grumbled, but the Prowlers caught her scent and either nodded in recognition of her presence or scurried quickly away. Which among them were loyal to her, she wondered, and which were members of the so-called underground?

Human males all through the club stared at her as she went, and some of the women did as well. Jasmine soaked up their lust and fascination. There was power in it.

In the far left corner of the club, not far from the stage, Alec stood with a small clutch of pack members, arms crossed, watching her approach. Jasmine smiled at him and Alec smiled back, though there was anxiety in both his expression and the way he held himself. He was afraid. Her face flushed with anger, and she realised that after the night was through, whether Alec survived or not, she was going to have to find herself another mate. He lacked the proper obedience and the proper respect. He *was* handsome, though, something exotic in his features and the dark curl of his hair. But there were always more-handsome males.

Her bodyguards stood aside as they reached that far corner. The other members of the pack also dispersed, giving her room to breathe. Alec tilted his head in an almost formal greeting.

"Good evening, Jasmine," he said.

"It is a good evening, isn't it?" she replied, her tone and the playful smile on her lips taunting him, mocking his caution. "Time for a party. Time to make a little mess."

Jasmine looked past him, to where Guillaume Navarre sat grimly between two more members of her pack. He had no restraints, save for the presence of so many of his captors and his belief—mistaken—that she still held his niece as well. With a coquettish smile Jasmine tossed her red hair back and went to sit beside him. One of his guards moved over, giving her room, and Jasmine slid herself along Navarre's body as she sat. Mischief in her heart, she kissed his cheek softly.

"Hello, bait," she whispered. "How long do you think before the mice arrive?"

Navarre—or Cantwell, as he preferred to be called—only glared at her balefully.

Alec moved in close and looked down upon them. He kept his voice low, but despite that and despite the music playing, Jasmine was certain the others heard him speak.

"Are you certain this is the way to proceed?" he asked. "There are safer ways. Easier ways. You could hold him anywhere in the city and put the word out, and still they would come."

A snarl escaped her throat and her lips curled in anger. Jasmine glared at him and knew then that she was going to have to kill Alec in the morning. "I don't have to explain myself to you, pup," she growled.

He stumbled back a step, as though driven by the force of her anger.

Jasmine sighed and glanced around at the members

of her pack gathered there. The others were spread throughout the club, in its shadowy corners, and mingling with the crowd, in search of their targets. They would arrive eventually.

"None of you were in Boston when these humans killed Tanzer. They aren't like other humans. Of course, we have our friend Navarre here, and he will keep out of things as long as his niece's life depends upon it. So he cannot aid them, but they also do not want him killed."

Of course, she knew that if he spotted Olivia, Navarre would try to aid her immediately, but that was why she kept him surrounded by those loyal to her. If he moved against Jasmine, her pack would kill him.

"Navarre's insurance, in a way, but we have a great deal more insurance than that. We have a lot of allies in this room. So do *they*. But you know what else is in this room?" With a grin, she glanced at each of them in turn. "No one? Look around. There are *victims* in this room. Cannon fodder. They cannot blow up the building or set fire to it or attack with guns from the outside. They have to come in to get him. If they want to hurt us, they have to come in to do it. And there are all these wonderful, juicy *victims* in their way."

Senses. It's all about the senses, Jack thought.

It was quarter after nine, and they had been inside for nearly an hour already. Thornbush were late going on, and each minute that ticked by before the music started was another notch up the paranoia scale for

him. The crush of humans and Prowlers—he made a
game of trying to guess which was which—mingled
their sweat and pheromones. They were counting on
that to keep Jasmine from being able to sort their scents
out of the hundreds of others stewing together in the
Voodoo Lounge. As far as they knew, she was the only
one among her pack they had ever encountered before,
the only one who would be able to recognize their
scents.

Their faces, though, that was something else. Jasmine
would likely have given descriptions to her pack. Winter
and Olivia had insisted that most humans looked much
alike to Prowlers, for they never focused too long on
their own false faces. Still, better safe than sorry.

Before coming to the Voodoo Lounge, Jack and
Molly had changed their appearance. The bouncers had
not given her a second glance, nor had they paid any
attention to Jack; not even to card them. Apparently the
owners of the club weren't terribly concerned about
getting busted for serving minors.

Now Jack stared at her and marvelled at how completely different Molly looked. They stood together by
the bar to the right of the stage and held abandoned
drinks they had snatched off the counter, unwilling to
directly address the bartender but wanting to blend in.
Though Molly's gaze drifted around the club as she surreptitiously scanned the place for Bill, Jack could barely
keep his eyes off her. With a quick dye-wash Molly had
bleached her wild red hair a deep, inky black, save for a
pair of tightly twisted pigtails that hung down on either

side of her face. These had been dyed purple.

Her hair was pulled back into a tight tail with half a dozen rubber bands, evenly spaced, so that it looked more like rope than anything else. Though she normally wore little make-up, a lavender eye shadow had been daubed liberally under, rather than over, her eyes. She wore a silk shirt tied in a knot beneath her breasts to show off her gently sloping belly, and she wore black leather pants supplied by Olivia's roommate, Mags.

As he watched she swirled the ice in her appropriated glass and glanced up at him. She blushed slightly and then glared at him.

"You're staring. Do I look that ridiculous?" she whispered, leaning in close to be heard over the music.

Jack smiled and moved closer to her, sliding his arm around her waist. "You kidding? You look amazing. Don't get me wrong. I'm glad the dye job's gonna wash out. But in the for-one-night-only category? You look smokin'."

A sly smile spread across her features and Molly turned away, trying to keep a straight face.

"What?" Jack asked, frowning.

Molly shook her head, but he poked her in the ribs.

"Nothing," she said. "Just sorry it's going to take longer for you to look like you again."

Jack opened his mouth, but no reply came out. He couldn't exactly be offended, since he agreed with her completely. With his sister's help he had cut his hair. Shaved it, more like. There was little more than a half-inch of hair left on his scalp. At the same time, he had kept the beard stubble on his face, using a razor to shape it so that it seemed like something he had done on purpose.

He had temporary tattoos up and down his forearms and wore an extremely tight blue cotton shirt and leather pants to match Molly's. Never in his life had he imagined circumstances in which he would have put on a pair of leather pants without a gun to his head, but here he was. From a certain perspective he knew that both he and Molly looked good, save for the scratch on his cheek. It was healing, but the wound was still obvious to anyone who looked at him. And yet that was the point. Jasmine and her pack would be looking for them to try to be unobtrusive, inconspicuous. To hide.

Instead, they were doing the opposite. Hiding in plain sight. Instead of wearing some sort of a disguise that would cover their features in hopes of going unnoticed, they had altered their features in such a way as to attract attention. And they did. Neither of them was really comfortable with the kind of looks they were getting from the guys and girls who passed them, but that was the very idea of it.

In unconscious imitation of Molly, Jack swirled the melting ice in his glass and scanned the club again. No sign of Jasmine or Bill, not yet, but in the crush inside the Voodoo Lounge it was not going to be easy to spot anyone.

Just as the thought crossed his mind his gaze fell upon his sister's face. Courtney looked slick and stylish, hair and clothes perfect, not like a club kid at all.

Bowden was at her side, and Courtney leaned into him as though the two of them were semidrunken lovers. The Prowlers would have their eye out for a woman with a cane, and so Courtney had left hers behind, using Bowden to keep from stumbling. Jack had been terrified to have her along, but she loved Bill and had already gotten her hands dirty in her quest to find and free him. He wasn't about to tell her to stay behind; as if she would have listened.

Besides, she had a role to play in this. They needed her.

Jack smiled at his sister. Her eyes gleamed in the semidark club, and a kind of electrical charge passed between them.

"I saw her," Courtney said, voice tight, her face a bit pale.

"Jasmine?" Jack mouthed silently.

Courtney nodded.

"Where?" Molly asked.

As surreptitiously as possible, Courtney inclined her head to indicate the opposite side of the room, the bar across from them, the whole club between them. Jack did not want to stare, but he could not help himself. He peered into the crowd, trying to see over heads and between bodies. The house lights were a golden glow, like the light of a full moon upon them. The roadies worked in darkness now to prepare the stage. Movement out of the corner of his eye caught Jack's attention. Someone carried a microphone stand out to the edge. A moment later another, larger figure carried out a crate that looked as though it might be a platform for the performers to stand on for solos or something. The crate was placed on the edge of their side of the stage, perhaps fifteen feet from where Jack stood.

He gazed again over the heads of the crowd, trying to see the other side. Dozens of people were milling around the bar, clustering there in an attempt to get drinks before the show started. There were two bartenders on either side, and he could see the two over there, eyes down, working quickly, grumbling. He knew from experience how they felt. Rows of bottles behind the bar glistened in the soft golden glow of the house lights.

Then, to the right, in the far corner of the club near the other side of the stage, a kind of clearing appeared in the crowd, and Jack noticed a block of grim-faced men and women who did not move to the beat of the piped-in music, who did not speak to one another, who only stared out at the sea of faces in the audience. They were a living wall, blocking off sight of whatever lay behind them like the entourage of some Hollywood celebrity.

"Over there," he said, just loud enough for Molly, Courtney, and Bowden to hear.

One by one they all glanced over and then turned away, not wanting to be too obvious about it.

"We can't be sure of that," Molly told him.

"I'm sure," Jack replied. He glanced at Courtney. "You ready?"

"Does it matter?" she asked.

Again some spark passed between them, some silent thing that defined who they were as a family.

"No," Jack said, unsmiling. "It doesn't." He turned his gaze upon Bowden and was distressed to see how afraid the Prowler seemed. Not that Jack blamed him. There was more on the line this night than merely their lives. The fallout from such a conflict could reveal the Prowlers' existence to the public, destroying the chance any of them had at living peacefully among humanity.

Somehow, despite his feelings for Bill, Jack couldn't summon too much sympathy. But he understood the trepidation he saw in Bowden's features.

Still, it was happening. And it was happening now.

"Let's do it."

Bowden nodded once, then reached under Courtney's chin, lifted her face to his, and kissed her. Jack bristled, and he could see Courtney stiffen awkwardly. But this was the signal they had agreed on.

A strangled cry erupted from the middle of the club, perhaps fifty feet away, back toward the entrance. It ululated, going on and on, and voices were raised in alarm as the patrons of the Voodoo Lounge decided if they wanted to move away from that spot or closer in to get a better view.

Mags, Bowden's roommate, had been watching him. The kiss had told her it was time for her to do her part. Though he could not see her, Jack knew that she had fallen to the floor and begun to simulate convulsions, as though she were having some sort of seizure. He smiled at the image, the oldest diversion in the world.

But Jasmine and her pack would immediately assume it was Olivia, or even him and Molly. And, as he had expected, Prowlers with dangerous looks on their human faces pushed through the crowd quickly, tearing people away to get a peek.

"Do it," Jack said again, voice low.

Bowden seemed laid back and amiable, almost a slacker Prowler. But before Jack had even completed the second syllable, he was in motion, swift and deadly. With all eyes on Mags's performance at the centre of the club, he leaped over the bar brandishing a wicked-looking hunting knife in his left hand. The blade had seemingly appeared out of nowhere, like a magician's sleight of hand. But there was nothing magical about what happened next.

With the music and the shouting and the crush of voices, Bowden slipped silently up behind the nearest bartender and slit his throat. The dead Prowler began to change even as he grabbed at his neck, but Bowden drove him to the floor, out of sight behind the bar. An instant later Jack saw Bowden lunge upward, wrap a powerful arm around the second bartender's neck, and drag him down as well.

"Jesus," Molly whispered in his ear.

Jack ran a hand over the thick stubble on his skull and glanced at her, seeing in her wide, haunted gaze what he imagined was a reflection of his own. Then he turned to look at Courtney.

His sister was no longer standing beside him. In the moment he had been looking at Molly, Courtney had climbed over the bar and taken up a place there. She grabbed a rag and began wiping down the counter, moving away from them, not even meeting Jack's eyes.

Farther along the bar Bowden did the same. Anyone looking at the bar from across the club, even walking up to it to get a drink, might notice that the staff had changed, but beyond that, they would have no idea that two inhuman beasts had just been slain. Jack knew that despite the odours of sweat and beer and perfume in the club, it was only a matter of time before one of the Prowlers caught the scent of the blood.

They would just have to hurry.

"All right!" a voice shouted. "Get the hell out of the way!"

Two huge bouncers—Jack figured they had to be Prowlers—lifted Mags off the floor and carried her, legs flailing, toward the exit. She protested, screaming that she had paid to get in, swearing and cussing, and everyone in the Voodoo Lounge watched the spectacle as she was physically tossed out the front door. No one made a move to stop it.

Jack scanned the club again, looked up nervously at the stage and then across at the clutch of bodyguard types who he was certain were shielding Jasmine. Two grim-faced members of that human wall had let curiosity get the better of them. They had stepped forward and craned their necks to try to see what the ruckus had been about.

Past them, sitting on the bench that ran along the walls of the club, he saw a mane of straight bloodred hair and a flash of smooth copper skin. Jasmine was stunning as always, dressed all in red like some dark and brutal goddess come to Earth. She wore a look of annoyed impatience as she whispered to a male who knelt on the ground before her as though bowing to a queen. Beside her, seated on the bench, Jack saw Bill.

"Molly," Jack said, voice a harsh rasp.

She moved to his side and squeezed his arm, letting him know that she had seen them as well.

Jack tried to mentally will Bill to look at him, but to no avail. There was only a moment when he could see his friend's face, and Bill was quite pointedly studying those nearest him in the crowd. *Looking for a familiar face*, Jack thought. *It's time you got to see one.*

Then, just as the pack began to gather around their Alpha and her prisoner again, about to block Jack's view once more, Jasmine glanced across the bar. Her orange eyes gleamed in the dim light as they focused on him. Jasmine narrowed her eyes, obviously not recognising him but clearly wondering who this was who was staring at her.

Jack smiled.

He waved.

Jasmine could not believe what she had seen. Her pack moved closer around her, blocking out her view of the guy standing in front of the bar on the other side of the club. In her mind's eye she tried to lay an image of Jack Dwyer over the face she had just seen. The scrub of bristly hair on his scalp, the shadow of a beard on his chin. No way to pick his scent out of all these mingling odours.

WILD THINGS

But that smile.

And he waved.

A flicker of anxiety, even trepidation, passed through her as she thought of all the stories she had heard about this hunter in the past months. But she had been there at the beginning, before the stories had been told. He and his mate, Molly, had killed Tanzer and nearly killed Jasmine herself, but they were only humans.

Only humans.

Why, then, did her trepidation not fade? That was the question she truly wished an answer for. Jasmine snarled, reached within her own heart, her own mind, and pushed those feelings away. They were replaced in an instant by the rage and hatred she had been kindling since that night months ago. She could picture it in her mind even now, the gunfire as the police moved in on their lair, herself and Tanzer forced to flee to the rooftop of a nearby hotel. Working their way down through the hotel, furious but also exulting in their escape, their freedom. Only to be ambushed at the door by this boy and his girl, these human *children* who were armed with guns and luck and had no fear that she could see.

And somewhere, down deep, a part of her wondered if that wasn't what gave her pause. She remembered that night so well, and she had not seen any fear in Dwyer or the girl. *No fear.* Jack the Giant-Killer, some of the whispers called him. But he had killed Tanzer, had created his own myth, and for her to achieve all she dreamed, she had to avenge that murder and remove

Jack Dwyer as an obstacle once and for all. And if he had built himself a myth, all the better, for that would make her slaughter of the boy all the more impressive to the wild ones. Jasmine would turn his reputation to her own purposes.

Damned child, Jasmine thought. *You'll watch your mate die, just as I did.*

"What's the matter?" Guillaume Navarre asked at her side. There was a playful tone in his voice, almost mocking. "You look like you've seen a ghost."

Her lips curled and she growled at him, though only softly. Jasmine rose and pushed through the gathered members of her pack, sniffing the air and trying to see if Dwyer was still at the other bar, and who else was with him. She thought she spotted the back of his close-shaved head, and she started for him.

Then the house lights went down, and the Voodoo Lounge was plunged into near-total darkness.

The music on the sound system cut off abruptly. In the darkness Bill tried to see past the Prowlers who had gathered all around him, Jasmine's pack, to see where she had gone. His skin prickled with the body heat in the club and the urge to change, to yield to the wild fury that wanted to tear loose from within him. Somewhere in the club he knew that Jack and Molly were about to start something. Nothing else would have garnered such a reaction from Jasmine. If either of their lives was endangered, he would be forced to act. But if he did, he would forfeit the life of his niece, the only blood relation he had left on Earth.

"It's a hell of a night, boys and girls," came a voice from all around.

No, Bill thought. *From the stage*. He glanced up there and saw six figures in the dark, shadows against shadows. *Thornbush*, he thought. *And the band played on*.

The crowd surged toward the stage, clustering there, whistling and applauding and shouting their support. Bill was jostled by Alec, Jasmine's mate, as the slender, dangerous beast uncoiled from the ground and tried to follow his lover.

"Jasmine?" Alec called. "Jas?"

On the stage a drumbeat began, a thunderous, marching rhythm that seemed almost a call to arms. The bass guitar began to fill the gaps in the beat with a jazzy syncopation that should not have worked but somehow did. These girls were good. Bill looked up at the still-darkened stage again.

"The rain's falling, the wind's howling. Winter's around the corner, but we thought maybe we could heat things up in here!" shouted the female voice, an echo filling the room. Too much reverb.

Then the bass and drum cut off abruptly. There was a moment of utter silence in the Voodoo Lounge, and then a beautiful, lilting acoustic guitar filled the club as a figure onstage picked out clear, strong notes that were part blues, part folk, part rock. In the dark the crowd was enraptured, and the guitar picking went on for nearly half a minute. Then with a single strummed note she stopped, and Bill could see the girl toss back her hair.

PROWLERS

The stage lights came up, the drummer brought her sticks down in a single beat, and then the band roared into an electric, shuffling rhythm with a jazz melody laid over it, a fusion of musical styles that was instantly engaging.

But Bill was no longer listening to the music.

He was staring at the girl onstage with the electric acoustic slung around her shoulders. Her long black hair draped across her eyes as she picked away at the guitar strings, swaying and grinding to the beat.

Olivia.

Bill Cantwell—Guillaume Navarre—smiled, but only for a moment. For centuries he had controlled the beast, practised holding it in. Never in all his life had he so relished setting his wild heart free. With a low growl that built in his chest, Bill stretched and his muscles shifted and expanded. With a shudder he felt his snout push out from his face, his fangs multiplying, sharp and gnashing. He tore through his false human skin as though it was a prison of flesh, and it flaked away like so much dust, leaving only the fur behind.

They were all staring away from him, either up at the band or searching the crowd for Jasmine. Alec was the first to turn. The expression on his face froze the instant he saw Bill.

"Oh, sh—" Alec started to say.

With a single thrust of his powerful jaws Bill ripped out his throat.

And the band played on.

CHAPTER 14

The moment the band had hit the stage, even in darkness, Courtney and Bowden had begun to go to work. Nearly the entire club had turned toward the source of the music, the women on the platform at the far end of the Voodoo Lounge. Only a few determined souls stayed at the bar, waiting for their drinks.

Courtney thought about Jack and Molly, wondering where in the crowd they were, if they had managed to place themselves where they needed to be in the audience. Focusing, she pushed the thought away. She had her own job to do.

Fast as they were able, she and Bowden served the stragglers at the bar. By the time the stage lights came up and the band tore into the first song of their set in earnest, bodies had begun to gyrate on the floor of the club. Some dancing, some merely moving to the music.

With a silent prayer, hoping the band was loud

enough to cover the noise, Courtney dropped a bottle of 150-proof rum, and it shattered on the floor behind the bar, not far from the corpse of the first Prowler Bowden had killed.

No one paid any attention.

Courtney glanced up at Bowden, and he smiled. Then, quick as they could, the two began pulling bottles off the liquor racks, anything one hundred proof or more. At first Courtney tried to pour them out, not wanting to draw any unnecessary attention.

"What the hell are you doing?" shouted a woman at the bar, halfway between horrified and amused.

"Mind your business!" Courtney snapped at her.

The woman held up both hands and backed away, then shot her the middle finger and pushed back into the audience. From that point Courtney just dropped the bottles.

A scream tore through the club, audible even over the pounding of the drums and the sweet melody of the vocals from the lead singer and from Olivia on guitar. Both Courtney and Bowden whipped around to try to see where it was coming from. Across the floor people had begun to draw away from the far corner, where Jack had seen that group of Prowlers. Like a wave the crowd swept back from that spot, but still Courtney couldn't see what was happening there.

The music never faltered.

Something was happening over there, though. They had run out of time. Courtney looked up at Bowden, about to ask if he was ready, but he was already brandishing a Molotov cocktail in his hands, a bottle of Wild Turkey 101 with a bar rag poking out of the neck.

Courtney slid a hand into her pocket, pulled out the lighter she had brought along, and spun the thumbwheel. A tiny flame appeared and she set it to the bar rag. It smoked black a moment and then blazed up like a torch on top of the bottle.

"Get back!" Bowden said.

She wasted no time. One hand on the counter to help keep her balance, Courtney rushed along the bar toward the stage. The audience had spread out, some still sitting on the benches along the walls. There was a gap of perhaps thirty feet between the end of the bar and the corner of the stage, and it was filled with people.

Courtney stopped there, turned to watch as Bowden reached the other end of the bar and then tossed the burning bottle of Wild Turkey underhanded back along the bar, where it shattered on the wooden floor amid the broken glass from twenty or more other bottles of flammable alcohol.

It exploded with a pop and a hiss of flames, and fire engulfed the middle of the bar. Quickly it began to spread.

"Oh, my God!" Courtney yelled. "Fire!"

Though she had helped to set the blaze, she did not have to fake the fear in her voice. Whatever happened now, there would be no slipping quietly out the door at the end of the night.

Other voices followed her own, cries of alarm. Across the club she could still see some sort of melee going on, a fight, and even as she glanced that way she saw Prowlers *turning*. Beasts emerged from within their human shells, and they began to attack other Prowlers. Claws tore at air and flesh.

Then Courtney's view was blocked by the shifting tides of the crowd as the shouts of alarm grew louder and people began to rush for the doors. Up on the stage the band stopped playing one by one, with a clang of cymbals, a screech of guitar feedback, and whispered cusses over the microphone.

A fire alarm began to blat loud and urgent as the blaze spread, engulfing the bar, and roared up the wall to begin licking across the ceiling of the club high above. Courtney stared in quiet horror and awe at the people shoving past one another, panicked into fleeing. But not everyone was trying to leave. In the midst of the receding sea of humanity stood tiny islands of three and four individuals who struggled to keep from being carried away by the waves sweeping around them.

Prowlers. They were not running away. They knew that this was only a precursor to something more. But the humans fled, and that was exactly the way Jack and Olivia had planned it. The house lights went on, dimly illuminating the chaos in the club.

Then, in the midst of the rush to escape, Courtney saw Jasmine stalking across the room, using her savage strength to slap down anyone who tried to move her, to carry her along with the exodus. The Alpha stared at the fire, fury in her orange eyes, which flickered with reflected flame. Jasmine turned to glance around, searching each end of the bar for the source of this fire. Her eyes settled upon Courtney, and Courtney understood immediately how she must look.

Jasmine would wonder why she was not running.

She couldn't run, even if she wanted to. Particularly not without her cane. But Jasmine wouldn't know that.

The Prowler's long leather coat swayed around her as she pushed through the crowd and moved for the bar. Courtney watched her come, not knowing what to do. There was nowhere for her to run. She turned to look around for Bowden, but he had disappeared into the crowd, ready to combat Jasmine's pack once most of the people had cleared out.

Above them, with the alarm blaring, the sprinkler system suddenly kicked in, and water began spraying down upon them from dozens of tiny heads, a cold shower that hissed as it hit the fire. Jasmine paused and stared up at the rain in annoyance. Most of the people had cleared away from the stage, and Courtney turned quickly and started to hobble that way, limping badly, trying not to stumble.

Up on the stage she saw Jack and Molly.

Before she reached them, she glanced back over her shoulder and saw Jasmine lunging through the straggling audience members toward her. The Alpha Prowler lashed out at a man in her way, and his neck twisted at an odd angle; he fell in a tumble of limbs on the now wet floor of the club.

"Shit," Courtney whispered.

But then she saw a tall, lanky figure step into

Jasmine's path. She could not see the white streak in his hair, but she knew that it was Winter. Courtney had no idea if he could take Jasmine on, but at the very least he would buy them a handful of moments. The rest of Jasmine's pack would just be realizing what was happening, and every moment counted now.

Alec was dead at Bill's feet, and he had snapped the neck of another member of Jasmine's pack before the others even began to notice anything was wrong. Even after Jasmine had taken off across the club, they had expected him just to sit there and let it all happen. In some ways that stoked the fires of his rage even higher, because he could not be certain it was not true.

But Olivia was up there on stage. She was all right. Not safe, perhaps, but in no more immediate danger than he was. Considerably less, actually.

"You should've left well enough alone, hunted the fringes like before," Bill snarled as he raked his claws across the chest of the nearest Prowler, spilling blood and viscera onto the wood floor.

They were all changing then, a ripple passing through them one by one as their human masques were cast aside, torn apart to reveal the monstrous faces of the Prowlers. Black fur and brown, blond and red, male and female, all sizes and body types . . . the tribes of millennia past had been erased and replaced by alliances of convenience and bloodlust. Together they began to move on him. One, nearby, was drooling copiously, tongue lolling out. Another gazed at him with one good eye, the other white and blind.

"You're a fool, Navarre," snarled the one-eye. "Jasmine's going to draw all the world's packs together, and then we will hunt wherever we like."

Three of them attacked at once. Bill felt claws slash his back, his thigh, and he saw a mouth full of gleaming needle teeth as one of them opened its jaws to tear into him. But they were off balance, in one another's way, and they fought like animals. Bill had lived as a human long enough that he was almost as much man as beast. He rammed his head forward and his skull crashed into the forehead of the one who had wanted to bite him. It cried out in pain and backed off, even as he shot an elbow into the chest of a Prowler rushing up behind him. The third tried to lunge at him, jaws gnashing.

Bill grabbed its snout in both hands, slipped his talons into its jaws, and yanked them open with all his strength, cracking bone and tearing muscle.

When he looked up at the others, he saw that they had reinforcements. Others of the pack had moved in to aid these, changing as they came for him, and Bill was cornered. Beyond them, though, something else was happening. He saw a familiar face, the human guise of a Prowler named Diego, a member of the underground in Boston. *But what's he doing here? Could he be with Jasmine?*

Diego transformed and lunged at the nearest member of Jasmine's pack. Behind him several others also changed and entered the fray. Bill's lips curled back from his teeth as he grinned and battered away a beast that tried to savage him.

"There's no going back, you idiots," he growled. "Only forward. All Jasmine's done for you is get you killed."

But his words were premature. So far there were more of Jasmine's pack than there were allies. His heart sank and he gritted his teeth. *Jack, whatever it is you're going to do, get to it!* he thought.

Which was the very instant he heard a familiar voice shouting about a fire. *Courtney!* And across the club fire blazed up the wall behind the bar, spreading quickly. Alarm bells began to jangle a second later, even as he slashed and bit and shattered the bones of his enemies. The music onstage stopped. The people screamed and fled madly, prepared to trample one another to escape. Some of them might well have done that. Already some had seen the melee in this corner, had seen the monsters tearing at one another. Bill could just imagine the newspaper headlines the next morning.

If they all *had* a next morning.

Claws raked his left shoulder, slashing to the bone, and he roared in pain and let the arm dangle at his side.

The sprinkler system went off, raining water down upon them, beginning to douse the flames. But the battle raged.

As soon as the fire was raging and the people began to race for the exits, Molly jumped up on the stage with

Jack close behind her. The music stopped with a dissonant clang of abandoned instruments. The two human girls in Thornbush took off backstage, heading for the rear exit none of the audience members would even think to search for in such a panicked state. The three Prowlers who had agreed to have Olivia join them onstage that night leaped to the floor and began to wade through the crowd toward where Jasmine's pack held Bill. They made it barely a dozen feet before Molly saw them intercepted by others.

Bodies changed, claws flashed, and blood was spilled.

A hand landed on Molly's wrist. She spun to see Olivia gazing at her, a dark gravity in her eyes.

"Hey," Olivia yelled over the din. "Come on. They'll be at us in a second!"

Molly nodded and turned to see that Jack was already upending the black-painted wooden platform that had been brought out onto the stage earlier. There was a latch on the raw, unpainted bottom, and he opened it with a twist, then lifted the hinged door and reached inside.

Jack pulled out a chopped-down pump shotgun, the barrel sawed off to get a wider spray with each pull of the trigger. *Spread the death*, Molly thought, and shuddered.

It had been a busy afternoon, and they had needed a great deal of help. But the word had gone out through the underground and touched off reactions from Prowlers all over the northeast like falling dominoes.

PROWLERS

They came in from Boston and Philadelphia and everywhere in between, all those Prowlers who had merged with the human race, who just wanted to live and let live, who had put together lives that they would lose if Jasmine fulfilled her own dream.

They came, this same underground from whom Bill had always gotten his information and his weapons, and they came bearing gifts, willing to put their own lives on the line. They had too much to lose to do otherwise.

"Olivia!" Jack shouted to be heard over the fire alarms. "You want one?"

The Prowler girl shook her head, and as she did so she changed. It was one fluid motion. She tossed her hair back and whipped her head around like a supermodel, but as she moved, the transformation came over her, and once again Molly found herself face-to-face with the lean, long-limbed beast with sleek black fur.

"That will never *not* freak me out," she called, surprised at her own words.

"Maybe that'll keep you alive," Olivia shouted back.

But Molly wasn't paying any attention to her now. The clock was ticking, and it would be only moments before the pack noticed what was happening up on the stage. She turned and went to Jack, knelt down by the wooden platform, and reached inside. She had always disliked shotguns, thought them too unwieldy. So instead she retrieved a pair of nine-millimetre handguns. She slipped one into the tight waistband of the leather pants she wore, the metal cold against her flesh, and thumbed the safety off the other. Then she nodded at Jack and Olivia.

The sprinkler system went off and water spilled from points all across the ceiling.

The Prowler girl grabbed the wooden crate and dragged it with one hand to within a foot of the end of the stage. When Molly glanced past Olivia, she saw Courtney stumbling toward them, stumbling on her bad leg, a stricken expression on her face. The fire had spread to engulf parts of the ceiling, but now the sprinklers were beginning to douse the flames. Across the floor the doors to the Voodoo Lounge were still jammed with people trying to escape the fire, and now the water as well, but fully half the club was cleared of human beings.

Among those who remained, most had already transformed. The club was filling with snarls and growls and roars of pain and rage. With the stench of animals.

Jack leaped down to the club floor and reached out for his sister, practically catching her in his arms. Then Courtney leaned against the stage, breathing hard. She glanced down at the sawed-off shotgun in Jack's hands and then glanced up at Molly, eyes wide and wild.

"Give me one of those things," she demanded, wiping a hand across her face.

Molly reached into the crate and came out with a pump shotgun, handed it down to Courtney. Then she reached in again and pulled out Courtney's cane. A smile crossed the older Dwyer sibling's features as she saw the lion-headed walking stick, but when Molly handed it to her, Courtney laid it down on the stage.

"Not gonna need that just yet. I'm gonna hold the

fort right here." Then Courtney looked back to her brother. "Winter's taking Jasmine on."

Despite the dim glow of the house lights above, the smoke from the fire and the spray of the sprinklers made it hard to see very well. Hard to breathe, too. Molly coughed and choked as she tried to get a good look at the various groups of Prowlers that were attacking one another in the club. Her gaze was drawn by a screeching and loud sort of howling from the corner off to her right, where Bill had been held. There were at least a dozen Prowlers there, and corpses already littered the ground, blood streaking the water on the wood floor. Molly could see that, and yet in the midst of that melee she could not tell if one of them was Bill.

"There!" Olivia said quickly.

She pointed into the chaos at a pair of monsters who circled each other warily. One was thin and quick with dark fur, and the other had a fine pelt of reddish brown. *Jasmine*, Molly thought.

Jack looked up at Olivia. "Go. I'll be right there."

"No," Olivia replied sharply. "My uncle—"

"Can take care of himself," Jack said quickly. "We want this thing to be over, we've got to kill Jasmine."

Olivia hesitated and turned to Molly, who was stunned to realize that the Prowler girl wanted her opinion. The gun felt suddenly heavy in her hand. Water dripped down Molly's face. Then she nodded at Olivia. "As long as Jasmine's alive, they've got something to fight for. We'll go for Bill. Bring him to you."

Olivia paused, stared at Jack a moment, and then

leaped off the stage and ran into the smoke and mist, lights strobing into that miasma of dark, inhuman shapes.

Jack grabbed Molly's hand. "Stay with Court," he said. Then he looked at his sister.

"Just go get him," Courtney said. "And watch your ass."

Jack nodded grimly and leaped off the stage, shotgun in his hands. Then he, too, was gone.

Molly slid down off the stage to stand beside Courtney, and even as she did Courtney raised the shotgun, pumped it once, and fired. The gunshot quieted the room for a moment. Startled, Molly looked up to see a Prowler blown backward, an enormous red hole in her chest. The female creature fell dead to the floor.

But there were others moving in.

Her throat dry, her heart pounding, Molly was amazed to find that her hands were steady as she raised the nine millimetre and began to fire.

Jasmine ducked low, lunged forward, and ripped a chunk of flesh from Winter's side with her teeth, blood sliding down the corners of her mouth. She tasted fur and spit it on the ground.

Winter clutched at his wound and backpedaled, but his eyes still blazed with defiance. His dark fur was matted with water from above, and the white streak on his head looked more gray in the smoke and mist. He did not growl, did not snarl, only gazed at her steadily, warily, looking for an opening.

Throwing back her head, Jasmine cried out to her pack. "Kill them all! The weak ones! They're tainted with the touch of humanity. Cowards. Tear them apart!"

The need to destroy Jack Dwyer and Molly Hatcher had receded for the moment, pushed out of the way by her bloodlust and fury at these others of her own race who dared to oppose her. She would kill those humans before the night was out, but first their allies. Like Winter.

"Betrayer," she snarled at him.

Winter glared at her, circled cautiously. "Better that than a fool. What you want is impossible. Your dream died in a bygone age, and yet it haunts you."

Jasmine lunged for him, slashing at his throat. Winter dodged her attack, slipped out of the way, and she landed on the floor a few feet past him. Her back was turned to him for just a moment, and Winter tried to take advantage of that. He drove her down, raised his right hand to tear her open with his talons.

With an almost giddy surge of laughter and power, Jasmine bucked him off. She shot up from the floor and leaped at him again. He tried to stop her, but she knocked his arms away and tore open his abdomen. Winter staggered, whimpering, and stared at her with wide eyes.

"Your legend has kept you alive, but not anymore. You have been a diplomat too long, Winter. This warrior's death I give you is better than you deserve."

Jasmine leaped on him as he fell to the floor amid

water and blood. Her snout darted down and her fangs tore his flesh, the warm crimson fluid of his life soaking her fur.

"Get up, bitch," growled a voice behind her.

Jasmine turned just as Olivia's claws raked across her back. The last of the Navarre bloodline did not just tear at her, though. Olivia struck her with a closed fist, fighting like a human as well. Then she lifted Jasmine off the ground and threw her against the smoldering remains of the bar. Jasmine's head struck the charred wood, and she lay there a moment, dazed.

"Tell you something, Jasmine. Tanzer got unlucky. From what I hear, he just went to the wrong town, killed the wrong kids. You, though? You're just stupid. All me and my uncle ever wanted, all most of us want, is to live our lives, be left alone."

Olivia walked toward her, sniffing the air, growling low. Jasmine lay, taking long breaths, letting her mind clear.

"We may want peace, but we're still Navarres," Olivia snarled. "You should have known better."

The girl reached her talons down to grab her again. Jasmine turned, lashed out, and dug long, bloody furrows in the fur on Olivia's face. The younger Prowler reeled, and Jasmine was up then, lunging at her, driving her down. Claws tore flesh. Blood spilled.

Outside, over the din of growls and grunts of conflict, Jasmine could hear sirens in the distance.

Careful not to slip on the water-drenched floor, Jack

ran through the smoke and the rain falling from the sprinklers above, shotgun held at waist level, finger on the trigger. He came upon a pair of Prowlers tearing each other apart and did not know which was his ally, which his enemy, so he simply passed them by. The monsters were too intent upon each other's destruction to pay him any mind.

Not far away, amid a circle of dead Prowlers—ripped open, decapitated, with heads and arms twisted at impossible angles—were five of the creatures, two females and three males. Jack saw the rich, deep brown on the largest one and knew it was Bill. Recognized him. One of the females fought at his side, two against the other three. Even as Jack ran toward them, Bill's companion was slammed against the wall, her throat ripped out.

"Damn it," Jack muttered.

His heartbeat was the loudest thing in the room, and he gripped the shotgun so tightly that his hands hurt. This was what had to be done, no way around it. If fighting to keep these things from slaughtering any more humans cost him his life, there wasn't anything he could do about that. Jack Dwyer was not stupid. He did not want to die. But he had come to understand that protecting the people he loved, combating these savage beasts, was perhaps the most important thing he would ever do. He could not have turned away, even if Bill's life were not in jeopardy.

Water streamed down his face, soaked his shirt, ran down his back. Spitting, Jack wiped a hand across his eyes to clear them. As he did a Prowler loomed up suddenly in front of him.

Jack swore under his breath and stopped short. His shoes slipped on the water and he actually slid a few inches but did not fall. He brought the shotgun barrel up and began to pull the trigger.

The Prowler raised his hands. "Jack, wait!"

"Bowden?" Jack asked, letting the pressure off the trigger. He shook his head and then ran on past the Prowler, letting Bowden fall into step beside him. "Almost got yourself killed."

"The night's still young," Bowden replied.

Side by side, the two of them stumbled over dead Prowlers. One of those attacking Bill looked up, spotted them, and lunged for Bowden. The two beasts fell in a tangle of flailing limbs and snapping jaws, and Jack ignored them.

Bill could barely fight. One of his arms was bleeding profusely and hung limp at his side. There were open gashes in his flesh that Jack could see even through the fur. Despite his wounds, Bill crouched low and glared at his two remaining attackers with damning eyes.

He growled and urged them to attack.

Jack couldn't fire. With the spray of a sawed-off he was sure to hit Bill as well. Scenarios raced through his mind, but he didn't have time for much strategy. Olivia had gone after Jasmine; Courtney and Molly were stuck in the corner.

And suddenly, from very far away, he could hear sirens.

Abruptly Jack shifted directions, cut diagonally across the room, though still toward the wall. He stepped over a headless Prowler corpse, eyes always on Bill. But Bill never looked at him, intent upon staying alive.

From the side Jack ran along the wall, slid up next to Bill, and raised the barrel of the shotgun again. The Prowlers were startled for just a moment.

It was all he needed.

Jack pulled the trigger, almost point blank, and the shotgun roared and bucked in his hands, tearing the Prowler in front of him nearly in half. A spray of bone and fur and viscera hit the ground in a shower only seconds after the torn-up corpse of the beast.

But as he swung the barrel to the left to shoot the other one, it leaped at him. His finger twitched on the trigger, but he was going to be too late.

With one huge hand Bill grabbed the surviving Prowler by the throat and hauled it out of the air. He stared into the other beast's eyes and whispered one word, low and cruel and merciless.

"No."

Bill snapped its neck and dropped it there on the wet floor. But when Jack went to his side, his friend was shaky on his feet. Bill shook himself suddenly, and a new focus came into his eyes.

"Courtney," he said. "I heard her voice."

Jack nodded. "She's here. And Molly and Olivia."

"And Jasmine," Bill snarled.

Together they started back across the club, amid the

dead. Jack looked around for Bowden, and a sick twist went through his gut when he spotted a grievously wounded Prowler—the one who had been attacking Bill—rising from the ground, Bowden's eviscerated body on the floor beside him.

Jack levelled the shotgun again and blew the monster's head off.

A sudden burst of gunfire from the other side of the room drew his attention. There were Prowlers all around still, but far fewer than before. Now, though, many of them perked up as the sirens grew closer. In alarm both allies and enemies began to run or limp for the door. Even as they went their bodies changed again, snouts withdrawing, fur buried beneath newly generated skin, the wild cloaked under a veil of humanity.

Jack started to go after them.

Bill grabbed his arm. "Forget them."

More gunshots, and Jack gazed across the room to see that not all the Prowlers were leaving. Six or seven of them were rushing at Molly and Courtney. Already several dead creatures littered the floor—Jack wondered exactly what kind of body count they were dealing with here, and how many of Jasmine's pack would survive the night.

Even as he and Bill ran to their aid, Jack saw Molly reach behind her back and pull out her second nine millimetre. She fired a couple of rounds into the nearest Prowler and it went down hard. But Molly did not drop the other, empty weapon. Instead she slipped it into the waistband of her pants, knowing that her prints would be on it and leaving it behind would be a bad idea.

That was when Jack knew that they could never go back from this. They were in this war forever.

Courtney pumped her shotgun and took down another Prowler. Molly shot two others, who didn't die but fell, wounded, and began to crawl hurriedly away.

"Hey!" Bill shouted.

The three who remained heard his voice and froze. They turned, backing away as they did so, cornered animals. Jack leveled the shotgun, but Bill pushed the barrel down. He stared at the others.

"Give me your throats and you can live."

For a second Jack didn't understand what he meant. Then the three Prowlers fell to the ground and lay on the wet floor, heads back, baring their throats to him, to this beaten, blood-covered creature, to Guillaume Navarre, and Jack understood.

"Bill, you can't . . .," Courtney whispered, for she understood too.

"I have to," he said. Then he stared at the Prowlers on the ground. "Get up, and get out of here. Come find me in Boston when you can. You're my pack now. I've got your scents. If you don't come to me, I'll come to you. And I won't be alone."

The monsters all glanced once at Jack, then back to Bill. They got up and fled the club, shape-shifting as they went.

"Olivia," Molly said.

They all turned at once. Only a few skirmishes were still going on, those Prowlers with such hate and bloodlust in them that they could not break off trying to kill one another, no matter the cost.

In the middle of the Voodoo Lounge, Olivia and Jasmine tore at each other. Both of them were bloody, but Olivia looked the worse off. She was strong, and impossibly fast, but Jasmine was older, a hardened warrior, and Jack doubted Olivia had ever really been a fighter, despite her strength and youth and speed.

Courtney let her shotgun dangle in one hand and picked up her cane, and the four of them hurried across the club, the sirens growing closer in the distance. As they approached, Olivia lunged in again, but Jasmine batted her away, then lashed out and slashed her ribs. Olivia went down in a tumble, whimpering, and Jasmine poised to leap upon her.

"Molly," Jack said.

With a steady hand Molly shot Jasmine once in the back, spinning the Prowler around. She went to her knees, but then looked up and saw the four of them coming, and slowly she rose, snarling, frothing at the corners of her mouth, jaws gnashing.

Olivia rose painfully and moved around Jasmine to cling to her uncle. Jack thought Bill might have been crying, but with the sprinkler system still showering down on them, he could not be sure.

"You're done," Jack told her. Molly moved up beside him, and he took comfort in her nearness.

"How?" Jasmine snarled, unsteady on her feet. Her fur was matted with blood and water, and even as she turned to glare at Bill her orange eyes had lost much of their gleam. "You are a coward. You truck with humans, even mate with them. You *love* them. Weakling," she spit. "Traitor."

"Give me your throat," Bill instructed her. "And I'll let you live."

"I am Alpha!" Jasmine snarled, but there was pain in her voice and she staggered a bit.

"Give me your throat!"

With a growl that sounded more like a scream of agony, Jasmine reared back and sprang through the air at Bill and Olivia, talons poised to tear them apart.

Jack and Molly fired simultaneously. Blood roses blossomed from Jasmine's fur, and she fell to the floor. She coughed once and then lay still, sprinklers raining like tears down upon her face.

epilogue

It all seemed surreal to Jack after that. They wiped down the guns to get rid of any prints and dropped them, then went up on the stage and out into the wings. The girls from Thornbush had left the stage door open, and they went out into the alley just as they heard the scream of fire engines pulling up in front. The police would arrive soon, but they weren't here yet.

Both Bill and Olivia were badly injured, but nothing that wouldn't heal. Whatever extraordinary biological functions made them capable of changing their physical form seemed to help them recover from wounds almost supernaturally fast. They had transformed now, taken up their human disguises again, but their clothes were soaked with blood and neither of them could move very fast because of their injuries.

Jack glanced at Molly and Courtney, then set off

along the alley with the others in tow. They had to get their friends off the streets without drawing too much attention. That wasn't going to be easy.

In silence, urged on by the knowledge that the Voodoo Lounge would soon be one enormous crime scene—the focal point of either one of the biggest news stories or one of the biggest cover-ups in modern history—they rushed along the alley to the public parking lot at the end of the block, where Bowden had parked his van. A van would have been a nice, inconspicuous way to transport Bill and Olivia, but unfortunately none of them had any idea how to hot-wire a car.

"We'll have to get to our rental," Jack said.

Molly stared at him. "That's fifteen blocks from here, at least."

They could hear police sirens, even thought they could see blue lights flashing off buildings, growing closer.

"If we find a dark place to stash them on the way, we'll do it and come back for them," he said, gaze ticking toward Bill and then back to Molly. "Otherwise, we'll just have to stick to the shadows."

One month later Jack and Molly stood on the sidewalk in front of the Lotus Club in Boston's Chinatown. A nervous energy burned through him, but when he looked at Molly, her calm, sparkling eyes soothed him. Jack had dressed for the occasion—which meant he was wearing pants other than blue jeans. The severe crew cut he had given himself had driven him crazy but now had almost completely grown back. Molly, of course, had washed the black and purple out of her hair within a couple of days. Tonight she looked radiant in a simple black cocktail dress and a soft, stylishly cut leather jacket he had bought for her.

"You up for this?" he asked her, hefting the shopping bag he held in his left hand. "This place can be a little intimidating."

Molly stepped in close, snuggling up beside him, and kissed him on the corner of his mouth. "Wouldn't miss it," she said, mischief in her gaze and the way her hand slid across his chest.

"Into the underground, then," he replied, and rapped on the door.

"We've been part of it for a while now. This is just the first time we've had something to celebrate," Molly told him.

The door was opened by a man whose face was not familiar to them. He bowed and stood aside to let them pass. Jack took Molly's hand, and together the two of them went inside the Lotus. The music was not nearly as loud as it had been the last time Jack was there, but people were still dancing, laughing, enjoying themselves. On the left side of the restaurant, where the tables were set up for dining, people milled about in small groups, sipping at drinks and conversing amiably. Chinese lanterns hung around the club, and streamers had been run along the walls and the bar.

"Over there," Molly said.

She pointed to a table near the back of the restaurant, and Jack smiled. Bill sat with his back to the wall on a chair that barely looked like it would hold him up. His arm was slung over Courtney's shoulders. Jack thought his sister had never looked happier than she did in that moment. Her cane was leaned against the table, forgotten, and she relaxed into the comfort of her lover's touch. Her hair was a bit shorter now and styled with simple grace that flattered her features. She wore a lavender dress that was almost elegant enough to be called a gown, though a gown would have been too much for the Lotus Club.

Olivia Navarre wore burgundy leather pants and a half-shirt that showed off her silver navel ring to great effect. She stood beside the table, in animated conversation with Eden Hirsch, who had her arms crossed behind her back, a posture that gave her the appearance of a little girl. Sweet and wide-eyed, almost demure, Eden pushed the long black ringlets of hair out of her face and smiled, blissfully unaware of how incredibly out of place she looked in the Lotus.

Jack swung the shopping bag at his side as he and Molly walked over to the table. As they approached, Jack saw another figure coalesce in the air behind Eden, a shimmering, translucent form. The ghost of Artie Carroll wasn't dressed for a party, but he smiled broadly.

"Bro!" Artie shouted. "What the hell took you so long? I'm dying of boredom here. No one to talk to."

"Sorry we're late," Jack replied, returning the spectre's grin.

"Hey!" Courtney said happily. "About time you guys got here."

Jack and Molly went around the table, exchanging the warmest of greetings with these people. When they got to Bill, Molly kissed him.

"Happy birthday," she said. "From both of us."

On cue, Jack handed him the shopping bag. "This is why we're late. Sorry we didn't have time to wrap it. Had a hell of a time getting them to do it in your size."

Smiling like a big kid, Bill slipped the tissue-wrapped gift from the bag. When he peeled the paper back, it revealed a thick cotton sweater of dark green knit. Bill held it by the shoulders and let it unfold, and on the breast was the name and logo of Bridget's Irish Rose Pub.

Bill smiled.

"You didn't tell me you were going to do this," Courtney said, obviously pleased.

"It's great, you two," Bill said. "Thanks."

Jack shrugged, glanced around the Lotus. "You've got a lot of responsibility these days," he said. An understatement, considering Bill was now Alpha to the largest Prowler pack on the eastern seaboard—but a different kind of pack, one whose members had vowed to live peacefully among human beings.

Jack's gaze returned to Bill, and he stared gravely at his friend. "I wanted to make sure you never forget who you are. Where you belong."

The expression on Bill's face was equally serious as he rose and pulled Jack into a bear hug. "I won't, Jack," he whispered. "Never."

The moment passed. Jack and Molly pulled up chairs, and soon enough they were all laughing together, enjoying the celebration of Bill's birthday. Molly sat close by Jack and was unusually quiet. Then, in the midst of a story Bill was telling, she leaned forward and spoke up.

"Sorry to interrupt, Bill, but the curiosity is killing me. It's your birthday, but you haven't said how old you are."

Bill and Courtney exchanged a long glance, then looked around the table. Everyone was watching closely, listening. Behind Eden even Artie's ghost was paying attention.

"Do you *really* want to know?" Courtney asked.

The question startled Jack, and he could tell that Molly was a bit unnerved by it. She thought about it, and so did he, and after a moment Molly shrugged.

"I'm not sure, actually."

"When you really want to know," Bill said, "ask me again."

"He's an old man," Olivia said dismissively. "What more do you need to know?"

Bill shot her a playfully menacing look. "Weren't you going to play your guitar?"

Olivia flapped her hands. "All right. Going!"

She rose and went to get her guitar case from an empty booth behind them. When Olivia pulled out the guitar and began to tune it, Courtney took that moment to slide a bit closer to Jack and Molly.

"We can talk more about this tomorrow, you two,

but I've been doing some research with my Internet contact, and I think we have another hot spot."

Jack felt Molly's fingers tighten around his. He glanced at her, and a kind of silent communication passed between them. Molly even sat up a bit straighter, though Jack doubted she was even aware of it.

"Where are we going this time?" Jack asked.

Courtney sipped at her drink, held the glass in both hands as if warming herself on it. "California."

Jack laughed. "Why do I think we're not going to Disneyland?"

about the author

CHRISTOPHER GOLDEN is the award-winning, *L.A. Times* best-selling author of such novels as *Straight On 'til Morning, Strangewood, Prowlers,* and the Body of Evidence series of teen thrillers.

Golden has also written a great many books and comic books related to the TV series *Buffy the Vampire Slayer* and *Angel.* His other comic-book work includes stories featuring such characters as Batman, Wolverine, Spider-Man, The Crow, and Hellboy, among many others.

As a pop-culture journalist, he was the editor of the Bram Stoker Award-winning book of criticism *CUT!: Horror Writers on Horror Film* and the co-author of both *Buffy the Vampire Slayer: The Monster Book* and *The Stephen King Universe.*

Golden was born and raised in Massachusetts, where he still lives with his family. He graduated from Tufts University. He is currently at work on a new novel for Signet called *The Ferryman.* There are more than four million copies of his books in print. Please visit him at www.christophergolden.com.